JENNY COLGAN

CHRISTMAS AT LITTLE BEACH STREET BAKERY

A NOVEL

WILLIAM MORROW
An Imprint of HarperCollins*Publishers*

CHRISTMAS AT LITTLE BEACH STREET BAKERY. Copyright © 2017 by Jenny Colgan. All rights reserved. Printed in the United States of America. No part of this book may be used or reproduced in any manner whatsoever without written permission except in the case of brief quotations embodied in critical articles and reviews. For information, address HarperCollins Publishers, 195 Broadway, New York, NY 10007.

Originally published in Great Britain in 2016 by Sphere.

First William Morrow mass market printing: November 2020
First William Morrow paperback printing: October 2017
First William Morrow hardcover printing: October 2017

Print Edition ISBN: 978-0-06-303615-4
Digital Edition ISBN: 978-0-06-266300-9

Cover art by Amy Halperin
Cover photograph © GreenArt/Shutterstock
Hanging Christmas balls illustration © Hallin/Shutterstock, Inc.
Author photograph by Charlie Hopkinson

William Morrow and HarperCollins are registered trademarks of HarperCollins Publishers in the United States of America and other countries.

20 21 22 23 24   CPI   10 9 8 7 6 5 4 3 2 1

To the dreamers, and your dreams, big or small.
Like, even if they're puffin-sized small.

"You'll never find peace by hating, lad. It only shuts ye off more from the world. And this town is only a cursed place if ye make it so. To the rest of us, 'tis a blessed place!"
—Brigadoon

Dear Reader,

Thank you so much for picking up this, the last in the Little Beach trilogy (probably). I have loved writing the adventures of Polly, Huckle, and a very naughty puffin called Neil so very much.

If you are new to these stories, honestly you don't need to know very much: Polly moved to the tidal island of Mount Polbearne when her business failed, and has built a new life there.

She lives in a lighthouse because she thought it sounded romantic (it is a MASSIVE pain in the neck, NB), with her laid-back American boyfriend Huckle and a puffin, obviously. She bakes every day for Mount Polbearnites and their guests.

Right, you're all ready to go!

A note on the setting:

Cornwall to me is a place of the imagination as much as a real home to lots of people, because I spent so much time there as a child.

To me, it is like a version of Narnia or any of the

other imaginary lands I liked to visit—I was absolutely obsessed with *Over Sea, Under Stone,* and of course the Famous Five and Malory Towers.

We used to stay in old tin miners' cottages near Polperro. My mother was a great Daphne du Maurier fan, and she used to put me and my two brothers to sleep in the little narrow beds and tell us bloodcurdling stories of shipwrecks and pirates and gold and wreckers, and we would be utterly thrilled and chilled and one of us, probably my littlest brother—although he would probably say me—would be up half the night with nightmares.

Compared to chilly Scotland, sunny Cornwall was like paradise to me. Every year, we were bought as a special treat those big foam bodysurf boards and we would get into the water first thing in the morning and bodysurf bodysurf bodysurf until physically hauled out, sunburnt along the crossed strap lines on my swimming costume, to eat a gritty sandwich wrapped in clearseal.

Later my dad would barbecue fish over the little home-built barbie he constructed every year from bricks and a grill, and I would sit in the high sweet grass and read books, and get bitten by insects.

And after that (because you get to stay up very late on your holidays), we'd drive down to Mousehole or St. Ives; eat ice cream strolling along the harbor walk looking at the art galleries; or hot salty fried potatoes, or fudge, the flavors of which I was constantly obsessed with, even though fudge invariably makes me feel sick.

They were blissful times, and it was such a joy to revisit them when I started writing my Mount Polbearne series. We went on a day trip—as required by law, I think, of anyone visiting Cornwall—to St. Michael's Mount and I remember being gripped and fascinated by the old stone road disappearing under the waves. It was the most romantic and magical thing I could possibly imagine, and it has been such a joy setting my books there. If I can convey even a fraction of the happiness Cornwall has brought to me in my life through my books—well, I'll be absolutely delighted.

Jenny xxx

CHRISTMAS
AT LITTLE
BEACH STREET
BAKERY

Chapter One

This story is about one particular Christmas, but it actually starts with a very Bad Thing happening the previous spring.

It's a bit of a shame that the Bad Thing happens in the spring and we're only going to look at it for a bit, because the Cornish tidal island of Mount Polbearne in the spring is an extraordinarily beautiful place.

There is a causeway leading to the ancient settlement, which used to be connected to the mainland until the seas rose up. Now the tides cover the old cobbled road twice a day, which makes it both a very romantic and an extremely inconvenient place to live.

There are a jumble of cottages and shops alongside the harbor and beach, including Polly's Little Beach Street Bakery, to distinguish it from the original bakery. You might wonder how such a tiny village sustains two bakeries, but then you obviously haven't eaten there, because Polly is to baking what Phil Collins is to playing the drums. Hang on, that might not be the best example.

Anyway, rest assured: she is very, very good at baking. Her sourdough bread is nutty and firm and has the chewiest of crusts; her baguettes are lighter and fluffier than air. She makes the densest, most delicious olive oil focaccia and delicate, sharp cheese scones. The scent of her baking—she tests things out in the kitchen at home in the lighthouse, then there are the big industrial ovens in the bakery itself, plus an amazing woodburner—floats across the town and brings the hungry and the curious from miles around.

In addition to the bakery along the harbor, there's Andy's pub, the Red Lion, which plays fairly fast and loose with licensing laws, particularly if it's a warm evening in the beer garden, which is strung with fairy lights and scented with the sea. Andy also runs a fantastic and mind-numbingly expensive fish-and-chip shop next door, so he's a busy man. In the harbor itself, the fishing boats rattle and chime; fishing, once the backbone of Mount Polbearne, is now the second most popular job in the tiny community, after tourism.

Up the hill ramble various little cobbled streets, where the same families have been living for generations. There were fears that the community was dying out, but Polly arriving to take over the bakery, after the graphic design business she used to run failed miserably, coincided with—some people say brought about—a new influx; there's even a posh fish restaurant now. Babies are being born, and there's a sense that things are definitely on the up.

The trick now is to keep it on the up without all the lovely tumbledown houses being bought as second homes by rich people from London and Exeter who never show up during the week and who make it too expensive for local people to live there. But with one or two exceptions, the lack of reliable Wi-Fi and the constantly shifting tides have kept the place more or less cut off from invasion—as it has been for hundreds and hundreds of years—so it could be worse.

Summer in Mount Polbearne is always mobbed and busy and a bit nuts as everyone tries to make enough money to get them through the long, cold winter. But in the spring, the tourists haven't quite started yet—or at least, there's normally a bit of a rush at Easter, when everyone turns up and hopes for the best and pretends that they aren't remotely disappointed when the wind that used to wreck ships on that treacherous stretch of southern Cornish coastline blows their candyfloss right back in their faces; that the picturesque bounce of the fishing boats that line the little harbor isn't done just to look nice in holiday videos but is actually the white-tipped waves hurling the boats about, with red-fingered fishermen mending nets or, more commonly these days, frowning at computer printouts showing shoals and movements and tallying up just how much they can take from the sea.

But once the slightly disappointed Easter holiday-makers (and the incredibly smug ones, I should say, who hang on until the second Tuesday and are rewarded with a golden day so exquisitely perfect and beautiful that they annoy their friends immeasurably for the next five years by reminiscing about it) have gone, Mount Polbearne has a short respite before the summer floods arrive: children with crabbing nets; adults dreaming of the kind of holidays they had as children, with wide golden beaches and the freedom to run around (until they realize that the causeway doesn't have any sides and the tide rushes in astonishingly fast, and what was perfectly okay for their parents to let them do in 1985 is now a bit horrifying; and, well, obviously they'll need good

Wi-Fi too, something Mount Polbearne can't provide, but they'll just have to make the best of it).

In April, then, Mount Polbearne takes a breath. Looking toward the mainland, you can see the trees starting to blossom out in great big garlands of pink and white. Days that start chilly and unpredictable suddenly get a darting bolt of sunlight, and the early-morning mist burns off, and the heat rises and releases that gorgeous aroma of everything growing and birds building nests and chattering to one another, and the light bright green of trees in bud and a particular buzzing, gentle loveliness that is England in early spring, at its very best.

Our story does not stay there.

But it begins there. And it should be a time of new beginnings, of cheery emerging from winter fleeces and television and blinking into the fresh light of the morning.

Mostly, though, it has Polly Waterford's best friend, the blond and sophisticated Kerensa, wife of Huckle's best friend, swearing wildly down the telephone.

"Stop swearing," said Polly sensibly, rubbing her eyes. "I can't make out a word you're saying."

As it so often did, the connection cut out between Polbearne and the mainland, where Kerensa lived in a huge and ridiculously opulent mansion with her wunderkind (and quite noisy) American husband, Reuben.

"Who was that?" said Huckle, waiting for toast to pop up in the sunny kitchen of the lighthouse they shared, a faded gray T-shirt pulled on over his boxers. It wasn't really warm enough for just that, but Polly absolutely wasn't complaining. It was a Sunday morning, her only day off; there was salted local butter waiting to be spread, or a squeeze of Huckle's own honey, sweet orange blossom to go with the gentle morning weather.

"Kerensa," said Polly. "She had some very busy swearing to do."

"That sounds like her. What about?"

Polly tried to ring her back, without success.

"Could be anything with Kerensa. Reuben's probably being a putz again."

"Well, I'd take that as a certainty," said Huckle gravely, standing over the toaster, watching it fiercely. "Oh, someone needs to invent a speedy toaster," he complained.

"A speedy toaster?" said Polly. "What?"

"Toast takes too long," said Huckle.

"What on earth are you talking about?"

"I really want some toast, and I put your sourdough in the toaster—which makes the best toast in the world by the way . . ."

"I knew there was a reason you were with me," said Polly.

". . . and then OMG, it just smells so good, it's like you can't wait, you have to eat the amazing sourdough toast straightaway."

He pressed the button, and two not-quite-toasted pieces of light golden bread popped out.

"See?" he said, attacking them crossly with a butter knife. The butter was still hard from the fridge and tore a hole in the soft crumb. Huckle looked down gloomily at his plate. "Every time. I panic and take it out too early and really regret it, and that's my toast experience totally spoiled."

"Make more."

"It doesn't work. I've tried it."

Regardless, Huckle popped another couple of slices in.

"The problem is, I'll have eaten the first lot before

the second lot is ready. It's a vicious circle. Exactly the same thing will happen all over again."

"Maybe," said Polly, "you should just stand over the toaster with your mouth open when it's about to pop up."

"Yeah, I thought of that," said Huckle. "Possibly with a kind of butter spray gun so it's all ready to go and you don't have to hack it on in a hurry because you need to eat all the delicious toast so quickly."

"I didn't think it was possible to meet someone more bread-obsessed than me," said Polly. "But—and I can't quite believe I'm saying this—I think it's possible you overthink toast."

"If I could just invent the Speed-E-Toaster," said Huckle, "we'd be richer than Reuben."

The toast popped up.

"QUICK! QUICK! QUICK!!!!"

And after that, they simply went back to bed, because Polly, being a baker, had to go to bed incredibly early every other day of the week, and Huckle, being a honey seller, didn't particularly, so their hours didn't always match up. And Polly sent a text to Kerensa saying not to worry, everything would be fine, she'd call her later, and then she turned off her phone.

This was to prove a terrible, terrible mistake.

Chapter Two

So let us be clear: none of what happened was truly Polly's fault, or Huckle's fault. It was obviously Kerensa's fault, as you'll see, and a bit Selina's, who wouldn't admit it in a million years but absolutely liked encouraging these things along (because some people are just a bit like that, aren't they? Stirrers).

But it was also a tiny bit Reuben's fault, because—and I can't stress this highly enough—even by *his* standards he was being the most unbelievable putz that day.

He had forgotten it was their wedding anniversary—their first wedding anniversary—and when Kerensa had pointed this out to him, he'd said, yeah, well, he'd done a lot of that lovey-dovey stuff in the past and they were married now, so that was all kind of fine, right? Like, he'd done it and now they were all awesome, and anyway, she had a dozen handbags, right, and by the way, he had to be on a plane to San Francisco to talk to his massive IPO base, and Kerensa had said she hadn't known that, and he'd said, well, she should read the schedule his PA emailed her, he was leaving in two hours, and she said could she come too, having heard that San Francisco in the spring was a magnificent place to be, and he said not really, sweetie, he'd be super-busy. Then he'd kissed her goodbye and suggested that seeing as they'd had a gym put in the house, why didn't she use it?

So. You see what I mean. He didn't mean it unkindly, that's just what Reuben is like: when he's working, he kind of turns into Steve Jobs and doesn't really think about anyone but himself, which is why he's pretty much as rich as Steve Jobs, more or less. It's a big number anyway.

So Kerensa stood in the completely empty huge luxurious hallway of their massive amazing house with its own beach on the northern coast of Cornwall and wondered about crying a little bit. Then she decided to be angry instead, because this had been happening more and more often, and Reuben never seemed to see that actually she didn't really like being contacted by his PA, who was cool and American and dressed very expensively and who Kerensa was slightly intimidated by, even though nothing much intimidated her, and ever since he'd kick-started his career last year after a near-bankruptcy, she'd barely seen him at all; he'd never been off a flight.

So she'd decided to get angry and in a frenzy called Polly, who was busy as it turned out guffing on about toast with Huckle on her only day off, and absolutely was not as sympathetic as a friend should be in those circumstances, which Polly regretted bitterly afterward.

So *then* Kerensa called their other friend, Selina, who had been through a terrible time being widowed two years before and could still be a little emotional on occasion, and Selina, who had lived on the mainland and always had a fashionable career before she'd accidentally fallen for a fisherman, said she had a great idea: she was bored out of her mind, why didn't they go into Plymouth, go to the smartest restaurant they could find, and drink the most expensive thing on the menu, then charge it to Reuben and say thanks for the lovely anniversary gift the next time she saw him?

And Kerensa liked this idea very much, so that was what they did. And what started out as lunch—and a lot, and I mean a *lot* of complaining about the men in their lives, or that had been in their lives—got a little out of hand, and they ended up meeting a bunch of other girls there on a hen night who immediately incorporated them into their gang, and they went to see a "dance show" with those girls and I will leave it totally up to your imagination what the dance show entailed, but there was quite a lot of baby oil on display, and some very tall men with Brazilian accents, and flaming sambucas, and then Kerensa's memory gets a bit hazy after that, but when she woke up in the morning in an incredibly posh hotel she dimly recalled waltzing into brandishing a platinum credit card at some ungodly hour, she remembered enough to know that if she could possibly have it surgically removed from her brain, she absolutely would.

He'd already left. Although there was a long black hair in the shower.

I know. I did say it was a Bad Thing.

And oh, it gets worse. Think of something slightly regrettable you've done on a night out, then multiply it by a factor of about a million.

Kerensa got home—with a sniggering, only mildly hungover Selina, who thought the entire thing was unutterably hilarious and had been careful to drink lots of water at the same time, as she is also that kind of a friend—to discover that Polly had felt so guilty about not seeing her that Huckle had phoned Reuben and basically ordered him to go home and be nice to his wife.

So Reuben had postponed his business in SF and flown all the way back, laden with every perfume in the duty-free shop because he couldn't remember what she liked. He'd marched back in the door—where a miserable Kerensa had been throwing up all morning and crawling along the tiles writhing with hung-over guilt and misery—grabbed her in his arms and declared his undying love for her, then attempted to dramatically carry her upstairs, which he couldn't manage as he'd been on a plane all night and Kerensa was two inches taller than him and also wanted to die; but they did their best together regardless, the early April light glowing through the huge floor-to-ceiling windows in their enormous circular bedroom, with its ridiculous/spectacular (delete according to taste) circular bed, and after that, he promptly whisked Kerensa away everywhere he went for the next six months.

So that is the terrible thing that happened in the spring.

And if this was a film, right, we would have reached the point where the ominous music crashes in and the credits start . . .

Chapter Three

Five weeks before Christmas

"This year," Polly was saying boldly, sitting up under the duvet, "I am making a LIST. A PLAN. This year everything will not be a disaster."

"When has Christmas ever been a disaster?" said Huckle, turning over, still sleepy and utterly unwilling to relinquish the duvet. Polly was getting up in the pitch dark, as she did for months on end in the winter, and their last heating bill had scared them both rigid, even though the house was almost never warm.

Polly had thought—and hoped—that heating the lighthouse would be like heating a gigantic chimney; that she could light the Aga at the bottom and the heat would permeate up the entire place. This was not the case at all. This was very far from the case. The kitchen was warm, but unless—and even after—they turned on the ancient clanky and very reluctant heating system for about five hours and tried to ignore the fact that they were living in a Grade I listed, non-insulated, not-meant-for-human-habitation building, running up and down the stairs was torture, a sport that took dares and bribery for anyone to accomplish.

Huckle did occasionally think longingly of the little beekeeper's cottage he'd once rented on the mainland, just across the causeway, which was a lot warmer simply by virtue of not being perched more or less in the middle of the sea. The beekeeper's cottage had had low ceilings and tiny windows and soft throws and cushions and curtains and two small bedrooms and had been cozy all winter long with one log burner and about four radiators.

And even further back, he thought of his childhood home in Virginia in the U.S., which was warm most of the year anyway—sometimes uncomfortably so—but when the cold weather did come in, his father would simply fire up the vast furnace in the basement and the whole house would heat up straightaway. The first thing his father had said to him when he found out he was moving to England full-time was, "You know they don't heat their houses?"

At the time, Huckle had thought this was a quaint and outdated expression, like the British not knowing how to drink cold beer or go to a dentist. But now he was beginning to have a great deal of sympathy with his pa and wondering what other advice he should take from him whilst he still had the chance, before hypothermia set in and robbed him of brain-stem function.

Polly was pulling a third sweater over her head.

"That's my favorite sweater," said Huckle. "It's kind of even more shapeless than the rest and gives you a sexy Marshmallow Man silhouette."

She hurled a sock at him.

"Still more attractive than the goose bumps," she said. "Anyway, I don't think you're listening to my excellent plans for a list."

"It's five a.m.," said Huckle. "You shouldn't even have woken me. It was vicious and cruel and I shall get my deadly revenge."

And he grabbed her ankle and pulled her closer, trying to get her under the warm covers, where he liked, in fact, having to burrow beneath the layers of heavy clothing, knowing that somewhere in there, deep underneath, were Polly's soft creamy curves, waiting to be discovered like buried treasure; visible, in general, to nobody else but him. He could already anticipate the shiver of his cold hand on her warm skin.

Polly giggled and shrieked.

"No! NO way! I have a million things to do and all anyone wants to order is gingerbread."

"You smell of gingerbread," said Huckle, sticking his head up her sweater. "It's awesome. It makes me horny and hungry all at the same time. They're going to ban me from supermarkets. I'm going to turn into Fru T. Bunn, the pervy baker."

Polly scrunched up her face.

"Oh God, Huck, I can't. I can't. Now that I'm up and have momentum . . . if I don't get going now, I'll get back into bed and never leave."

"Get back into my bed and never leave. That's an order."

"And we'll starve to death."

"Neh, we'll live on nothing but gingerbread."

"And die early."

"So worth it. Where's Neil?"

Neil was the puffin Polly had inadvertently adopted when she'd nursed him back to health after he had broken his wing as a puffling. By all accounts, he would soon fly off home to join his flock. It hadn't happened yet.

"Outside."

They looked at one another. As ever, Huckle had that slow-burning, amused look in his eyes, as if the world was a funny game; that eternal sunny side of him that made him always think that everything would turn out for the best. His dark blond hair was scruffy. He slept in his old college T-shirt and smelt like warm hay and honey mixed together.

Polly glanced at the alarm clock, which Huckle covered up with his hand. She had deliveries, invoicing, paperwork, baking, serving . . .

"What happens one day," said Polly, getting dressed again in a tearing rush, trying to text Jayden, her assistant, to tell him she was running late, "after we've been together for ages and everything, and sex kind of tails off?"

"That won't happen."

"Well, it does."

"Not to us." Huckle gave her a warning look. They had gotten engaged in the summer, and every time he mentioned the future, Polly changed the subject or fretted about being too busy. He knew he had to sit down and properly talk to her about it; he knew she was busy, but he didn't understand why it seemed to be a problem. To Huckle it couldn't be simpler—they loved each other, they wanted to be together forever, they wanted to raise a family. Of course, he sometimes reflected, he loved Polly because she wasn't like other girls. But he couldn't help thinking that most other girls, surely, would have been happy with that.

He decided, once again, that this wasn't the time. He grinned at her.

"Can't you enjoy just one thing for five minutes?"

Polly smiled back. "Yes," she said. "And I think it was longer than five minutes." She frowned. "Mind you, I kind of lost track of time."

"Fine. Deal with it. Be happy. Everything lasts forever. I'm going back to sleep."

And he did, even as Polly pulled on her thick woolly socks, his face completely smooth and relaxed in sleep, and Polly loved him so much she thought her heart would explode; she was terrified by how much she loved him. It was just everything that came next that scared the life out of her.

Downstairs, she stoked up the Aga for Huckle later, grabbed a quick coffee and ran out of the lighthouse door. The rain threw itself violently at her face. She could always tell by the wind whistling through the windows how bad the weather was, but you had to steel yourself for it when it truly arrived, and now that it was nearly December, it was definitely here, with no end in sight.

That was what you got, Polly supposed, when you lived on a lump of rock in the middle of the sea, with houses built on steeply winding streets in gray slate, the same color as the stone itself, leading upward toward the great ruined church at the very top. The ancient causeway that led to the mainland was dangerous to navigate, although possible, but mostly the many tourists parked at the parking lot on the other side and walked the cobbled road, squealing if they mistimed it and the tide rushed in closer and closer. The fishermen who made their living on Mount Polbearne had a handy sideline in rescuing the stranded and acting as a highly expensive taxi service.

There had been a movement a year or so ago to build a permanent road to the island, but it had been defeated by the villagers, who liked its unique character and didn't want Polbearne to change from the way it had been for hundreds of years, regardless of how inconvenient it was.

The sandwich shop Polly also ran up the road was closed for the winter, but the bakery continued, as busy as ever, as villagers and off-season tourists queued to get the freshest, warmest bread from the oven, not to mention the hot tasty pasties for the fishermen to take out in their boats; the flaky croissants that Patrick the vet would devour in his sunny office, waiting on his barking clients; the cream cheese brownies adored by Muriel, who worked in the little grocer's that sold every single thing you could possibly want; the doughnuts for the construction workers doing up the posh new second-home extensions, with their glass-walled balconies and steel wires; and the jam tarts for the old ladies who had lived here all their lives, whose voices had the low hum and musical cadence local to the region, whose own grandparents had spoken Cornish and who remembered Mount Polbearne without electricity or television.

Polly braved the incredibly high winds on the shell-embedded steps that led down from the lighthouse—then battled her way across the promenade, with its low stone wall, crumbling slightly from the years of pounding waves, and down the seafront to Beach Street, the cobbled road that faced out to sea.

Buying the lighthouse had been an act of temporary madness, she knew, triggered by the astonishing fact of it coming up for sale. There was far too much work that needed to be done, and they absolutely couldn't afford to do it, but still, she couldn't get over how much she loved it, or the great feeling of pride she experienced when she saw it beaming out through the darkness (the top, working segment still belonged to the government), its red and white stripes a cheerful bulwark at the very edge of the village. The light didn't reflect back into the house—it was the only place on Mount Polbearne where you couldn't see it shining—and from the sea-ward side there was a completely unbroken view out across the Channel. In Polly's eyes, the ever-changing panorama—sometimes angry and dramatic, sometimes stunningly restful, and sometimes, when the sunset hit, the most radiantly beautiful thing on earth—was worth every penny of the horrifying mortgage and the freezing early starts.

The only lights on this early, apart from one or two lanterns along the seafront, were, of course, in the bakery. Polly ran around to the back door and slammed inside.

The kitchen was gorgeously, ravishingly warm, and she took off her gigantic parka with a sigh of relief. Jayden looked up inquiringly. Polly went pink, and it wasn't just from the heat in the kitchen; she was remembering with a smile what had made her so late.

"Um, hi!"

"The cheese twists are in," said Jayden self-importantly. He'd grown a moustache for Movember the year before, and it had suited him so much he'd ended up keeping it. That, combined with his white apron and a rapidly increasing girth through stock sampling and

eating far more from the bakery than Polly would recommend that anyone do, gave him the look of a jolly
tradesman from about 1935, and it suited him rather
well. Jayden was madly in love with Flora, a local girl
who had an incredibly light hand with pastry, and she
was feeding him up too, despite being very thin herself.
They looked like a couple from a nursery rhyme.

At the moment, though, during the winter closure,
Flora was at college on the mainland—the first time
she'd ever spent much time there—studying at a patisserie school in Devon. Jayden was absolutely miserable
about it; he couldn't bear her being away and humped
around like a sad walrus. Polly thought their romance
was very touching but wished he wouldn't be quite so
miserable with the customers. He used to flirt with them
and cheer them up no end.

"Thanks, Jayden," she said, topping up her coffee cup
from the machine.

They'd recently started selling hot beverages, and
Polly had spent a very long and over-caffeinated day at
a trade fair trying to find a machine that could dispense
drinks that weren't absolutely disgusting and tasted all
the same. She'd found one eventually—you could tell it
straight off by the way everyone was clustering around
the stand trying out the freebies, even people who were
trying to sell other coffee machines—but of course it
was by absolutely miles the most expensive one there.
She'd be lucky to make her money back on it if she kept
it for thirty years. There was a limit to how much you
could charge a freezing fisherman who'd been on the
water for eighteen hours for a hot Bovril, and it only just
covered their costs. But it was nice to have it.

Except for the hot chocolate. Nobody could make
hot chocolate properly in a machine. After it had ar-

rived, Reuben, their loud American friend (some might say pain in the neck, but Polly had grown quite tolerant in the last couple of years), had marched in shouting, "I make the best hot chocolate ever. Don't even think of doing it in a machine, otherwise this friendship is totally at an end," and brought her several tins of his specially imported Swiss chocolate.

No slouch in the kitchen himself, he'd shown her how to make it, with gently warmed milk and whisked cream and the chocolate folded in until it became a thick, warming syrup that tasted like liquid joy, finished off with special small American marshmallows, a touch of whipped cream and a Flake.

Polly charged for those separately and only served them in the winter, but there was absolutely nobody in town—and for a long way around—who didn't think they were absolutely worth it, much to Reuben's complacent happiness. In fact, the start of the Little Beach Street Bakery's hot chocolate season was, as far as many local inhabitants were concerned, the first bell of Christmas.

"There's a sou'wester out there," observed Jayden sadly. "I hope Flora's all right."

"She's in a centrally heated hall of residence, on a campus, on the mainland, and will still be in bed for another three hours," said Polly. "I think she'll be fine."

Jayden sighed. "I miss that lass."

"She misses you too! That's why you get so much post."

As if worried he wasn't getting enough baked goods, Flora was sending Jayden the results of her efforts through the post every couple of days. Some made it in fairly good shape—the French cakes were a particular highlight—but others, like the croquembouche, were something of a disaster. Dawson, the postman, was threatening to sue them for repeatedly ruining his trousers. He was already furious because he was always either missing the tide or getting caught in it. Mount Polbearne wasn't the jewel in a postman's round, to be honest. On the plus side, they'd all agreed that he could bin the junk mail at the recycling center on the mainland, so that helped everyone. Until Flora's cakes had come along. Jayden had offered to share the results with him, but Dawson had declined the first time and was too proud to change his mind now. If they came out particularly nicely—the cream horns had been surprisingly unspoiled—Polly put them on sale and posted the proceeds back to Flora. This annoyed Dawson too, especially if she put coins in the envelope.

"Morning, Dawson," said Polly now, answering the back door and taking the pile of bills and one slightly soggy jiffy bag from him. "Want a cup of coffee?"

Dawson muttered to himself—he'd obviously had to come extremely early this morning, on his bicycle, in the pitch black, to catch the tide, and he really wasn't happy about it. The post delivery tended to vary between six a.m. and two o'clock in the afternoon.

"On the house?" added Polly. She worried that if Dawson ever got too cold and miserable, he'd simply stop coming altogether and throw all their post into the sea. Mind you, she thought, leafing through the usual pile of endless bills, some days that wouldn't necessarily be the worst idea.

Dawson muttered some more and retreated into the inky darkness. Polly shrugged and shut the back door.

"It's amazing how well I've integrated into the community after a mere two years here. Accepted everywhere."

Jayden sniffed. "Oh, Dawson's always been like that. I was at school with him and he used to cry if they made him eat gravy. So we used to always give him our gravy, like. That seems wrong now, looking back on it, I suppose. We used to call him Ravy Davy Eat Your Gravy. Yeah, I think that might definitely have been wrong."

"Oh!" said Polly, pulling out a letter from a plain brown envelope postmarked Mount Polbearne, which meant Dawson would have had to pick it up from the old-fashioned red pillar box on the town's little main street, cart it over to Looe, then bring it all the way back out with him again. "Well, it's funny you were talking about schools . . ."

Jayden and his contemporaries—now in their mid-twenties—had been the last generation of children educated on Mount Polbearne, in the little schoolhouse on the lee of the island that was now used for village get-togethers and parties. The tables and wooden desks were still stored there, rather forlornly, and the old signs carved into the lintels on each side of the tiny building, marking the entrances for "BOYS" and "GIRLS," were still visible, even though, like everything else on the tiny island, they were gradually being eroded by time and tides and heavy weather.

But now here was a letter from Samantha, who, despite only having a holiday home on Mount Polbearne with her husband, Henry, always liked to get her fingers into as many pies as possible. She'd also had a baby last year and had started making worrying noises about schools in London and nursery prices and children being too jaded and sophisticated in the big city (even though Polly and Kerensa had thought that being jaded and sophisticated was absolutely Samantha's favorite thing). The letter was a typed circular, announcing a meeting to discuss the possibility of appealing to the council to reopen the village school, seeing as there were now upward of a dozen children being bussed to the mainland every day—expensive—and lots more babies on the way.

Jayden smiled when he saw it.

"Ah, school was fun here," he said. "You know, except for Dawson, prob'ly."

"It would certainly improve the children's attendance in the winter," said Polly, who had noticed how often they couldn't go because of bad weather making the crossing too difficult.

"Well, go to the meeting then," said Jayden.

"No way!" said Polly, for whom the idea of giving up a winter's evening wrapped round the fire and Huckle before falling asleep at 8:30 was sacrilege.

"You should," said Jayden. "You'll be having babies one day. One day soon, I reckon."

Polly glanced down at the fourth finger of her left hand—it was still awaiting the ring Huckle was having made for her, the seaweed engagement ring he had put there the previous summer not having proved as long-lasting as they hoped their union was going to be.

"Hmm," she said, feeling a slightly familiar wobble of panic that came over her whenever she thought about the future.

It was true, she wasn't getting any younger. But she was so crazy busy holding both the businesses together, and she couldn't possibly afford to employ someone else and take maternity leave. And that ridiculous lighthouse they'd thought was such a hilarious idea at the time . . . How on earth could she look after a child? How on earth did anybody do it? She had absolutely no idea.

And Huckle would probably want to get married first, and truly, she had enough on her plate . . .

Even though it was still almost pitch dark outside, the first customers were lining up expectantly. The older people still started work early after lifetimes of toil at the very edge of the British Isles, and the fishing boats came in to hit the fish markets so that the restaurants and chippies could get the very best and freshest from the cold, salty water. In the summer, Polly would head out and watch the sun coming up and sit out in the dawn in a sweater, chatting with the fishermen. In deepest, darkest winter, they all simply had to charge in at the speed of light, closing the door behind them as quickly as possible.

The old ladies bustled in with their dogs, and Archie, captain of the fishing boat *Trochilus*, turned up looking utterly freezing. There was a local saying that there was no such thing as bad weather, simply bad clothes, but all the fishermen had the best high-quality gear there was, and even then it was a tough old life out there, particularly when sometimes you needed to use your stiff, freezing fingers to untie knots, or gut fish, or open the freezer compartment. Archie's were mottled red and white and took a while to unfurl as Polly handed him his incredibly strong tea in the special mug she kept for him in the back kitchen.

"Good catch?" said Jayden, who used to work with Archie and had never gotten over how grateful he was not to have to do it any more.

"Aye, not so bad," said Archie, head down, inhaling the steam from the tea. That, from Archie, meant things were definitely looking up.

Old Mrs. Corning, one of Polly's regulars, marched up to the counter.

"Where's your calendar?" she said, pointing with her walking stick. Brandy, her tiny dog, yapped as if to back her up.

"My what?" said Polly, confused.

"Your Advent calendar! Advent starts today. Or weren't you raised in a Christian society?"

"I haven't seen her at church," said another of the old ladies who was busy chatting to Jayden.

Polly rolled her eyes. She'd slightly hoped that everyone's opinion on her comings and goings and what she did and didn't do might have died down since she'd gotten engaged to Huckle, but, if anything, it appeared to have gotten worse. Polly had grown up in Exeter, quite a large city, and had found village living agreeable but certainly different.

"Mattie and I get along very well," she pointed out. Mattie was the vicar who came over from the mainland every couple of weeks to hold a service. Polly tended to skip the service—in season she was working; out of season she was fast asleep—but Mattie often popped down for a coffee since she and Polly were roughly the same age and had quite similar outlooks on things.

Polly paused and froze. No wonder she'd been so funny with Huckle this morning. No wonder.

"Is it really the first of December today?" she said.

"Yes. First day of Advent. You know. To celebrate the birth of Our Lord, Christ the King. That's what Christmas is supposed to be about." Mrs. Corning, who was a kind old stick really but rather felt the world was running away from her—even in rural Cornwall—peered at Polly through her thick glasses. "Are you all right there, me lover?"

Polly blinked. "Sorry. I didn't realize the date. November was so gray and endless, it all felt as if it were sliding into one another . . . all the days . . ." She wrung out her tea towel. "I'm not making sense. Sorry, Mrs. Corning. Well. Anyway. It's . . . it's my dad's birthday."

It didn't feel right calling him that. He wasn't her dad; dads were people who turned up.

"Ah," said Mrs. Corning, who lived in a world where almost all the men had died, and she and her small battalion of ladies, with their thin permed hair and their sensible beige BHS anoraks bought on irregular trips to Looe, stuck close to one another and looked out for each other and spent far longer discussing the ailments of their small dogs than they did looking back on the past, and their handsome sixties Teddy boys, back from their National Service, grinning over their John Players. "Has he been gone long?"

"Oh yes," said Polly.

Even then she didn't want to tell the truth: that he'd never been there to leave in the first place. The only reason she knew his date of birth was because she'd written it on her passport application form. That had been literally all she'd ever had from him, according to her mother, apart from some basic maintenance. A ne'er-do-well. Someone whose presence wasn't missed. You couldn't miss what you'd never had, after all, her mother had pointed out to her.

Polly wasn't sure about that, not at all.

The cold of the day brought punters in in shedloads, relieved to get out of the wind and pick up some warm pecan and cinnamon buns. The hot chocolate stayed simmering in its pot, getting richer and thicker with every new cup that was poured, and the till dinged satisfyingly all morning.

Huckle wandered down about three o'clock as Polly swept up the mail ready to take back to the lighthouse. She would do her paperwork by the Aga as she tested out a new Christmas cake recipe, even though the idea that she was making different types of Christmas cakes had raised eyebrows throughout the village.

"Hey," she said, pleased to see him.

Huckle looked at her, still a little concerned after what she'd said that morning.

"You all right?"

She nestled reassuringly into his arm as he leafed through the post, stroking her hair gently.

"I'm okay, really," she said, muffled. "I just needed a quick cuddle. Mrs. Corning wanted to give me one, but I was worried she'd break a hip."

"Did you call your mom?"

They exchanged a look.

"The usual?"

"Yeah."

Huckle sighed. Polly's mum wasn't really one for answering the phone. Or going out. Polly had never noticed until she'd left home how reclusive her mother actually was; she never invited friends over, never had people in, very rarely went out, only socialized with her own parents, both now gone. Because that was how Polly was raised, it hadn't even occurred to her to question it until she'd gone out into the world and discovered loads of other people actually having fun.

"Just tell her to come down here! Breathe some fresh air, take some walks, get some color in her cheeks. It'll do wonders for her."

"She can't," said Polly. This was not the first time

they'd had this discussion. "Seriously. It's impossible. Last time I tried to get her out, she told me she couldn't because she'd miss *Doctors*. *Doctors*," she went on to an uncomprehending Huckle, "runs on BBC One five days a week and has done for about seventy-two years. You can watch *Doctors* or you can actually have a life, but it's tricky to do both."

"She should see an actual doctor," said Huckle, and Polly grimaced. They'd been there before, too. Her mother wasn't sick, she was just . . . introverted. That was all. It was all right to be quiet in a world full of shouting social-media extroverts, wasn't it?

"Well, call her again when you get home," said Huckle. "Hey ho," he added, picking up Samantha's letter. "What's this?"

"Meeting for a possible school," said Polly. "Have you seen Neil?"

Huckle snorted. "Have I *seen* him? He's practically sitting in the Aga. I have never known a bird so fond of his home comforts. If he isn't careful, we're going to end up roasting him for supper."

"That's not funny," said Polly, who had a total blind spot as far as the cheeky puffin was concerned. "Still no sign of Celeste?"

Celeste was Neil's girlfriend; or rather, he had mated with another puffin and they had been nesting around the back of the lighthouse. Their first egg, to Polly's absolute dismay, had not hatched. Celeste had been fairly grumpy with them to begin with, so this tragedy hadn't necessarily changed her attitude that much, and then one day she had simply upped and left. Polly had been so heartbroken, Huckle had had to put her to bed. It had taken all his powers of persuasion to convince her that birds couldn't actually imagine the future and therefore Neil had absolutely no idea what he was missing out on, though even now she didn't exactly quite believe him.

It was true, though, that as the weather had turned colder, Neil was quite happy to *eep* until the door was opened, then march in and settle himself down cozily in front of the stove for a snooze. He seemed more or less entirely unfussed about his longer-term prospects.

"Puffins shouldn't even be this hot!" Huckle had said, looking at the bird stretched out contentedly in front of the oven. "They're going to die out as a species!"

Polly had skritched Neil behind the ears fondly, and he had fixed Huckle with a beady eye.

"Okay, okay," said Huckle, who was mostly pretty good at hiding his feelings about sharing his life with a small black and white seabird.

They locked up the bakery and headed out into the already darkening afternoon. As they rushed across the pebbled esplanade and up the steps to the lighthouse door, the clouds scudded across the sky and handfuls of rain and seawater hit them in the face.

"Guh," said Polly. "Seriously. Why couldn't we have opened the Little Caribbean Beach Street Bakery?"

Huckle smiled.

"We still could," said Polly. "We could get Neil a very, very small straw hat."

They shut the door behind them, and Polly took off her wet boots and put the kettle on.

"Oof. Right. I am not moving out of here tonight."

Huckle was standing by the door, still studying the letter he'd grabbed from the counter.

"Are you *sure* we shouldn't be going to this?"

Polly frowned. "A town meeting?"

"Yes, well, *our* town meeting."

They looked at each other.

"What's this about?" said Polly suddenly.

"Well," said Huckle. On the small kitchen table was a large ledger book. "The honey . . . I mean, the honey thing isn't going too well . . ."

"That's all right," said Polly. "I'm not taking off this coat till spring. You can also sew me into my underwear if you think that would help."

Huckle poured tea for them both and indicated she should sit down.

"Listen, I've been thinking."

"Uh oh," said Polly, her heart starting to beat a little faster. "I've been thinking" was one of those phrases, like "we need to talk" or "you'd better sit down," that brought about a modicum of panic. It reminded her of her horrible break-up with her ex, Chris, and the loss of the business they'd built up together. She hated those kinds of conversations.

Huckle took her hand in what was clearly intended to be a reassuring manner but that unfortunately had completely the opposite effect.

"What is it?" she said in alarm.

"Oh. Well . . ."

There was never any rushing Huckle. He was a slow-talking, laid-back boy from the American South who could normally calm Polly down in any circumstances, no matter how frenetic she got. She hoped he would manage it now.

"I was just thinking 'bout our wedding."

After Reuben and Kerensa had had the most over-the-top crazy themed wedding ever not that long ago, Polly and Huck had vowed never to do that, telling each other that they'd have something small and intimate. But small and intimate was proving harder and harder, seeing as how literally everybody in the village thought they would be invited, plus Polly's family and all her old friends from home, who complained they never saw her these days since she'd moved away to the back end of beyond. She could have pointed out it was only two hours away but didn't need to, as quite often people turned up with a carload of buckets and spades to spend their summer holidays at her house, which was lovely but could get a little tiring when she had to get up at five a.m. and her guests were carousing till all hours and begging her to join them.

She told herself that was why she didn't like to plan ahead. She didn't really want to think about what else it might be: that her own mother and father . . . that they'd never been a family. The only families she knew had failed so badly.

"Uh, yeah?"

Huckle cast his eyes down as he thought about what he wanted to say. He'd given up a good corporate job to move to the UK, almost on a whim, after a long-term relationship had fallen apart due to their crazy working habits. His initial idea had been to de-stress, downsize for a little bit, get himself some breathing space somewhere far away from home—he loved working with his bees—and his father's British nationality had made it a cinch.

Then he'd accidentally fallen madly in love with this strawberry-blond whirlwind of baking powder and capability, and that had been that.

Except he was stuck in an extremely remote, if utterly beautiful, corner of Cornwall, far away from reliable broadband and transportation and normal jobs. Last year, when Polly had lost her job temporarily, he'd tried commuting back to work in the States, but it had nearly torn them apart. He couldn't be a management consultant again, he just couldn't. It felt like it ate his soul from the inside. Even if Polly had been willing to move to America, which she wasn't. There wasn't much for her to do in Savannah, he knew; there probably wasn't room for another artisan bakery in the beautiful old-fashioned town.

And anyway, Mount Polbearne was where she belonged, however much she complained about the weather. They'd both become part of this community through good times, as businesses thrived and the town was a happy place, and bad, like the previous year, when a fishing boat and its young captain, Tarnie, had been lost, breaking the hearts of everyone in the area. They were a part of it now.

But oh my goodness, he couldn't make any money. A few jars here and there of his exquisite honey, which he sold to wholefood shops and beauty salons, wasn't enough. It wasn't nearly enough to pay for a wedding, even one a million times less flash than Reuben's.

He held Polly's small hand, muscular from kneading bread, with white crescents of flour beneath the tidy unpolished nails, and she looked up at him, concern in her eyes. He cursed himself for simultaneously thinking that money did and didn't matter. It shouldn't when it came to how you spent your days—free and creative, out in the fresh air or experimenting in a kitchen, as opposed to shut up in some ghastly air-conditioned office listening to boring managers and filling in spreadsheets for ten hours a day.

"You know, about the wedding?"

Polly winced. It seemed like it didn't matter what they did, this wedding was going to be a big deal regardless.

"Don't wince!" said Huckle. "Seriously, that is not a good look for talking about, you know, marrying me."

"I know," said Polly. "It's just . . . you know. Getting your family to come all that way, and it'll have to be something really nice and special, and my family too, and it's just so much and we're so . . ."

She didn't want to say "skint," but she didn't know how to avoid it. She never, ever wanted Huckle to go back to that high-paying job that made him so miserable. It wasn't worth it, not at all, ever. They got by. They got by absolutely fine, they needed so little. Well, the lighthouse needed a lot, but it had stood for nearly two hundred years so far; it could survive a couple of winters more.

"Okay," she said. "I'm listening."

"Well, I was thinking," said Huckle. "You know, you are thirty-three . . ."

"Thanks."

". . . and, well, I figure we seem to be giving ourselves a ton of stress with thinking about a wedding. And cash and other stupid things that we don't really want to think about."

He held her close to him.

"You know," he said softly, "I couldn't love you any more than I do. I couldn't."

Polly looked up at him, blinking.

"I love you too," she said. "So much."

"Good!" said Huckle. "Okay, this feels like a good start. Okay, listen. Without me ever under any circumstances not wanting to marry you, all right?"

"Uh huh."

"What would you think if . . ." He gripped the letter a little tighter. "What would you think if we, like, maybe did it the wrong way round?"

Polly blinked, not sure she understood him straight-away. Then gradually it dawned.

"You mean . . ." she said, and her heart started to beat very fast. It wasn't that she hadn't thought about it; it was just she felt it was very far off. After the wedding, maybe, and everything, when the shop was stabilized and . . . She felt suddenly panicked. Rushed.

She realized she'd been putting it off.

"I mean," said Huckle, "it's not like we've not been practising the stuff you need to do to kind of *make* a baby."

"I know that," said Polly. "But . . ."

Outside the sea crashed against the rocks, and spray flew upward. But inside everything was warm and cozy, the fire lit and a candle burning in the window. She and Huck weren't superstitious, but the fishermen were, and Polly knew they liked to see the little light flickering as they returned to harbor, guiding them safely home.

She looked into Huckle's face: his blue eyes, which always had an amused look about them; the broad, generous lips, always so ready to break into a smile. He wasn't smiling now.

She reached out and took his hand.

"Do you think we're ready?" she asked.

"No," said Huckle. "You'll feed them on nothing but cake and make them obese and grumpy, like Celeste."

"Oh," said Polly.

He stroked her cheek. "But I don't think anyone's ever ready. I don't think that's how it works."

Polly swallowed down her fears and indecision. After all, she should be thrilled, shouldn't she? A man she loved dearly, to whom she was engaged to be married, had just asked her if she'd like to have a baby with him.

"You can think about it," said Huckle, noting how anxious she was. He didn't want to rush her.

"Okay," said Polly. "Okay. Thanks." She turned to him awkwardly. "I mean, we could go upstairs now . . ."

Huckle shook his head. "I hope that isn't a ruse to get out of going to the town meeting."

"Rumbled," said Polly, though in fact she'd been trying to change the topic of conversation as much as anything else. "I thought maybe if I took you upstairs and did that thing you like, you might not make me leave the house again. Because I am never leaving the house again, like I told you. Once I'm in for the winter, I'm in. Summer we can stroll along the beach and eat outside and enjoy paradise. Winter time I am going to put on four stone and never change out of my sixty-denier tights and possibly not shave my legs, and you're just going to have to deal with it."

"I *will* deal with it," said Huckle, "and I will deal with *you*, young lady, in absolutely no uncertain terms. After the town meeting."

"Noooo!"

"Get your coat on."

"My coat's wet!"

"I'll take you for chips afterward."

"I don't care."

"Come on! And if you don't, I'll get Samantha to come around and sign you up for the committee."

"I can't believe I'm supposed to be joining my life together with such a bad, bad man."

Huckle grinned. "It's my innate drive and decisiveness. Move your ass."

Chapter Four

The village hall was surprisingly crowded—or rather not surprisingly when you considered how organized Samantha liked to be, and how relentless her pestering was if she didn't get what she wanted.

It was vicious outside, rain seemingly dancing all ways in the sky, with a distinct promise of snow on the air. It didn't snow much on the island, simply because they were surrounded by too much salt water, but it wasn't unheard of, and the icy wind definitely seemed to make it feel like a possibility. Huckle put his arm around Polly, but it didn't help that much as they trudged up the hill to the old schoolhouse at the top, Huck clutching a box under his other arm. Polly had okayed Jayden to make some extra apple turnovers that afternoon and pretend they were leftover stock so they could donate them, though that only made lots of people tut at her and tell her about stock control and how she shouldn't be so wasteful if she was going to run a successful business, so she pretty much wished she hadn't bothered.

There was lots of chatter and some crying in the hall.

Muriel from the grocer's was holding baby Cornelius, and Samantha had brought her daughter Marina, so the place sounded quite lively. Most of the village was there, it seemed to Polly, including lots of the older residents, who were out for a free cup of tea and a bit of excitement—nothing wrong with that; as well as Mattie, the part-time vicar, and a stern-looking woman Polly didn't recognize, obviously the council worker from the mainland. She had a sour look to her.

Samantha cleared her throat, ready to call the room to order.

"Welcome, everyone, to the Mount Polbearne town meeting . . . You will find agendas and minutes on your seats . . ."

Everybody pretended to look at them.

"Now, tonight we're here to talk about the possibility of reopening the village school. As of the next calendar year, we'll have nine babies ready for nursery and a total of fourteen children up to the age of eleven. As this would be the largest school roll in Mount Polbearne in over twenty years, we feel the time is right for the county council to allocate us school services."

She continued in this vein for rather longer than was probably necessary, extolling the virtues of Mount Polbearne "not as a monument of ancient Britain set in aspic, but as a living, breathing, growing community," and Polly, as she listened, rather found herself falling under her spell.

Mount Polbearne had grown and flourished for hundreds of years, the generations continuing through fathers and sons, mothers and daughters. It was only recently that the place had started to die, as holidaymakers traveled further afield and people began to favor convenience in their lives over all things. Was it possible, thought Polly, that now they could reverse the process? Keep alive their little corner of the world, with its inconvenient access, winding roads, inclement weather, terrible broadband and lack of home delivery services?

She had been up for a very long time, and it was warm in the hall. Samantha's soothing tones washed over her, and she found herself snuggling under Huckle's large arm, her eyelids drooping. Huckle nudged her and smiled.

"This is where ours will go one day," he whispered in her ear, and she smiled sleepily.

Then, abruptly, Samantha stopped speaking, and after a short pause, another voice started up. This one was harsh and abrasive, and Polly jerked awake, blinking.

"We have a responsibility in our district to ensure the health and safety of all our customers," said the annoyingly nasal voice. "Now I can see here that two years ago Mount Polbearne fought very strongly against a new bridge to the mainland that would have enabled ambulances and other vehicles to get through in a timely fashion. I simply can't see a situation in which anyone would allow a school to function in this place."

And it's all your own fault, the voice implied, even if it didn't actually say it out loud.

There was a clamour of dissent, and a raft of questions, but the woman—whose name was Xanthe— simply closed her very thin lips and shrugged her shoulders. It was not going at all well.

Polly suddenly discovered that actually she did care, more than she'd realized, and she sat up straight and wondered how you would make a case for a child who fell over in the playground and couldn't get to a hospital on the mainland if the tide was in. One option would be to have the GP there more often, but the local doctor wasn't fond of the Polbearne beat either—that old time-keeping issue.

She sensed that Xanthe thought they were all totally ridiculous, clinging to a rock in the middle of the sea and refusing to move to modern identical boxes on the mainland, all neat and tidy and squared away for the convenience of the NHS and the local council and the postman and the people who picked up the bins. It made Polly quite determined to do the opposite. This was a free country, wasn't it? Why should they toe the line and conform just so some suit from the council could tick a bunch of boxes about health and safety? She sat up straighter.

"Couldn't we just have the school open when the tides are favorable?" she asked. Huckle glanced at her, grinning. Polly never could keep her natural enthusiasm down for long.

"I don't believe schools get to pick and choose their hours," said Xanthe, smiling thinly.

"Course they do," said Polly. "It's not written on holy tablets that they're shut during August, is it? It's not, like, the law."

"School hours *are* the law," said Xanthe. She might as well have said "*I* am the law," and Polly started to bristle.

"Laws change," she said.

"You think we should change the laws of England to accommodate Mount Polbearne?"

"Well, that escalated quickly," murmured Huckle. "What is this, a coup d'état?"

Polly sat back, fuming. "I just think that if you wanted to find a way, you could."

"We have budget cuts to make and staff to keep safe,"

said Xanthe. "The world doesn't begin and end with Mount Polbearne. Even if the road does."

"I hope she misses the crossing cut-off tonight," muttered Jayden, sitting just behind them. There were small noises of agreement and the kind of shuffling that denotes a large group of people who are quite tired now and want to go home or to the pub.

Suddenly the door to the hall burst open, and everyone turned to look as Reuben and Kerensa marched in, Reuben looking as usual extremely bullish.

"Hey!" he shouted, as if everyone weren't looking at him already. Behind him, Kerensa looked uncharacteristically deflated and a little pale, Polly noticed. She hadn't seen her friend in a while—Kerensa worked sporadically and Polly on her own admission had very much gone into hibernation the last month or so. The idea of getting dressed up to go out somewhere when you first had to take off the seven layers of clothing you were already wearing didn't seem to appeal. They'd texted, of course, but the unpredictability of the Mount Polbearne signal meant they'd hardly spoken on the phone. Now Polly perked up to see her, but she couldn't help being slightly worried at the same time.

"Hey?" She waggled her eyebrows in Kerensa's direction, but got no response.

"Hey, everyone," Reuben went on. "Great news! Glad tidings and all that stuff! So, anyway, we're totally having a baby!"

Polly jumped up. Huckle rolled his eyes. Only his showboat of a friend would use a public meeting to announce something like that. Nonetheless, everybody clapped and cheered, happy to hear good news. Reuben and Kerensa might live in a huge mansion on a private beach, but new babies were new babies and, right now, very welcome.

Polly ran up to hug her friend.

"I am going to kill you for not telling me," she said fondly. "Seriously. I am going to absolutely kill you."

"I wasn't going to tell anyone," said Kerensa, sounding horrified. "I haven't got my head around it myself yet."

"How far gone are you?"

"About eight months, apparently."

"You're NOT!"

"I am. I know. Don't kill me."

"But that's not even possible." Polly was absolutely stung. "Why didn't you tell me?"

Kerensa shrugged. "I didn't know. I didn't realize."

"You didn't *realize*? How thick are you? Didn't Reuben guess?"

"Not until tonight."

There was something strange about Kerensa. Polly turned to look at her, then glanced over at Reuben.

"Is he handing out cigars?"

"I told him not to do that."

"Are you feeling sick?"

"Sick, fat, everything."

Polly stood back. This wasn't like Kerensa in the slightest.

"Seriously, Kez. Why . . . why didn't you tell me?"

But Kerensa just shrugged, and Polly, hurt, made her promise to come over later, because Reuben was insisting on taking everyone to the pub and it looked like it was going to be quite a noisy night.

"So in conclusion," said Xanthe, obviously annoyed that attention had been diverted away from her, "I have to say that the case for a school in Mount Polbearne has not yet been successfully made."

Reuben raised his hand to stop the hubbub and turned around.

"Oh yeah, you should have a school here," he said. "That's an excellent idea. I'll send my kids over. Nice. Brilliant. Okay, that's sorted."

"Well, Health and Safety say the local council couldn't recommend a school facility on these premises," said Xanthe thinly.

Reuben stared at her for a moment.

"Who cares?" he said eventually. "I'll buy it and open my own school. No problem. Private school, we can do what we like. Free to local residents, of course. Then we'll charge a fortune to gullible Russians and I'll end up even richer than I am now. Which is very rich."

The room applauded. Xanthe looked horrified.

"But the hours . . ."

"My school, my hours," said Reuben, and on this general wave of cheerfulness, the meeting broke up and the villagers swarmed out into the biting cold and down to the warmth of the pub, except for Jayden, who had to get the taxi boat out to take a furious Xanthe back to the mainland, where she had self-importantly parked her car on the forecourt rather than in the designated parking lot, and thus found it up to its axles in seawater.

"I can't believe how you can live out there," she hissed, once she'd finally got it started.

Jayden looked at her, blinking, and to his credit didn't say, "Because it's not full of people like you."

Chapter Five

The next day, Polly left Jayden touting doughnuts to the blearily hungover and headed straight out over the causeway to visit Kerensa.

Reuben and Kerensa's mansion had recently had a complete overhaul and was now freshly redecorated. Reuben had been going through something of a *Game of Thrones* phase, so the place had gone from frenzied gilt to a kind of peculiar medieval mishmash, full of tapestry and gigantic wooden throne-style chairs. Tartan curtains hung from wrought-iron poles, and great oil paintings had been shipped in. There were also lots of candles. Polly thought it was spooky. Kerensa was just pleased she'd managed to talk Reuben out of getting a kestrel.

Polly rang the ridiculous deep-clanging bell and was let in by Marta, the maid.

Kerensa was half lying on a dark purple chaise longue next to a huge roaring fire that looked like it should have a pig over it roasting on a spit. She still wasn't smiling; she still looked pale and wan.

"Last night was quite fun!" said Polly, who'd had two glasses of wine and considered herself almost ready to get into the Christmas spirit. "How are you? Still feeling poorly?"

She hadn't even confessed to Huckle how hurt she felt at being left out of Kerensa's news. So they'd been away a lot, but . . . eight months? Before she could think, she blurted out "Who doesn't know they're having a baby for eight months?"

"Loads of people," said Kerensa defensively, as Marta came in and set out the tea on a side table. Polly would never get used to this kind of thing. "Some people don't know they're having a baby till they actually poo it down the toilet."

"Okay," said Polly. "Okay, okay, okay. It just seemed . . . Okay." She looked at her dear friend. "You just . . . I mean, are you happy about it? Your mum must be over the moon."

"She is," said Kerensa. She stirred her tea.

"What's up?" said Polly, suddenly worried. Where was her mouthy, exuberant friend?

Kerensa let out a great sigh, and Polly moved forward on the huge overstuffed sofa she was sitting on.

"What?" she said. "Weren't you ready, Kez? I mean, neither of us is getting any younger . . ." She was conscious that she was trying out some of Huckle's arguments on Kerensa. She was also curious as to whether her friend felt as ambivalent about the whole thing as she did.

To her horror, Kerensa suddenly dissolved in floods of tears.

"What?" said Polly, rushing to sit next to her. "What is it? What's happened? Don't you want the baby? What is it?"

Kerensa could barely choke out the words.

"Do you remember in the spring . . . when Reuben was being such a putz?"

Polly cast her mind back. The problem was, Reuben was so often completely insufferable, it was hard to remember just one occasion.

"D'you mean that time when he booked that band to play in the garden for his birthday then insisted on getting up and singing all the songs, and he was terrible and started yelling at people for not enjoying it?"

Kerensa shook her head. "No, not that."

"Was it the time he fell out with the telephone company and hired ninety-five people to cut the wires into their building, and MI5 thought he was planning a terrorist atrocity and he had to get himself that incredibly expensive lawyer?"

"No, not that one either."

Kerensa sighed.

"Remember our anniversary?"

"When he flew back from San Francisco because he felt guilty?"

"Yes," said Kerensa, hanging her head.

"And took you to loads of places and whisked you off to the States with him and it was all lovely and romantic?"

"Yeah, all right," said Kerensa. "But leading up to that, he'd been totally awful."

"And . . . ?" said Polly.

"Selina and I went out one night."

Polly blinked, trying to remember.

"Oh yes, she said you were really drunk. I don't like people who tell other people that someone's been really drunk."

"She didn't say anything else?"

Polly remembered there had been an excited gossipy look on Selina's face, but she hadn't wanted to know about other people's daft exploits—she had plenty of her own—and had just kept on working.

"No," she said.

"Honestly?" said Kerensa. "I was too . . . Well. I didn't want to . . ."

"Is this why you haven't been in touch?" said Polly. "I thought it was because I was working too hard and didn't make enough time for you."

"God, no," said Kerensa. "No. No. It wasn't that."

There was a long pause.

"I sort of . . . and it was only that one time, and I was really cross and a bit drunk and . . . Well. I. Well. I maybe . . . slept with someone else." Kerensa hung her head.

Polly drew back, too shocked to speak.

"You did *what*?"

"I was really upset."

"So upset you *fell on a willy*?" Polly immediately felt bad about saying that. "Sorry. Sorry. Sorry. And also, sorry."

Kerensa wasn't listening; her face was full of pain.

"I don't know what I was thinking. I was so annoyed and I went out to a bar and I had a couple of drinks and he happened to be there . . ."

Polly was shaking her head.

"Why didn't you just come and see me and vent?"

"Because exactly this!" said Kerensa. "Because I tried and you were off being ooh blah blah blah the most loved-up person in the world, and also you would have been so judgy, so, like, oh Reuben bought you a new car and a big house, you should be completely grateful, 1950s housewife style, that someone else is making all your decisions for you, instead of my perfect life where I'm running a business and have a devoted partner who respects me!"

The tears were coursing down her cheeks now. Polly shut her eyes.

"But it's okay now, though, right? It was a stupid mistake that came and then went away again. It doesn't mean anything. You managed to deal with it and forget about it and just not do anything stupid like that again, right? You're not here to tell me that . . ."

They both looked at the bump at the same time.

"Oh no," said Polly.

"It was only once," said Kerensa. "Well. One night."

"Yeah?"

"I've . . . I mean, I woke up and felt awful and came back, and we made up straightaway the next day. He flew back. We were fine. We ARE fine."

She started to sob. Polly leaned over to hug her.

"Oh for CHRIST'S sake," said Polly. She was surprised how overwhelmed with sadness she was; how upset. Selfishly, she'd hoped Kerensa's joy—her presumed joy—would rub off on her, make her more ready.

"I know," said Kerensa. "Can we just handle the fact that I'm a terrible, horrible person and kind of move on?"

Polly swallowed hard. Kerensa had always been there for her; had provided her with a home, for God's sake, when she was bankrupt and had nowhere to go. She owed her everything. They were best friends. But this: this was so big. Huge.

"Tell me . . ." she finally managed to say. "Tell me he was short with red hair."

Kerensa shook her head, tears spotted all down her cheeks.

"Nooo," she said. "He was Brazilian. Six foot four. Quite hairy. Very hairy. Dark hairy."

"Fuck a duck," said Polly. "And can't you find out?"

"Not till he's born," said Kerensa.

Silence fell.

"Did he look hairy on the scan?" asked Polly finally.

"It's actually quite hard to tell," said Kerensa.

And they sat there letting their tea get cold.

"You're very quiet," Huckle said later. "How's Kerensa? We should have them over."

"No we shouldn't," said Polly. She was making stollen and kneading it far more than it actually required, just for the happy thump of dough on wood, taking out her mood on it a little bit.

"What's wrong?" said Huckle. She hadn't seemed quite herself since he'd first mentioned this stupid wedding again, and the baby thing. He didn't normally rush anything in his life; he hadn't thought he was rushing this. He'd had a little vision of Polly pregnant, round and glowing like the moon; how beautiful she would look . . . and now she was hammering the bread board like she wanted to karate-chop it in two.

"Nothing. Busy. Work," she said.

She knew this was unfair, and not a nice way to talk to Huck, but she couldn't help it. Kerensa had sworn her to deepest darkest blood secrecy forever, particularly from Huckle. It would be beyond awful if he felt he had to tell Reuben. It was the kind of black-and-white way men looked at things, Polly thought: that it would be too unfair if a man had to raise a child who might possibly not be his own, even though the statistics suggested that that was the case for quite a lot of babies.

On the other hand, the entire situation was just a disaster. And even though it wasn't Polly's direct disaster, it felt strangely somehow as though it was; that into their safe, cozy little world a wolf had come, quietly padding over the snow in the dark woods of winter and lying down just outside their door.

Chapter Six

After a week, Huckle was still worried about Polly's mood. She seemed withdrawn and a little strange about things. He hoped it wasn't him. She had hurled herself into work with abandon. Perhaps it was his suggestion that they try for a baby. He'd thought it was a great idea. After all, surely it was the natural next stage? He'd made his decision; he'd crossed the world and decided to make his home here—a bit cold and drafty, but they could handle that. He loved their life, and he would love a baby. To Huckle, life was pretty simple. He just couldn't understand why Polly was so confused.

Polly felt horrible, like her stomach had dropped out. She couldn't imagine what Kerensa must be going through. She wanted to call her, text her, but she couldn't think of the words. She was having trouble sleeping, which wasn't like her at all—Polly slept like the dead normally, as Huckle had had cause to point out. And she could understand, couldn't she? People made mistakes. Life was made up of loads of mistakes.

But she thought of Reuben, and his many, many

kindnesses to her—he'd sent her the oven to start up in her first-ever bakery; he'd supported her when she'd gone out on a limb and bought a van; even when he didn't have any money, he'd always been there for them, however annoying he might be sometimes.

How could she stand by and watch him care for a new baby that might not be his; that might not look anything like him? To be complicit in all that deception? And it could last for years. She wished in a way that Kerensa hadn't told her.

But then she'd told her because she'd needed a friend—really really needed one. This was a true test of friendship. And Polly was failing it, right here, not even picking up the phone.

"You look like you've lost a penny and found a farthing," said Jayden, bagging up a large collection of Empire biscuits. "I have no idea what that means, but my grandmother always says it and I don't think it's good."

"Oh, just lots on my mind," said Polly.

"Yeah, I know," said Jayden. "They've started on you already, haven't they? They've got to you."

"What do you mean? Who's got to me?"

"For the Christmas fair."

"What Christmas fair?"

Jayden stared at her.

"Where were you last year?"

"I went to my mum's. What are you talking about?"

"The Christmas fair," intoned Jayden seriously. "Highlight of the Mount Polbearne social calendar. Revived, as all these things are, by Samantha and her All-Cornwall Social Committee."

"I should have guessed," said Polly. "What is it?"

The bell on the door rang, and Samantha herself bustled in.

"Ah, Polly!" she said, beaming. "I hoped I'd catch you."

Polly didn't point out that there was absolutely nowhere else she was likely to be.

"Hi, Samantha," she said. "Hello, Marina."

The toddler looked up from her buggy and grinned gummily. She had inherited Henry's high color, but it rather suited her; she was a rosy-cheeked, bonny little thing.

"Now!" said Samantha. "Here's the thing. We're reviving the Christmas fair."

"So I hear," said Polly.

"She's been miserable about it all morning," chipped in Jayden.

"Excuse me, I have not!" said Polly. Jayden and Samantha exchanged looks.

"So I wondered if perhaps I can put you down for a stall?" said Samantha.

"Um, what would that entail?" said Polly.

"Well, just what you normally do, but up in the village hall."

Polly looked at her. "And I give you all the money?"

"Well, quite, that's the point."

"And it's on a Saturday?"

Samantha nodded. "Yes! Then we get lots of people visiting from the mainland and they can do their Christmas shopping, do you see? We're going to have all sorts—craft stalls and books and bric-a-brac!"

Polly nodded. The thing was, craft stalls and books and bric-a-brac were absolutely great and fine and everything, but this would be a whole day's profits she'd be expected to donate, and it was tough enough to stay afloat as it was.

"And what's the cause?" she said.

"Well, it was going to be the school development fund," said Samantha. "But that all seems to have been sorted by that wonderful friend of yours with the loud voice, isn't that magnif? So we'll have to think of a new one."

She turned and was on her way out again before Polly had time to give her an answer.

"I'm guessing that's a yes," said Jayden.

"Hmm," said Polly. "It looks that way."

"You know, you could ask other people to bake cakes and have a competition," said Jayden. "On your stall. Without you in it, of course."

Polly smiled. "Or Flora. She'd wipe the floor with everyone."

"She would," said Jayden, looking moist around the eyes. "But you know. Everyone else could get stuck in."

"Wouldn't it cause the most terrible fights and bad feeling?" said Polly.

"Totally," said Jayden. "It'll be hilarious."

Polly picked up her phone and checked it, regardless of whether she'd got a signal. There was nothing from Kerensa. She felt horrifically guilty whichever way she looked at the situation, but the longer she left it, the worse it got. Then something occurred to her.

Selina, who'd gone out with Kerensa on that fateful evening, lived upstairs in Polly's old flat. She was Tarnie's widow and helped Polly out in the bakery from time to time. She was new to the village—even newer than Polly herself—and didn't really know Polly's friends all that well. She'd had a tough time getting over the death of her husband at such a young age, but living in the village had seemed to bring her some of the peace she'd been searching for. Polly didn't think she'd be there forever, but for now it seemed to comfort her to be near Tarnie's family and friends, even though she was a city girl born and bred. No wonder she'd jumped at the chance to take Kerensa out.

Selina tended to sleep late in the morning, so at about ten o'clock, Polly made a big fancy latteccino (the sort of drink most of the locals had absolutely no time for), put some hazelnut syrup in it and headed upstairs.

Selina was floating about in light loungewear. She'd done up the ratty old flat with its uneven floors and holes in the roof that let the rain in. Now, instead of the cozy cushions and warm rugs Polly had strewn around the place, it was a calm oasis of white walls and stripped-back wood, with what to Polly's unpracticed eye looked like quite expensive art on the walls. Selina's plump cat, Lucas, whom Polly had distrusted ever since he'd mauled Neil the previous year, lay resplendently on a cushion.

Selina was all right for money and was taking a kind of correspondence course in jewelry design on the mainland. Thankfully, Tarnie had had a really good life insurance policy, and though it didn't make up for him not being there, not for a second, it was typical of his thoughtfulness that he had made sure she was looked after. Fishing was still one of the most dangerous professions in the world, even these days.

Polly still missed him terribly. She couldn't imagine what it was like for Selina.

"Hey," said Selina. "Is that for me! Oh wow, thanks!"

"And!" said Polly, producing a warm cheese twist from her apron pocket like a conjuror. "Don't give any to Lucas; he looks fatter all the time."

"No way!" said Selina. "You know, I have to hold my

nose every time I go past the shop to stop myself going in and just guzzling everything. I thought I'd get used to it, but no. Fresh bread, every morning. It's not fair!"

Selina was absolutely tiny and took being absolutely tiny extremely seriously. Polly's theory was that she gave all her cravings to Lucas.

"I should say that given your willpower, you're the best person in the world to live here," she said. "Which is why you're allowed a cheese twist every now and again."

Selina looked at it severely.

"I'll go halves with you."

"You're on," said Polly.

"Is there skimmed milk in the—"

"Yes!"

"So, what's up?" said Selina, as they sat down on the angular white sofa.

Polly bit her lip. "Am I that obvious?"

Selina nodded. "Yup. Otherwise you'd be up here all the time."

"I'd like to come up more," said Polly. "I'm just . . . I'm so busy."

"I know," said Selina. "I'm not."

"I'd love you to work for us again in the summer, you know that," said Polly.

Selina nodded. "So, anyway. What is it? If it's the sodding Christmas fair, count me out."

"But your jewelry . . ."

"I know," said Selina. "I was slightly hoping I could make myself sound tough enough to be convincing to Samantha, but it won't work, will it?"

Polly shook her head.

"You know she wants my entire profits for the day," said Selina.

"Mine too," said Polly.

"I mean, I wanted to do this for a job."

"Exposure?" suggested Polly weakly.

"That's what she said," scowled Selina. "And *you* don't need the exposure. You're literally the only baker in town. What are people going to do, start getting their bread delivered by drone?"

"I quite like having someone bossy around," admitted Polly. "I even miss Mrs. Manse." Mrs. Manse had been the original, rather dragonish, owner of the Little Beach Street Bakery. "I just like the idea of someone else knowing exactly what's to be done, and insisting that it is. I only get really worried when I don't think anyone's in charge."

Selina nodded. "I know what you mean," she said. "What are you doing for Christmas?"

Polly rolled her eyes. "Hopefully nothing."

The previous year she and Huckle had gone to Polly's mum, in her small house in Exeter. Polly's mum was scared of anything out of the ordinary—Polly breaking up with her fiancé and moving to a tidal island to set up her own business had been quite a challenge for her—so it had been a quiet Christmas. Fortunately, though, she'd taken a shine to Huckle, who was very easy company and didn't mind not doing very much, which was just as well given Polly's mum's reclusive nature. Polly knew that she should persuade her to come down and spend a few days in Mount Polbearne, but she was aware how hard she'd find it, and she hated making her mum unhappy.

"What are you doing?" she asked Selina. "Tarnie's family again?"

Selina nodded. The awkwardness of the arrangement was far outweighed by the pleasure it brought Tarnie's mother, having a connection to him in the house. They would drink too much at dinner, and then sit afterward and watch old videos of him as a child, and then they'd watch the wedding video and everyone would cry for hours.

"Worst conceivable day of human existence," said Selina. "But I tell you what: if there is a heaven, I'm getting in." She took another sip of coffee. "Man, this is good. It's nice to drink real milk once in a while. Although I'm probably lactose intolerant."

"Probably," said Polly.

"Oh my God, you're agreeing with me even though you don't believe in it!" said Selina. "How bad is this thing?"

"Right," said Polly, steeling herself. "I really need someone to talk to. And Kerensa's busy. I mean, I like you just as much . . . Um. Anyway. Listen. What do you think? I've got a friend back in Exeter. From school. You haven't met her; I don't see her very much. She's married and everything. And now she's pregnant. But. But she thinks it's somebody else's."

"Oh my God," said Selina, sitting up straight. "Is it Kerensa? From that night? Oh my God, it is, isn't it? It's Kerensa. The dates totally work."

"What?" said Polly. "Of course it's not Kerensa. Don't be stupid. I just said someone you'd never met."

"Yeah, but you're forgetting I was there!"

"What? No, it's not her! How could it be? She totally wouldn't. It isn't like her at all!"

Polly felt her face grow hot. Selina didn't say anything, just kept watching her for a while.

"Okay," said Polly. "Look, it's my cousin, okay. The family is falling apart. Please, could you not mention it? I know some families are all right about this kind of thing, but not mine . . ." She looked down, but kept an eye on Selina to see if she was buying it. Thankfully, it seemed like she was.

"Okay," Selina said eventually. She paused. "Is it you?"

"Of course it's not me!"

"Only you have form."

"Don't bring that up," said Polly, and she meant it. During a period of temporary estrangement from Selina, Tarnie had slept with Polly without telling her he was married. It had been awful for everybody. "Look, this is a nasty family problem, but I can take it elsewhere if you don't want to treat it seriously . . ."

"Okay. Sorry," said Selina, who wasn't a bad stick really. "I'm preparing myself for a month of being unbelievably thoughtful and lovely to everyone. Just getting the last of it out."

"Okay," said Polly. "Look, it's just . . . I mean, I feel really bad about it. Even though it's not officially my problem."

"Do you know the husband?"

"Yes . . . uh, a little bit."

Selina looked at her shrewdly.

"And is he a dickhead?"

"Sometimes," said Polly. "Does that matter?"

"Does he have other women?"

"No! I don't think so."

"Hmm," said Selina. "And are you good friends, you and your cousin?"

"Yes," said Polly. "I want to be. But this is . . . it's so awful."

Selina leaned forward. "What do you think you have friends for?" she said softly. "This is why. Have you the faintest idea how many people abandoned me when

Tarnie died? I lost so many friends over it. How is that fair? People . . . they didn't know what to say, blah blah blah. What's to say? You just say, it's a fucker. Then you maybe apologize in case you say the wrong thing in the future. It's not rocket bloody science. Then you start being friends again."

Her jaw looked fixed.

"Some people stayed. Some people," she looked at Polly when she said this, "some people came. But some just vanished completely, as if by being miserable I would infect their cozy, perfect little worlds. Does that make sense?"

Polly nodded. It did. It made perfect sense.

"That's when friends need you more than ever. When something awful happens. And here's the crucial thing: even if the awful thing that's happened is your own fault. *Especially* when it's your own fault. Do you see?"

Chapter Seven

W ell, get in then."

Neil loved going in the van. Well, he preferred
Huckle's sidecar, where he would perch and enjoy the
wind ruffling his feathers, but he loved the van too.

The rain had cleared, leaving in its wake a bitter cold,
but Nan the Van warmed up quite quickly, and Polly
wanted to get moving before, as normally happened,
people started queuing up in front of it for a pasty or a
Marmite twist.

When she'd lost her job at the bakery the previous
year, she hadn't stopped baking; she'd simply bought a
van and moved her operation into that. It had worked
far better than she'd expected, and she'd kept the van
on, partly for transport and partly because she could use
it in the summer for coffees and sandwiches and keep
everything bustling over. People's faces lit up when they
saw her out and about in it, and more than one person
had asked if she'd consider a delivery service. But it
was also her only mode of transportation when the rain
came in.

She rocketed across the causeway—she'd done the crossing so often now, she no longer had the fear she used to have, that the van would swerve and she would simply drive off the side and down into the depths; you could still see, moving under the waves to their own current, the tops of the trees that had grown there when Mount Polbearne had been connected to the mainland all the time. Somebody had once sat under those trees, had thought and dreamed about their life. And now they were down deep beneath the sea, as one day Mount Polbearne itself would be, reclaimed by the ocean along with everything they now held dear.

It was a short drive across the thin end of the county to Cornwall's north coast. In the spring, summer and autumn, the beach Reuben and Kerensa owned was a perfect private surfing spot, coveted throughout the county. Reuben often let the local lads use it, in return for doing a bit of bouncing and keeping out the pushy weekend surfers, who drove down from the cities with their loud voices and stupid hipster vans and entitled manner.

But now, in the heart of winter, there was a touch of frost on the sand that had not rinsed away, and the entire beautiful, desolate beach was completely deserted. Reuben's beach hut—which had a full working kitchen and bar—was shuttered for the season; the turnoff to the private road was even harder to find than usual.

Polly drove along the bumpy track at the top of the dunes and on up to the house itself. She'd thought it was crazy the first time she'd been here, and time and circumstances hadn't changed it: this was a mad place.

The house was very contemporary in style, with a lot of steel and glass, overlooking the unbeatable views of the wild coastline. There was a round turret almost entirely glassed in, which Reuben had requested because he'd seen it in an *Iron Man* film. This pretty much summed up the madness of the project. Film companies were always asking to use the house, and Reuben generally said no, although he'd started saying yes if it was an actor Kerensa liked.

Polly was now starting to doubt the wisdom of being here. Then she got cross with herself for even thinking it. Oh God, what a mess. And it wasn't as if she'd never made a mistake herself. She'd slept with Tarnie without even knowing he was married. They'd been careful, but maybe she'd just been lucky. Maybe she'd have been raising Tarnie's baby right now . . . Maybe, she thought, everyone was only ever two feet from disaster, and it was luck, not fundamental goodness, that made all the difference.

She'd stopped the van in the nearby town, which was full of chintzy gift shops selling driftwood with HOME written on it at highly inflated prices, and gone into the third one she saw. She'd chosen an incredibly overpriced, but very plain, cream cashmere blanket, then picked out all the wrapping bobbins, which seemed to cost just as much again, and handed over her credit card with her fingers crossed. Kerensa forgot sometimes that other people had to think about money, but this wasn't about that. This was about buying something lovely— and it was an apology, not a gift.

She rang the bell, not even sure if Kerensa would be in. It was often hard to tell, given how many cars they had parked on the gravel driveway around the peculiar fountain sculpture. She hadn't heard from her at all—normally they texted and spoke every day more or less—and she didn't blame her. She hadn't wanted to let Kerensa know she was coming, in case she told her not to. It wouldn't have surprised her; would have felt like what she deserved, really.

The vast door already had a thick wreath of holly hanging from it. They actually paid people to do the Christmas decorations in this house. Polly hadn't even known that was possible; that that was a job.

The maid didn't come to the door; instead, it was Kerensa herself.

She looked even worse than before, all her natural buoyancy gone. She was washed out and pale, with great dark circles under her eyes.

There was a silence between them. Kerensa looked sullen, like a dog waiting for a blow.

"Is Reuben in?" said Polly.

Kerensa shook her head. "Why?" she said, looking terrified suddenly. "Is that who you've come to see?"

"No," said Polly. She handed over the present. "Kerensa, can you forgive me? I'm so, so sorry."

There was a roaring fire in the hallway and they sat beside it, underneath a Christmas tree that looked to be about thirty feet tall and filled the three-story turret.

"That tree is mad," said Polly.

"That's what I said," said Kerensa. "Then he ordered one that was about four times bigger on purpose."

They both smiled ruefully. Kerensa stared at the floor as Marta brought them hot chocolate.

"I'm sorry," said Polly. "I'm sorry. I was just so

shocked, that's all. The fact that you kept it from me all that time . . ."

"YOU were shocked?" said Kerensa bitterly. She looked up at Polly, eyes full of pain. "I didn't expect . . . I didn't expect you to turn away."

"I was wrong," said Polly. "I was so, so wrong. Kerensa, you're the best friend I've ever had. I shouldn't have . . . I shouldn't have done anything except tell you it's going to be all right."

"How can it be all right?"

"I don't know," said Polly. "Things work out. You love each other, right?"

"I think we'll find out when I have a six-foot olive-skinned baby with thick dark hair," wept Kerensa.

"Don't be stupid, you'll drag up a relative from somewhere. Why don't I start seeding the conversation?"

"What, hey Kerensa, remember that Spanish grandfather you never mentioned before?"

"Exactly," said Polly. "That great-uncle who came back from sea very rarely."

Kerensa perked up slightly. "Well," she said. "There is that side of the family . . . I mean, we hardly see them." Her father had died four years ago, but her parents had been divorced for a long time before that.

"Exactly!" said Polly. "Just don't bring it up when your mum's about."

"I could say it was something of a scandal at the time . . . marrying a foreigner."

"Will he buy that?"

"Reuben thinks Spanish means Hispanic. He'll buy it."

"That's incredibly racist."

"Who's incredibly racist?" Reuben marched in, whistling cheerfully. "Where's the gorgeous mother of my baby, huh? Huh?"

He chucked Kerensa under the chin, and she did her best to smile at him.

"She's been so sick," said Reuben to Polly. "Honestly. I thought she'd be, like, too awesome to be sick, but, huh, apparently not. She's sleeping in the spare room because she throws up every five minutes."

"It's very common," said Polly. "Kerensa was just saying you're a big fat racist."

"Did you bring me some hot chocolate?"

"No," said Polly. "But I did bring you some Sacher torte."

Reuben's face brightened. "That'll do. Yes, I am racist. I hate everyone."

"Why?"

"Because at my school for advanced and gifted children I took a pounding on a regular basis by blacks, Chinese, Asians, Caucasians, Hispanics, Arabs, Jews, Catholics and Zoroastrians. So I just totally hate everybody."

Polly looked at him.

"Are you absolutely a hundred percent sure it wasn't, like, maybe possibly a tiny bit you?" she said.

"Don't be a putz," said Reuben, eating all the Sacher torte without asking either Polly or Kerensa if they'd like any. "It was them. Everyone. I hate everyone. Except you," he added, speaking directly to Kerensa.

"Ahem," said Polly.

"Yeah, whatevs," said Reuben. "Did you bring me anything else to eat?"

They followed him through into the vast, gleaming kitchen, which was flooded with light even on a cold gray day like today. It contained what appeared to be every single appliance in the history of kitchens, all of them shining and mysterious and mostly untouched. There was, incredibly, another kitchen downstairs where the chef cooked.

"You know about food: what should a pregnant woman be eating? To make her glow. I want one of those hot, glowing pregnant wives with utterly gigantic breasts."

Polly smiled. "I only know how to make toast, I'm afraid. Although it might help a bit."

"I'm fine," said Kerensa. "I just need to juice some more."

"That juicer cost four thousand bucks," said Reuben. "You totally should. But also you'd think at that price it would do it for you."

"Gosh, Kez, I wonder if the baby will look like your dad's side of the family," said Polly. It was out of the blue, but she was doing her best.

"No," said Reuben shortly. "It'll look exactly like me. I look exactly like my dad and he looks exactly like *his* dad. Finkels have been getting rich and marrying absolute knockouts for generations, but we still get short freckled redheads. Who can pull knockouts."

Kerensa looked as if she was about to start crying again. "Show me how the juicer works," said Polly in a hurry, but Kerensa didn't know, so they had to leave it.

Reuben went upstairs to answer his emails, and Polly held Kerensa whilst she wept silent tears all over the cashmere blanket.

"It'll be okay," promised Polly. "It'll be okay. I'll be here every step of the way."

"Good," said Kerensa. "Because I think I'll be raising this gigantic swarthy baby by myself."

Reuben came charging back down the stairs.

"Crud!" he was shouting. "CRUD CRUD CRUD CRUD CRUD."

Kerensa blinked in alarm.

"What is it?"

Reuben sniffed. "Oh, my entire family has just decided to come for Christmas. Man, they're going to hate my small paltry house."

He sighed.

"This is going to *totally* suck."

Chapter Eight

"You said what?" said Huckle.

"Ah," said Polly.

"I mean it, seriously. You didn't want to check with me?"

"Ah," said Polly.

"I mean, I have no say in this?"

"Yes, but—"

"Sheesh, I know you don't know these people, but let me tell you, I do. And."

"And what? They aren't good people?"

"They're rich people," said Huckle. "Good or bad doesn't really come into it for them. They've all got lawyers for that kind of morality stuff anyway, so it's kind of beside the point."

"What is the point?"

"The point is sitting around telling you how rich they are. My God, they make Reuben look like Mother fricking Teresa. With the witty conversation of Stephen Fry. Oh Polly, how could you?"

Polly knew she was in the wrong. But the look

Kerensa had given her had been so full of yearning and sadness that she hadn't even considered not immediately offering. Actually, it hadn't even been a case of offering, not really; Reuben in his inimitable way had simply turned round and announced, "Hey, you guys can come."

"I think . . . I think we have plans," Polly had stuttered, even as Kerensa coughed loudly.

"What plans? Sitting in a freezing tower on your own watching a bird fly round and round," said Reuben with some degree of accuracy. "That will totally blow. I'll have a chef in and the biggest turkey, goose, whatever you people eat here . . . you won't have to lift a finger. Except to talk to my pop, so I don't have to. That's it. That's the sole thing you'll have to do all Christmas."

"Well," said Polly.

"Great. It's settled. And also I'll need you to . . ."

"What?" said Polly.

"Neh, I'll tell you later."

"I'm so glad you're coming," Kerensa had said, and she'd looked so happy and relieved that Polly hadn't had the heart to protest.

And now Huckle looked sad, which he rarely did, and Polly hated to see it. His crinkly blue eyes turned down at the corners.

"Only," he said, "I saw us . . ."

Polly came and sat next to him, putting out a hand to reach him.

"Sleeping late, you know. For once. Not getting up till it's light."

"Light!" said Polly.

"Yeah. And maybe not even then. No ovens, no dough, no baking."

"No fresh bread on Christmas morning?"

"No," said Huckle. "Because we would have some of that coarse brown bread left over, you know? The squishy stuff? With fresh salty butter and loads of smoked salmon on the top . . . and a bottle of champagne in bed. You and me."

"And then what?" said Polly.

"What do you mean?" said Huckle. "That's it. What on earth else do you need to do on Christmas Day? I'll give you a small present . . ."

"Is it honey?"

Huckle grinned. "It . . . it maybe might be honey, yes. Of some type or another."

"That's great," said Polly. "I love honey."

"And maybe you could give me . . ."

"A croissant?"

"Perfect. That's exactly what I wanted for a present."

"Seriously, what *do* you want?"

"Seriously, I have everything I want," said Huckle. "Except . . ."

He made a mischievous grab for her, and Polly giggled and pretended to shove him off, which didn't exactly work.

"Well, why can't we do all that stuff and *then* go over to Reuben's?"

"Because AFTER all of that," said Huckle, rubbing her shoulders gently, "we open those big bags of chocolate coins you do here and put the television on and then we watch movies all day eating candy."

"What about Christmas dinner?"

"Can't I just have more smoked salmon? And some cheese? And then the rest of the chocolate coins?"

"Oh GOD, that sounds good," said Polly, thinking about it. What with cooking for the Christmas fair, crossly, with Selina making jewelry downstairs in companionable fashion, and stocking up the freezer in case the weather turned bad, and having to think about dealing with Kerensa, and Reuben's family, and Christmas, everything had suddenly seemed to come at her like a freight train.

"I think we might need two bottles of champagne. For when we wake up from our nap in the afternoon ready for more champagne and more movies and more chocolate coins. And if we're feeling really, really energetic, a long, hot bath. And then another snooze."

Polly, who'd never been a morning person in her life, let out a sigh.

"We couldn't turn up after that," pointed out Huckle. "I'd be too drunk to drive the bike and you'd be too drunk to get out of the bath. And we'd both be asleep. We have a really, really busy Christmas Day schedule. Tell him."

"You tell him."

"You started it."

Polly closed her eyes.

"You know what he's like. He won't take no for an answer. He's so insistent."

"You're pretty insistent," said Huckle, moving closer to her. Polly turned her head and surrendered happily to him. Maybe they could put off making the decision for another day. Maybe she could put off all the decisions.

Chapter Nine

Polly looked at the printout and let out a groan. It was a full and packed schedule that Reuben's PA had sent her for Christmas Day at the Finkels', including two hours of charades, some round singing, whatever the hell that was, a full ninety minutes of gift exchange, walking to church—which was ridiculous, as Reuben had never set foot in a church once in his entire life and had been married by a rabbi—plus various mysterious entries such as "Finkel family pageant" and "The bringing in of the beasts," which Polly didn't even want to speculate on.

It just looked like so much *work*. Also there was a present list of about sixteen people on the email, all of whom Polly knew were terribly rich. She wasn't sure of the protocol, though: did that mean they liked fancy presents, or did it mean they had everything and barely even noticed if they got a Christmas present or not? Well, regardless, she had a tiny budget for that kind of thing. In fact she was seriously considering simply making two dozen fruitcakes and handing those out instead. Everyone liked fruitcake, didn't they? Mind you, this being Reuben's family, someone would be allergic to something. She'd never met a more Piriton-dependent man.

She sighed and looked up from serving old Mrs. Larson, who bought half a loaf every day, ate four slices for her tea with soup and sprinkled the rest for the birds, even though the local birds were tiger-sized seagulls who would eat a rabbit if they could get it to stay still long enough. Polly was worried that one day one of them would swoop down and do for Mrs. Larson, who was tiny and frail and whose eyesight wasn't as great as it had been and who was entirely capable of mistaking a gigantic seagull for a beautiful lark that was closer than it looked. And just at that moment, Reuben banged through the door, looking cheerful.

"Hey!" he said. "Right, so I've got this list."

"What list?"

"A list of, you know. Stuff we want to eat at Christmas."

Polly took the list and scanned down it. Warm baguettes . . . gingerbread men . . . a gingerbread house, full-sized . . . 16 loaves of rye bread . . . 14 loaves of wholemeal . . . 60 latkes . . .

She looked up.

"I thought we were invited to your house for Christmas?"

"Yeah, of course you are," said Reuben, completely unabashed. "It's going to be great!"

"But I don't want to be catering at Christmas time! I don't want to be working at all. It's Christmas. I want to take some time off and mostly stay in bed and not go to work!"

"But Polly," said Reuben, his face creasing in incomprehension, "we're going to need baked stuff. You do the best baked stuff. I don't know how to say it more clearly than that."

His face lit up.

"Man, I wonder what you're going to charge me to bake at a really inconvenient time for you."

"No, Reuben," said Polly.

"I think it would be a really horrific amount of money. I mean, seeing as my only alternative would be to helicopter in supplies from Poilâne in Paris. So you guys would have to charge me something totally disgusting. Man, it's really going to hurt me in the wallet. I mean, ow. Ow, that is such a painful amount of money. Even to me. Oww."

"Stop it, Reuben!" said Polly.

"Well, of course if you don't really need the money . . ."

"Stop it! I just want one quiet Christmas without being up to my eyeballs in flour!"

"I thought you liked baking."

"I do like baking! As a JOB. As a JOB I like it."

Reuben raised his eyebrows as he backed out of the shop.

"You know," he said. "They say people who love their jobs never work a day in their lives."

"Shoo," said Polly. "Get out of here! I mean it!"

"Don't worry too much about the ninety-six bagels," added Reuben. "I think I'll just get them sent over from Katz. No offense, Polly, but your bagels pretty much suck."

"GET OUT!"

The queue of old ladies looked at Polly with disapproval in their eyes.

"Isn't that the young man who's going to rebuild the school?" said one.

"Yeah, all right," said Polly, cross and conflicted.

"*And* he's going to be a father," said Mrs. Larson, sniffing. "You'd think he'd deserve a little kindness."

Polly began to fill up bags slightly lighter on the doughnuts than they usually were.

How on earth would she break it to Huckle? On the other hand, there was absolutely no doubt about it: they were completely skint. His honey just didn't cut it. They didn't need much, but the lighthouse mortgage was big and . . .

She heaved a frustrated sigh. She knew that in the scheme of problems—Kerensa's, for example—this wasn't much. But she so longed for a quiet time this Christmas. Last year with her mother had been slightly awkward—not her mum's fault, she knew. And the year before that had been heartbreaking, with Huckle away in the States and her entire future hanging in the balance. All she wanted was a bit of a respite. Just the two of them, celebrating the huge next step they were about to take.

She knew she should be happy and grateful. That it was really selfish to wish for more than she had, when she had so much already. But she had imagined everything proceeding nice and relaxed, just as it was, for a little while. Then at some point in the future, when things weren't so hectic and mad, she'd enjoy the stage, and babies and things, but in a while.

This was, she knew, utterly ridiculous. They were engaged. He was committed. He was the love of her life beyond measure.

It was stupid to care about it. And she'd never really seen herself as a bride; it wasn't the kind of thing she dreamed about. Everything she dreamed about was here in the Little Beach Street Bakery: the tinkling of the bell as customers came in; the never-ending pleasure of the scent of fresh bread; the satisfaction of baking and feeding people. That was her dream.

Anyway, that was hardly the most pressing issue. First she had to break it to Huckle that she'd basically ruined his dream Christmas. Or else turn down Reuben's money. And she knew it would be a lot of money. Enough to pay to get the windows sealed up against the January storms, or . . . No. She still didn't want to do it.

On the other hand, imagine having to spend Christmas at Reuben's with the entire conversation circling round how selfish she'd been for not making the bread and the cakes—basically for not having done all the catering.

To which Huckle would say, great, let's not go at all, and Kerensa would give that tragic washed-out sigh and make those puppy-dog eyes again to show how horribly sad she was, and the wind would continue to blast through the bedroom windows.

The old ladies had left, and Selina snuck in tentatively through the back door.

"Have the biddies moved out? Man, they give me such a hard time about whether I've found a nice young man yet."

Selina had had a brief torrid affair with Huckle's brother DuBose, but they tended not to mention it.

"They just want everyone to be happy," said Polly weakly, given that she'd just fended them off herself.

"They don't," said Selina darkly. "They want stuff to happen so they can gossip about it and say it's awful."

"That too," admitted Polly. "Oh Lord, what should I do?" She explained her dilemma about Christmas, skipping the Kerensa part.

"Don't go," said Selina promptly. "Are you nuts?

Why would you do that? You're not starving. Okay, you bought a stupid house; that's your fault. Rent it out or something. But it's Christmas; for heaven's sake, just enjoy yourself. Somebody has to."

The bell tinged, and a man burst through the door. He was broad and sandy-haired, with bright blue eyes. Selina immediately perked up.

"Ooh, did I just make a wish I didn't know about?"

She turned around and smiled.

"Hello, can I help you?"

"Selina!" said Polly. "You don't actually work here at the moment."

"This is more or less my house," said Selina.

"Less," said Polly firmly.

The man looked agitated.

"I'm looking for . . . I'm looking for the lady with the puffin."

"Ha," said Polly. "Um, sorry." She wiped her floury hands on her apron. "Hello. I'm Polly Waterford."

The man shook her hand. He was about thirty-five, weather-beaten, but in an attractive way. His eyes crinkled a lot when he smiled. He had an Australian accent.

"Hi," he said. "Look. We need money."

Polly looked at him for a long time.

"Well then," she said, "you've totally come to the wrong place."

Chapter Ten

They made coffee and eventually calmed the man down a bit. He told them that his name was Bernard, and that he was the head of the puffin sanctuary up on the north coast, near Reuben's house. Polly had tried twice to release Neil into the wild up there; both times it had been an epic failure, much to her deep and profound relief. Neil, it turned out, was not at all a fan of the wild, although the last time he had at least returned with Celeste.

"We just heard," he said, shaking his head despairingly. "Kara told me."

Kara was the capable New Zealand girl, Polly remembered, who'd taken Neil both times to release him.

"Heard what?"

"They're cutting our budget," he said. "Government cuts. Apparently puffins aren't a priority in our austerity culture."

"What?" said Polly, shocked to the core.

"I know," said Bernard. "They're endangered, you know."

"How are they endangered?" said Selina. "I thought you had like two million or something."

"Yeah," said Bernard. "But fewer and fewer all the time. The sea's getting too warm."

"Didn't feel like that this morning," said Selina, looking outside to where the wind was still blowing.

"Yeah, well, local weather isn't anything to do with it, is it?" he said, with a sudden flash of anger.

"Ooh," said Selina. "You're feisty. I like that."

"But what about the school parties?" said Polly. "I see them all the time."

"Neh," said Bernard. "The schools have all had their budgets cut too, haven't they? No more of that kind of thing. And the kids aren't really interested any more. Either they're all off playing Laser Quest or . . ."

He looked as if he was going to sob.

"They've got kestrels down the road," he said, deeply wounded. "A birds of prey exhibition. You can hold a hawk and launch a falcon."

"Oooh," said Polly. "That sounds . . . I mean, that doesn't sound anything like as interesting as what puffins do."

"Puffins don't do anything," said Bernard bitterly. "They don't do tricks. Unless you count swimming at forty kilometers an hour and flying at twice that speed and having the best air-to-weight ratio of almost any living thing and mating for life and—"

"You know a lot about puffins," said Selina. "Watch out, Polly likes that in a man."

Bernard didn't seem to hear her.

"I mean, just because I haven't got . . . stunt puffins."

The bell tinged and Huckle wandered in, wondering if Polly would be free to have lunch with him, a hope that faded as soon as he saw her face. Neil was with him; since Huckle had let the fire go out, he'd thought he might as well go for a bit of a hop. When the little bird saw Polly, he *eep*ed loudly and marched over to the counter, where he fluttered up in stages—he was getting rather too lazy and fat to fly—until he made it on to her shoulder, whereupon he leaned into her hair affectionately until she gave in and absent-mindedly rubbed him behind the ears.

"Yes!" said Bernard. "Like that! That's exactly what I need! How did you train him to do that?"

"I didn't," said Polly, surprised. "He just did it."

Without thinking about it, she passed Neil a crumb of brioche that had fallen into her apron pocket. He chomped it up cheerfully and leaned against her hair again.

"There you go," said Bernard. "But how are we going to train up all those puffins?"

"What are you talking about?"

He turned his blue gaze on her.

"You don't want the puffin sanctuary to close, do you?" he said.

"Of course not," said Polly.

"I mean, it would be the end, probably, of puffins in Cornwall."

"That would be . . . that would be awful," said Polly, meaning it.

"We need a star attraction."

"NO WAY," said Polly.

"That's it!" said Huckle. "That's what you have to start saying to people! Say it again!"

Polly barely glanced at him.

"I mean, he could turn things around," said Bernard weakly.

"You're not having him," said Polly in a warning voice. "Don't even think about it."

Neil *eep*ed and edged closer to her hair.

"C'mon, Polly, shall we take Neil out of here?" said Huckle.

"Yeah," said Selina. "I can stay and look after Bernard. It's no trouble."

"Jayden will be back in a minute," said Polly.

As she passed Bernard, she looked at him grimly.

"You can't have him," she said again.

As if things couldn't get any worse, Jayden arrived just as she was on the point of leaving. He was blushing all the way down to his moustache.

"Um," he said. "Can I have a word?"

Polly looked at him.

"Of course."

He rubbed the back of his neck.

"Um, I wanted to ask . . . Can I have a raise?"

Polly blinked. Both of them took the absolute minimum out of the bakery. She was planning on raising prices a little during the summer; the holidaymakers who came over from the mainland had plenty of money and were inclined to spend it, and people who had tasted her delicious fresh offerings had assured her repeatedly that her wares would fetch much higher prices in London or Brighton or Cardiff.

The problem was that the local people were on fixed incomes or pensions or low wages—like the fishermen, who worked harder than anyone she had ever met and still found time to pull shifts for the RNLI. She couldn't have a two-tier pricing structure; it was against the law. And she absolutely wouldn't compromise on the 00 flour, or using local butter in the croissants and cakes.

You got out what you put in, and Polly only put in the absolute best.

But it meant there was very little left over.

"Oh Jayden," she said in disappointment.

Jayden nodded. "I know, I know," he said. When he'd started at the bakery, the wages had been more than he got for fishing, in much more agreeable conditions.

"What's changed?" Polly asked.

Jayden blushed even redder, if that were possible.

"Um," he said. "It's just . . . Flora finishes college soon . . . And I thought. I thought I might put a ring on it."

He mumbled this last bit, as if embarrassed to say it out loud even just to Polly, whose eyebrows shot up.

"Oh my God! Jayden! But she's only twenty-one! And you're only twenty-three!"

Jayden looked confused at that.

"Happen," he said. "That's older than my parents when they got married. And Archie too."

Polly reflected on the tired-looking captain of the *Trochilus*, whose three young children made him look considerably older than his years.

"I suppose so," she said. "But Jayden . . . You see what we take through the till every day."

Jayden nodded.

"I know. I just . . . I wondered. Because Flora will be getting a job, you know, and I thought . . . I thought it might be time we settled down."

"Are you going to stay here?" said Polly.

"I'd like to, aye," said Jayden. "But we'll see. Getting a place to live . . ."

Polly nodded. She understood completely. Jayden lived with his mum still, but of course he'd want to find a place of his own one day.

She had the oddest sense that everyone else seemed to be happily moving along with their lives, whereas she felt like she didn't want to move at all; that she was being carried forward against her will. She knew why on one level. But it didn't help her to feel much better.

"I just can't," she said. "Not at the moment. Can we see if we have a good summer? Flora can run the other shop and we'll get the van open for ice cream and see how we do."

Jayden shrugged.

"Sure," he said, and deftly started clearing up the crumbs in the back kitchen, returning the room to pristine perfection. He was a brilliant member of staff. If Polly could, she'd have given him his raise and then some. She felt like a bad boss; like a mean person. The fact that Jayden wasn't even complaining made her feel even worse.

Polly was so frustrated by the time Huckle got her out of there that he frogmarched her down to the Red Lion and ordered her a hot toddy. There was a roaring fire in the grate and a few fishermen on night shift sitting sleepily beside it playing dominoes. There wasn't a jukebox in the pub, as most of the locals liked to sing a song or two after a night out, which meant the only sound was the ticking of the large ship's clock over the mantelpiece thick with local holly, and the occasional snuffling noises from Garbo, the pub's gigantic shaggy lurcher, who lived rather magnificently on a diet of fish and chips and the occasional spilled beer. He was less dog, more pony on the whole. That lunchtime he was stretched out in front of the fire, his paws twitching as he chased rabbits—or, more likely given the size of him, gazelles—across imaginary plains.

"What's up?" said Huckle.

"Oh God," said Polly. "I'm so, so sorry. Everything's kind of gone . . . gone absolutely rubbish."

She looked up at him and began to tell him about her day. Huckle tried to remember a time in his life when all that was important was whether the queen bee was fertilizing the hive properly and whether he had enough boiled jars in stock.

"That's terrible, sweetie," he said when she'd finished.

"Do you think Reuben would fund the puffin sanctuary?"

"What?"

"Do you think Reuben would fund the sanctuary?" Polly repeated. "I mean, all those people will lose their jobs and nobody will look after the puffins and the sea will grow too warm and ALL THE PUFFINS WILL DIE."

She looked a bit wobbly and as if she might burst into tears, and Huckle vowed not to buy her any more hot toddies.

"Look," he said. "You're doing too much. I said it all along. Just calm down. We're taking Christmas off and that's that."

Chapter Eleven

That weekend, Huckle simply insisted that a walk was going to happen. Polly hadn't been outside properly in daylight for about four weeks. And there was nothing like a walk for clearing heads.

"And Neil needs the exercise," Huckle added.

"So do I," said Polly. She was happy to go, especially as there might be a tea shop at the end of it. Or a pub.

"No, you're fine, it's that puffin that's fat," said Huckle, checking his phone. "Can Reuben come?"

"No," said Polly. "I'm planning on bitching up him and his relations for several miles."

There was a pause. Huckle tapped at his phone. Then he looked up.

"Ah," he said. "So, anyway, he's coming."

"Don't tell him where we're going!"

"Ah," said Huckle again.

"HUCKLE!"

She looked down.

"We've got our sweaters on now," said Huckle.

"Hmm," said Polly.

The sun was just about visible through a misty haze. Great pools of fog gathered in the fields, where birds swooped in hopeful fashion around newly planted seeds in the brown turned earth, and sheep tried to nibble the grass under heavy frost. The sky was a hazy pink, the days having the shortest possible attention span at this time of year; making the least effort. You had to get out and grab it while it was there, otherwise the wind and rain would tear in again and then you were stuck.

They were cutting through the north of Cornwall, the Tintagel path, which would take them out along the headland—it was hard where they lived to do anything really without a view of the sea—ending up just past the puffin sanctuary. Polly wanted to pop in and see how they were doing. Neil had his blue foot ribbon on just in case he decided to go off and play with his old friends, but he showed no inclination to do anything except lie in his paper bag in Polly's backpack, which rather negated the purpose of the walk: getting a fat puffin some exercise.

But Polly didn't care as she walked along trying to match Huckle's long strides, breathing the cold, invigorating air. Winter had more to recommend it, she realized, than she remembered. Or rather, this part of winter. February she could more or less take or leave. Once Christmas was over, it just turned into a waiting game. But now, out here in the harsh air, the sun glistening off the frosted fields, the waves pounding into the cliffs far below, Huckle's dirty blond hair dishevelled beneath his beanie hat, she could see why it was some people's favorite season.

"I like seeing roses in your cheeks," said Huckle, smiling at her. "I'd forgotten what you look like out of doors."

"Me too," said Polly. "It's nice. I should come outside more often."

Huckle smiled.

"I miss the summer, too," he said. "When the bees are buzzing again, rather than sleeping. I feel like a spare part kicking around."

"A very sexy spare part," grinned Polly.

"I need to earn more money," said Huckle. "I need to throw myself into that beauticians' circuit. I really do. There's lots to be made from organic products."

"But who'd look after Neil?" said Polly. "Who'd look after *me*?"

They walked on hand in hand, until a stray brown terrier ran up cheerfully to say hello and Huckle tousled its rough fur.

"Hello, buddy!" he said. "How are you?"

The dog wagged its tail furiously, and Huckle gave Polly a look.

"No," said Polly. "Seriously. We're not getting a dog. Neil would pitch a fit."

"How do you know?"

"Don't want to risk it," said Polly.

From inside the rucksack came what seemed to be little bird snores. The dog started sniffing around it.

"Shoo," said Polly. "You do *seem* to be a nice dog, but Neil's already been in a fight or two and he doesn't come out of them terribly well. I think it might be quite easy to chomp him by accident."

The dog scampered off to be with some children heading in the opposite direction. They laughed and jumped up and down with their pet, then the elder boy ran to a tree and started hanging off it upside down by the knees. Huckle went quiet again and watched them, and Polly looked at him in trepidation. He felt her eyes on him and looked away. He didn't know, truly, what her problem was, but he didn't want to press her on it. He didn't want to make it too much of an issue. Huckle didn't really like issues. On the other hand, some things were important.

Polly blinked as the children's shouting and laughter reached them.

"Nice place to bring up a family," said Huckle softly.

Polly nodded. "I suppose so," she said stiffly. She was actually relieved to see Reuben and Kerensa appear, coming the other way on the path.

"HEY!" shouted Reuben. "We're out to see if my pregnant-but-still-totally-hot wife can perk up a bit."

Kerensa shot Polly a tight smile. Polly felt sick. This was awful. Such a horrible burden to be carrying around, and of course it was even worse for Kerensa.

"Hey, you guys!" she said, more cheerily than she felt, and linked arms with Kerensa. "Come on. Only three miles and there's a pub that does the best cheese and ham toasted sandwich in Cornwall. And I know this because I have tried them all."

"You're only trying to make me feel better because I can't have any hot cider," grumbled Kerensa.

"You can have a tiny bit of hot cider," said Polly.

"Nope," said Reuben, overhearing. "No way. You're not damaging this baby. This baby is going to be the most awesome kid ever. I'm not having him born with fetal alcohol syndrome. You shouldn't eat the cheese either."

"Is he being like this the entire time?" said Polly. She could say it in Reuben's earshot; he was impenetrably thick-skinned.

"Yeah," said Reuben. "For our perfect baby."

Kerensa didn't answer him back cheekily like she normally would. Instead she dug her hands into her pockets and trudged on. Reuben raised an eyebrow at Huckle.

Polly let the men get ahead and hung back with Kerensa. The ground was slippery and muddy from all the recent storms and wind. The two chaps made a funny combination ahead: Huckle so tall and broad with his slow nod; Reuben talking up to him nineteen to the dozen, arms flailing.

"How's it going?" said Polly, although she could see from the body language pretty much exactly how it was going.

Kerensa shook her head. "It's like someone gave me a precious globe, made of glass or something, and told me to carry it safely. And I haven't. I dropped it and I broke it and it's shattered into a million pieces. There's absolutely no way I can put it together again. I've done something so awful. And one day—it could be any day, probably soon—he's going to walk in and he's going to find out; he'll look at the baby. And I'll have broken everything. Everything in my perfectly lovely life will be ruined and shot and I'll have to raise a baby on my own and my life will be over and I'll have lost this brilliant, clever, sexy, funny man I really, really love . . ." She collapsed into tears.

"You couldn't . . . you couldn't explain?"

"How?" said Kerensa. "How could I? God, Poll, I didn't even know I was pregnant for months, I was in such denial. He was the one that noticed my tits felt all different and brought me home a pregnancy test. He was so excited . . . Oh God."

The men turned round, but Polly waved them on. She put her arm round Kerensa's shoulders.

"You never know," she said. "I mean, it could be his, couldn't it?"

Kerensa nodded. "Yes." She sniffed.

"But why didn't you tell *me*?"

"What, with you all happy and loved up and living in a perfect fairy world?"

"I don't live in a perfect fairy world!" said Polly crossly. "I work my tits off and I'm completely skint and . . ." Her voice trailed off and she realized that she was going to cry too.

"What?" said Kerensa.

". . . and I don't even know if we can afford a baby. With everything."

"Oh no," said Kerensa, for whom money was never a problem. "Oh Poll. Don't be daft. You're doing all right."

"We are doing just about all right," said Polly. "As long as we never buy anything. Or go out. Or try and have a baby that I have to give up work for. Or try and fix anything in that stupid too-big house I bought by mistake."

"You wouldn't have to give up work," said Kerensa. "You could have a bakery baby. Just sit it up on the counter and give it a croissant to suck."

"Is that how it works?"

"I dunno, do I? I don't know anything about babies."

They looked at each other, and at Kerensa's huge bump.

"Oh GOD," said Kerensa. "How have we managed to fuck everything up so completely?"

Polly burst out laughing.

"God knows," she said.

"At least you still get to drink cider," said Kerensa darkly.

The little pub just off the trail was perfect: cozy and warm with firelight and old brasses gleaming on the walls. They used local cheese and homemade bread for perfect toasted sandwiches, just as Polly had said. The four of them flexed their chilly toes and sat in a cozy booth. Polly sat next to Reuben and decided, as Huckle had suggested, just to come out with it.

"Reuben," she said. "I need some money."

"Well, cater the Finkel family Christmas," said Reuben equably.

"I don't want to," said Polly.

"Well then, we have a situation."

"Listen, it's not for me. It's for the puffin sanctuary."

"That stink hole?" said Reuben.

"What? What do you mean?"

"It's just up the coast from us. I can smell the fishy bastards when the wind's going in the wrong direction. Hey, why? Is it up for sale?"

"No," said Polly in alarm. "But they're having trouble keeping it open."

"Well, this is great news," said Reuben.

"No, it's terrible news! They're an endangered species."

"They can't be, there's millions of the pricks. Shitting all over my beach."

"Reuben! You can't be serious. Neil can hear you."

"He's all right. The rest of them can get eaten by cats

for all I care. Hey, I want another cheese melt. These things are awesome. Get me another one!"

"Two won't be more awesome than one," said Polly, slightly horrified at his greed.

"Course they will," said Reuben, rubbing his hands cheerfully.

"No, look. Can't you donate to keep it open?"

"No," said Reuben. "I'll make them an offer for it, though. Hey, I could build a nice summer house there."

"A mile away from your actual house?"

"That would be just about right for my parents," said Reuben. "Although I could probably still hear them. Plus, I could have both beaches. Hell, yeah, I can see this coming together."

"Nooo," said Polly. "Huckle, tell him."

"I think I've known Reuben long enough to never try to tell him anything."

"Well why don't you buy it and move the sanctuary and put all the puffins somewhere else?" said Polly.

"What, and ruin someone else's beach house? Yeah, good luck with that, taking ninety-five years to get through court and ruining everybody's lives."

Reuben's second sandwich arrived and he fell on it with gusto.

"See," he said. "One is good, but more is better."

"Reuben!" said Polly in total dismay.

"What?" said Reuben. "I'm celebrating getting rid of those stinky puffins."

By the time they'd finished lunch, the light was fading and absolutely nobody was talking to Reuben. They made their goodbyes in silence, Polly hugging Kerensa for a long time. As they headed back along the cliff path, Huckle looked at Polly with concern. They were approaching the puffin sanctuary, and as if by unspoken agreement, they both turned toward the entrance.

The place was just closing up as they got down there. Bernie and Kara were walking round checking water levels and fencing to stop local wildlife getting at the birds.

"Hey," said Bernard.

"Hey there, is that Neil?" said Kara. "Hello, little fella!"

Neil, who'd seemed to sense where they were, had hopped out on to Polly's shoulder. Now he fluttered around the area cheerfully before returning to his perch, rubbing his head against her neck in case she was considering leaving him there again.

"Don't worry," she said, patting him reassuringly. "You're not going anywhere. You're staying here with me."

"*Eep,*" said the little puffin.

"How's it going?" Polly asked Bernard.

Bernard looked glum.

"We tried to organize some Christmas parties here," he said. "We thought maybe offices would like to come down, you know."

"Come down and look at birds in the cold?"

"Yeah," said Bernard. "For Christmas, like."

"In the dark and the cold? Look at birds on the sea?"

"We've got a café."

They had a horrible café, which sold cold greasy fish and chips to parties of schoolchildren under fluorescent lights. Polly looked at it.

"Hmm," she said.

She looked at Huckle, and Huckle looked at her.

The room itself was actually rather nice: classically proportioned, with big windows overlooking the rocks and the ocean; birds flying everywhere. It had horrible formica tables and chairs. Polly wondered what it would look like with great big long traditional wooden tables and benches. And fresh baking and . . .

She shook her head. That was ridiculous. She didn't want to expand. She couldn't.

She thought about Flora, about to finish her patisserie course. She thought about the number of young unemployed there were in Cornwall. She heaved a sigh.

Huckle glanced at her. Polly mentally shook herself.

"How much money," she said to Bernard, "do you need to see you through? If we could look at it again, maybe in the summer."

Bernard looked momentarily startled, then delighted. Polly worried in case he thought she was rich. People did when they saw the bakery. She bit her lip.

Bernard named a figure. "It'd take us through to the summer," he said weakly. "And then, hopefully, it'll pick up again with the season. Especially if we maybe changed our caterers . . ."

Polly blinked. It was a lot. It really was a lot.

She looked around the empty facility. The moon had come up—low, still, given the time of year, but it was a clear, cold evening, and the moonlight shimmered on the waves. Under the stars, slowly popping out even at this hour, she could see the birds dancing, whirring and diving in the sea, crossing the sky, the cold nothing to them with their heavy oiled wings. Up on the cliff there were nests on every available surface, thousands of birds banding together, chattering, diving, heading out for fish; small pufflings stamping up and down in that funny way they had that reminded Polly of toddlers wearing wellington boots.

She heaved a sigh and pulled out her phone.

"What are you doing?" said Huckle.

"I'm invoicing Reuben in advance for catering his Christmas," said Polly.

He read over her shoulder; it was the exact amount the puffin sanctuary needed. He took the phone off her and adjusted the total.

"What are you doing?" said Polly.

"It means we might get a holiday out of it," said Huckle, kissing her. "Cor, there's no messing about with you when you've got an idea in your head, is there?"

"Thanks for being so understanding," said Polly, nuzzling into him. "I don't deserve you."

"You don't," said Huckle. "But hey, here I am anyway. Dealing with the fact that my very, very, very busy fiancée has just taken on a massive extra job."

"Look on the bright side," said Polly. "If you sous-chef for me, you won't have to spend any time talking to Reuben's parents."

Chapter Twelve

The next few days passed in a blur. Polly engaged Selina, who had a tendency to get distracted but when she applied herself was perfectly capable, and taught her, painstakingly, how to turn out perfect buns and rolls and croissants, doing most of the prep herself and leaving the selling to Jayden, who was desperate for any scrap of overtime he could get.

He was still planning on buying a ring for Flora when she got back from college. Polly still thought they were far too young, but she didn't mention it. In fact she was slightly admiring. The idea of organizing anything as complex as a wedding was far too much for her to consider at the moment; Jayden's confident attitude was impressive in its own way.

She knew she ought to buy Huckle a present, but she didn't know when or how. Online stores didn't really deliver to Mount Polbearne without a hefty surcharge, and even when they did, it was still something of an ordeal to deal with Dawson complaining about having to heave stuff across the causeway, so the best thing to do was to go to a big town. She managed finally to sneak an afternoon off with Kerensa. She was going to attempt some shopping in Exeter so she could go and see her mother, too.

Polly was aware that her family was strange. Kerensa had been raised by her mother, Jackie, entirely on her own, and it had all worked out fine. She knew the circumstances of why her dad had left, and she even saw him from time to time. It was tough, but it was how it was.

It wasn't like that in Polly's house. There, a mysterious shroud of silence covered everything. Her grandparents, with whom they had lived when Polly was little, had stiffened if Polly ever mentioned her father, so she had learned early not to ask questions, although she'd been extremely curious.

And unlike Jackie, who had dated and eventually married a lovely man called Nish, for whom Polly and Kerensa had been giggly, rather naughty bridesmaids, Doreen had never moved on, nursing her parents until they'd died within six months of each other, using them as an excuse not to have a social life really, or have any friends of Polly's around. The house was always quiet. Not much changed there: the same cross on the wall; the same school picture of Polly at six, with her strawberry-blond hair and missing tooth, against a bright blue background; her mother's circled *Radio Times* in the tidy magazine rack beside the floral sofa.

It was school that had saved her. There was a local school that had been founded for orphans hundreds of years ago. Now it was a posh private school, but it still had a mission to take in fifty or so children missing a parent every year on scholarships. Her primary school had suggested it, and she'd managed to pass the exam.

The school itself was academic, backbitey, a tough environment with lots of clever children jostling to take first place. And the gulf between the paying pupils and the parentless charity cases was absolutely huge, socially unbridgeable.

But Polly soon found she didn't care about that, because in the intake of scholarship children she made so many friends, among them Kerensa. They became an almost impenetrable group who bonded closer than glue. They felt affinity with the young motherless princes; as they became teenagers they got drunk on Mother's Day and Father's Day in each other's basements; they looked out for one another and stuck together because they had all experienced something children shouldn't have to.

That was one of the reasons it had been so shocking for everyone when Polly had upped and moved to Cornwall. Thankfully Kerensa had moved too and kept in touch. It was also why what was happening now was so awful. If Reuben found out, and if he decided to have nothing to do with the baby, then the cycle would start again, and both Kerensa and Polly knew how much they wanted to break it.

And it was why Polly was finding it so very difficult to take the next step with Huckle.

The little red terrace was spotlessly clean as always. Frosties, her mother's cat, who was pure black with cream paws that looked like they'd been dipped in milk, was sitting on the windowsill behind the net, watching her carefully. She was not an affectionate cat. Polly thought her mum should get a little dog like the old ladies in Mount Polbearne, something that would jump up and down and yap and be happy to see her and give her enthusiastic licks and cuddles. But Frosties lived up to her name and treated her mother with a casual disdain, like much of the rest of the world.

Unlike Kerensa's mother, Doreen had never dated again, despite looking perfectly presentable for her age (and even if she hadn't, Polly thought, plenty of people found other partners later in life). Her existence had contracted to the local street, the church, the high street shops. Polly didn't know if it was a bad life, but it was certainly a small one. Her mother was scared of everything: the internet, public transport, people who weren't the same color as her, everything. In contrast, amongst Polly's peer group, they dared each other, expanded their horizons, traveled far. Because they knew life was fragile, they embraced it rather than retreated from it. And that had opened up a great chasm between Polly and her mother. She couldn't even ask, really, what her father had been like, or her mother would start to cry.

Best not to, then, all things considered.

So she nipped in quickly whilst Kerensa was in John Lewis, and said hello, and invited her mother to Reuben's for Christmas, and Doreen of course immediately declined. Then they sat in near silence, and Polly felt, as ever, how much there was to say and how little ever actually got said. She wanted to ask her mother, "Should I get married? Should I have a child? Is it worth it? What do you think? Would I manage it? Could I?"

But Doreen had nothing to say on the subject, and Polly didn't know how to ask.

Chapter Thirteen

The phone ringing at night was a horrible thing.

First of all it was so freezing, and only Polly would ever wake because Huckle was so used to her keeping weird hours late at night. So there was no point in her prodding him, even though statistically speaking it was far more likely to be his parents forgetting the time difference.

Also there was the panic factor. Already Polly could feel her heart beating far too fast. Phones shouldn't ring late at night unless you were expecting something nice, like your friend having a baby in Australia or something. Polly was not expecting anything like that.

She experimentally stretched her foot out of the bed. The cold air felt sharp, like a knife. She hoped they weren't going to get ice on the inside of the windows again. Neil had tried to sleep in the fireplace.

She made a grab for one of Huckle's enormous sweaters and leapt into some Ugg boots. She had a massive and, she felt, very valid objection to Ugg boots on aesthetic grounds—she had once seen a picture of a celebrity wearing them on what had looked like a really sweaty beach and had been opposed to them ever since—but the Cornish climate had somehow allowed them to worm their way in when Kerensa had given her a pair, seeing as she had six pairs and was feeling sorry for her poor relation. Kerensa looked fine in Ugg boots; she had legs like sticks. They did not suit, Polly felt, the more curvaceous lady.

However, they were very useful under the circumstances, she thought now as she ran down the cold stone stairs. One of these days she was going to miss a step and trip and slip all the way down, but for now she knew every inch of them; every missing lip and worn section where generations of lighthouse keepers' boots had marched patiently up and down.

The phone was not stopping. Probably not a wrong number then, she thought glumly. Her mum was all right, wasn't she? She'd seen her a couple of days ago, and it wouldn't be like her to be up after nine p.m., unless *Midsomer Murders* was on, a program Polly thought entirely unsuitable for her nervous mother, though she wouldn't be told.

The phone was an old-fashioned thing they'd inherited when they'd bought the property, with big buttons that used to connect it to the RNLI. It looked quite excitingly cool, like a sixties retro piece of spy kit, and had a satisfyingly deep bell, which now thrummed through Polly's chest like a chime of doom.

She picked up the receiver anxiously.

"Hello?"

The voice on the other end sounded tremulous and nervous. Polly desperately hoped they were about to ask her for a minicab so she could go back to bed. They didn't.

"Hello . . . is your name Polly Waterford?"

"Yes," said Polly, feeling a horrible ominous cold shiver run through her. "Who is this?"

"My name's Carmel."

The voice was shaky, but deep. The name meant nothing to Polly.

"I'm . . . I'm . . . a friend of your father's."

Her father. Polly flashed back to herself as a small child, asking her mother where her daddy was, drawing pictures of him at school, and being told that there was nothing to ask about; that they were a family and that was all that mattered, wasn't it?

And Polly would say of course, they were totally a family and it was all fine, anything to stop her mum from getting too upset, moving the subject on as quickly as she possibly could so as to keep things nice and calm and happy.

Then, as she got older, she would go into the kitchen and whip up yet another batch of bread, kneading the dough so furiously her knuckles went white.

She knew that her parents had been together very briefly and that her father had cut off contact before she'd been born; that he paid some money on the condition that he never saw her—something Polly found particularly difficult—and that Doreen often said she didn't want his stupid money, but of course they needed it nonetheless.

And that was all she knew about him. She didn't know where he lived, she didn't know what he looked like or what his relationship with her mother had been like. She had never received a letter or a present from him. She assumed he was just some Jack the Lad who'd come to town, had his fun and probably never given it another thought.

As she'd grown older, she had wondered why her mother had never met someone else. Doreen had only been twenty-four when Polly had been born—plenty of time to start again. People did it all the time. She didn't think her father had been abusive, and she knew they hadn't been married. It was like her mum was stuck on this thing that had happened to her when she was very young—a man had got her pregnant and hadn't stayed—as if this was 1884, not 1984.

Throughout her schooldays Polly had seen absolutely loads of her friends' parents remarry or couple up again—some more than once—with occasionally hair-raising results. But it had never happened to her mother.

When she was in her teens, she'd kind of gone looking for her father online, but every time she found someone who might be him—Tony Stephenson wasn't an uncommon name, after all; Waterford was her mother's name—she'd panicked and hadn't dared take it any further.

She didn't know what was out there; she didn't know what she might uncover. What if he had an entire family who looked like her but who he'd stayed with, who he loved? How would she feel about that? Would they even want to know her? Did she mean anything to him other than a long-forgotten direct debit? Did he ever think about her? Or was she just a night of fun he barely recalled, now too busy with all his other children having happy loud Christmases round the fire while she sat with her mum, her nana and occasionally her awkward Uncle Brian watching BBC One, as Nana didn't trust the other channels.

School had helped so much—she could pretty much

pretend he was dead, it didn't make much difference—
and then first pouring herself into the business with her
ex, Chris, and after that the amazing surprise of moving
somewhere so out of the way and finding so much happiness doing something as basic as baking bread for a
living, something she actually cared about: all of these
things had changed her beyond recognition and she had
been too busy living her own life and being an adult
to care any more. Sometimes, when she saw a father
tenderly pick up his daughter and carry her proudly on
his shoulders, she might feel a tiny pang, but it had been
going on too long now for it to hurt much. Some people got two parents, some started out with two and lost
one; everyone was different. But you couldn't lose what
you'd never had, and she wasn't going to let it get in the
way of her happiness.

Well, that was what she'd thought, until now; until
this telephone call.

"I'm so sorry," came the voice again. "It's just . . . I'm
afraid he's not well. And he's been asking for you."

Polly swallowed.

"Where are you?"

"Ivybridge."

Devon. No distance away, not at all. Basically just
up the road. All that time. He'd have seen her maybe;
in the *South West Post*, where they'd run an article last
year. Had he read it and thought about her? Or . . . well,
who knew?

"Whereabouts?" she stuttered.

"In the hospital, darling," said the tremulous voice.
"He's in the hospital in Plymouth."

Polly blinked. She felt a rush of emotion that at first she couldn't quite work out. Then she realized. It was part worry and sadness, but a lot of it was anger. How dare he come into her life right now, making emotional demands on her like this? How dare he?

There was a pause at the other end of the line. Then the voice again, which was sweet, with a Welsh tinge.

"I would . . . I'm sure he'd . . . Polly, I'm sorry. I would totally understand if you weren't in the least bit interested."

Polly's anger was growing.

"Who are you?" she asked, quite brusquely. Behind her she felt a touch on her shoulder. It was Huckle, groggy and confused-looking at the fierce expression on her face.

She pressed his hand with hers to let him know she appreciated it, then shooed him away with a serious look.

"I'm . . . I'm his wife," came the voice.

"Right," said Polly. "So he married you and you don't actually have a clue about him at all? He didn't bother to tell you any of this stuff when he finally grew up? That he already had a daughter? That didn't cross his mind?"

"No," said the woman. "No. We've been married . . ." There was a sob in her voice. "We've been married thirty-five years."

Two years longer than Polly had been alive. And then she understood.

Chapter Fourteen

It was 4:30 a.m. Polly would have been getting up shortly in any case. She was in two minds. She hadn't phoned her mum. She hadn't phoned anyone. She was in Huckle's arms, wishing she could just stay there forever and never have to move. His touch, his lovely smell tightly wrapped around her; it was the safest place in the world, the only place she wanted to be.

She laid her head against the golden hairs of his chest and sighed. Huckle knew about her dad, of course, or at least as much as she did, which wasn't much. His own family were noisy and affectionate, and apart from DuBose, his black sheep brother, they seemed nice and pretty normal, so she didn't know if he could possibly understand. It wasn't like losing a father, losing someone you loved. It was the weirdest sensation out there: that somebody, a person you didn't know, shared various things with you—Polly's unusual red-gold hair, for example, didn't come from her mother's side at all. You were half a person you'd never met.

Most of the time she never even thought about him.

Sometimes she did. But she'd never gone looking for him; never been particularly interested in trying to make up the pieces of the puzzle. She knew friends from school who had, and in general, they'd been severely disappointed, as well as upsetting the parent who'd actually brought them up. And it wasn't as if she had memories. He'd gotten her mother pregnant, that was all.

And now, somehow, he'd tracked her down—Huckle agreed with her that it was probably the piece in the paper they'd done last year; a nice journalist had come and asked all about the bread van Polly was running, and recommended it to everyone, and she had felt like quite the sensation for a week or so.

He must have seen it. That must have been it.

Polly blinked hard. She looked up into Huckle's eyes. "What do you think? Should I go and see him?"

Huckle shrugged. "It's up to you," he said.

Neil had woken and had stalked across the kitchen counters as he usually did, leaving floury footprints behind him. He jumped up on to Polly's shoulder, knowing instinctively as he always seemed to that she needed him there for comfort.

"Don't tell me that!" said Polly. "Tell me to do something one way or the other and that will help me decide!"

"Okay, well, I think you should go."

"I don't want to go! He never knew me! He never cared for me! Not a Christmas card, nothing!"

"Okay, don't go."

"But this might be my one chance to meet the only father I'm ever going to have!"

Huckle was still holding her tightly, even though Neil was breathing fish fumes in his face.

"Okay, so go."

"But I don't owe him anything! You know, my mother never moved house her entire life. He'd have known where to find her. I think that's *why* she never moved. And he never once bothered . . ."

Huckle nodded.

"No, you're right. Don't go."

Polly stood back.

"You are absolutely no use at all."

"I'm not, I know."

Polly breathed deeply.

"Okay," she said. "I know what I'm going to do."

"Toss a coin?"

"No," she said. "I'm going to get in the van and drive there. Then when I'm outside the hospital I'll see if I know what to do."

"You're putting it off? How does that even work?"

"I don't know," said Polly. "I'll figure it out as I drive. I'll call Jayden and wake him; he can get Selina down to cover the basics."

She grabbed her big parka and went to throw it on over her pajamas.

"I'm just saying," said Huckle carefully. "I'm just saying that if you decided to go in, you probably wouldn't want to be in your pajamas. But also if you want to, that is completely fine too."

"Gah," said Polly. "No, you're right."

While she ran upstairs to get changed, Huckle grabbed a clean shirt and washed in the sink.

"What?" she said when she came downstairs to find him dressed.

"I'll take you."

"What do you mean? No, I'll be fine. What if I change my mind? You'll lose an entire day."

"Yeah, right, for something that might actually be

quite important. You can change your mind. But I don't like you thinking about it whilst also sitting in traffic. I don't like that at all."

"You know if you're taking the bike . . ."

"I know, I know."

Neil loved the sidecar.

"I still might change my mind."

"Well, if you aren't changing it now, you'll need to get a move on. The tide is turning."

The tiniest glimmerings of dawn could be seen as they trundled across the treacherous causeway. It was strictly forbidden to cross it at night, but nobody paid the slightest bit of attention to that. Huckle steered the motorbike with its ancient burgundy sidecar carefully along the cobbles, the water lapping at the sides of the ancient narrow road.

It was freezing in the sidecar, even under the water-proof cover; Polly curled her fists into the sleeves of her sweater. Her hair was whipping out behind her under-neath the old-fashioned helmet. Neil didn't mind the cold, of course, and Huckle was concentrating on the slippery, treacherous road beneath them. She shrugged down further in her layers and gazed out toward the dawn, enjoying the sense of motion beneath her and the quiet emptiness of the road ahead. Not quite empty, of course; this early in the morning there were tractors and farmers out and about; milkmen and postmen and, of course, bakers. The lighthouse flashed behind them—Polly hardly noticed it these days—then switched itself off as the pink spread across the sky and the morning was fully there.

It was too noisy to speak, but occasionally Huckle

would turn his head to the left as if to check on how she was doing, and she would blink back to indicate that she was all right and he would power on.

But was she? She sat rigid in the sidecar, trying to examine herself to see what she actually thought. Was this all connected? she wondered. The way she kept brushing Huckle off whenever he tried to talk to her about children. She kept telling him they were too poor, or too busy . . . but was that true? Or was it all down to the fact that she didn't know how to be part of a family? Not a full one anyway. She didn't know how a father should be.

She had a nasty memory, suddenly, from out of the blue. When she was very small, hardly older than Year 1, she had developed a huge pash for the school janitor and had to be told not to throw her arms around him or follow him about. Even at that tender age, she had been hopelessly humiliated as the head teacher had spoken gently but firmly to her mother, telling her to make sure it didn't happen again.

What had that been, she wondered now, but a sublimated desire to attach herself to a father figure?

And every dead end in her heart; every time she'd stopped thinking about it, or cut herself off. Had it changed things? Made them go away? Of course not. Just because she stopped herself spending a lot of time dwelling on things, that didn't mean they had disappeared. She was just putting off confronting them for another day, and then another.

And now that day was here.

She realized that part of her felt flattered, oddly vindicated. As if, yes, you *did* think about me. It *did* matter to you, whatever you said or didn't say, however much you didn't pay me any mind or make contact. I was there all the time. I did exist for you. I was real in your eyes.

Although did that matter in the end?

Her heart was beating dangerously fast.

She had to see him. Didn't she? But what kind of a state would he even be in? Perhaps he was raving. Completely crazy.

And what would her mother say? This terrible thing, this elephant in the room, how would they move beyond it? Perhaps Polly wouldn't tell her. Yet would that not just add to the family secrets that bore down on them so heavily, that kept her mother's heart so sad even after all these years?

She sighed out loud, but Huckle didn't hear her. The sun was up properly now. It was going to be a ravishing English winter's day, the sun slowly rising over fields carpeted with frost; beasts turned out in the fields; a pause in the beat of the farming year as the world held its breath, waiting for Christmas, the darkest, quietest time—or at least it was meant to be—followed by the full bursting of spring. It was quite lovely.

They could go somewhere else: watch the cold crashing waves; find a deserted out-of-season hotel; eat scones in front of a roaring fire. Jayden already had the shop covered, and it didn't take much to persuade Huckle to bunk off. They could just have a lovely day, the two of them.

But how could she, when all she'd be thinking about was this?

Instead, they neared the busy outskirts of Plymouth, already clogged with angry-looking commuters—was it worse, Polly thought, commuting to work on a mucky day or a beautiful one? She hadn't ever thought about it when she used to drive to the graphic design office she ran with Chris. It was traffic and parking and fuss. It was what it was. Nowadays she ran thirty meters along a cobbled promenade with trays of warm buns in her arms; that was her commute.

She looked at the angry drivers, most of whom turned to stare at the motorbike—it garnered attention wherever they went. They looked stressed, their shoulders and bodies tense over the steering wheel; groups of noisy, disruptive schoolchildren in the back; radios blaring.

It was funny, she reflected. When she thought about how tough it was working for yourself—the long hours, the paperwork, the worries that kept you up at night—she never considered that she no longer had to get to work, and how grateful she was for that.

They queued through the traffic and finally turned in to the hospital. There was nowhere to park, but Huckle popped them up on a grass verge: nobody minded a motorbike, even if it was as wide as a small car. He stilled the engine, and suddenly the world became a lot quieter.

Polly started to shake. She felt incredibly sick. She should have eaten before they left. Or maybe that would have been worse. Huckle blinked. Even his blinking, Polly thought sometimes, was kind.

"Well?" he said in that slow drawl she loved so much. "Whadya reckon?"

She sat there, not moving. Huckle didn't feel the need to fill the silence, or indicate what he'd rather do either way. He was perfectly happy to wait, or to come, just as she needed him. Although if he'd heard her plan to take the day off and have a picnic, he'd probably have liked that the best.

Finally Polly turned to him, her face pale and anxious.

"We're . . . I mean. I suppose. We're here now," she said.

Huckle shrugged. "That doesn't matter."

"But I don't . . . I don't know what I'm supposed to

do. I don't know what I'm supposed to feel. Three hours ago I thought I didn't have a dad, or rather that it didn't matter. Three hours ago my life was totally happy."

"Well that's good to hear," said Huckle, politely not mentioning the snit she was in about Christmas, or the puffin sanctuary.

"But now . . . I mean, everything's been turned upside down."

"*Eep*," said Neil.

"Thanks," said Polly. Huckle tried not to roll his eyes.

Stiffly Polly pulled herself out of the sidecar. It wasn't the easiest of maneuvers. She stretched her legs.

"Well?" said Huckle.

"Well," said Polly. "Nothing ventured."

"You're very brave."

"I'm an idiot."

"Do you want me to come?"

"Yes. No. Yes. No."

"Don't start this again."

Polly heaved a sigh.

"I feel this is something I need to find out by myself. Maybe. In case it all goes wrong."

"Okay." Huckle nodded. "Oh," he said. "Look. I know this isn't exactly the time, but . . . I bought you something. Well, something I owed you. Selina made it for me. Well. For you. For us."

Polly blinked.

"What do you mean?"

He handed her a little box.

"I was going to keep it for Christmas. But I decided I couldn't."

"When did you decide this?" said Polly.

"Five minutes ago," said Huckle. "When you couldn't decide anything, I decided something."

Polly took the box and opened it gently.

It was a beautiful engagement ring. Silver, the metal carved so that it looked like a tiny twist of seaweed; exactly what he'd proposed with in the first place. It was quirky and precious and entirely them, and suddenly Polly loved it more than anything in the world.

"Oh!" she said, slipping it on. It fit perfectly. "I love it," she said.

"It goes very well with . . . whatever it is you're wearing." Polly had gotten dressed in a hurry.

She kept staring at the ring, her eyes full of tears.

"You're part of my life," she said, slowly. "The most important part. Maybe you should come after all."

"The thing I love most about you," said Huckle, "is your decisiveness."

She didn't smile, just kept staring at the ring, shaking her head. Then, finally, "Okay, stay," she said. "Look after Neil. I'll call you if I need you."

Huckle pulled her forward, and she buried her face in his chest once more.

"Are you sure?"

She nodded and attempted a weak smile.

"And if I come out shouting GUN IT!, we break for the border, okay?"

"Okay," said Huckle.

He watched her small frame disappear into the vast hospital, looking very alone. Her head was held high; you wouldn't have known from looking at her the turmoil she was in. That's my girl, he thought.

Neil *eep*ed inquiringly.

"I don't know either," said Huckle. And he left the bike on the grass verge and went off in search of coffee.

Chapter Fifteen

It was slightly absurd, Polly thought as she looked out for Carmel, who'd said she'd be waiting for her by the entrance, that it had never crossed her mind that she might be black. Too long living out in the country, no doubt. It didn't matter, though, as the soft-voiced woman with the very short hair came directly toward her. Her face was drawn.

"Sorry. Sorry, are you . . . are you Polly?"

That was it, Polly thought later. The final chance; her last opportunity. She could have lied, could have said no, sorry, you must have someone else in mind. She could simply have turned around, walked back out into the exquisite December morning.

The woman's hands were trembling, Polly noticed. Trembling almost as much as her own, which she'd jammed into her jeans pockets.

She cleared her throat.

"Yes," she said quietly. "Yes, I am."

The hospital was vast. Endless pale, identically lit corridors. It reminded Polly oddly of a ship, crewed by men and women in green scrubs and white tops, sailing— well, where? From birth to death, she supposed. Traveling on. Pregnant women walked slowly up and down, interspersed with the elderly; people were wheeled around, some missing limbs, many pale and gray-faced. Carmel didn't seem to notice. But then she wasn't desperately trying to hang back as Polly was; wasn't trying to spin out time before some kind of reckoning had to be met.

"He saw you in the paper," said Carmel. "He stared at it for ages. I didn't know what was up with him."

She looked at Polly, really looked at her. Then she laughed.

"What is it?" said Polly, thrown. She twiddled her new ring, a talisman to remind herself that things weren't so bad, no matter how strange the situation she found herself in.

"You . . . I mean, it's undeniable. Do you remember when Boris Becker had a baby in a broom cupboard?"

Polly didn't say anything, and Carmel's face dropped.

"I'm so sorry, love. I'm just nervous." She swallowed hard. "I knew I'd say the wrong thing. I'm so sorry. I'm . . ."

She looked at Polly again, then turned her face away, shaking her head.

"You see, until the paper . . . and until he got sick the first time . . . I had absolutely no idea you existed."

Polly hadn't wanted to hear it, but there it was. She was invisible. She had been airbrushed out of his life completely, just as she had always thought. She came to a halt in the middle of the corridor.

"You didn't know?"

Carmel stopped beside her.

"No. Not until two weeks ago."

"You never knew anything about me?"

Carmel shook her head. "I thought he told me everything." She paused. "Turned out I was wrong."

"What did he say?"

Carmel sighed. "Oh Polly, I wouldn't want to . . . I mean, your mum . . ."

"Forget about my mum," said Polly, shaking with anger. "*He* did. Tell me. What did he say?"

"He said it was a one-night stand," said Carmel. "He was a traveling sales rep. He said it had just happened . . ." She gave Polly a look. "We were married very young. He traveled about. His family . . . They didn't want him to marry me in the first place. Things were a bit different back then."

Polly nodded.

"He calmed down, you know. After the children. He just got married young and he was a good-looking chap, and there was a lot of opportunity . . ."

It sounded like she was trying to convince herself.

"My mum was not an *opportunity,*" said Polly, with barely concealed fury.

Healthcare workers and patients were having to move around them, standing stock still in the middle of the floor.

Carmel shrugged.

"No. No. I'm sorry. I'm saying the wrong thing again. You're right. It was just . . . I'm so sorry. I think it was just one of those things that happened."

"*I'm* just one of those things that happened?"

"Oh dear," said Carmel. "I'm making things worse. I'm sorry. You have to realize this was as much of a shock to me as it is to you. And when he saw you in the paper . . . He'd been ill already, and he just gave the biggest sigh. Like it was a weight on his chest. I have never known a man to apologize so much."

Polly blinked in fury.

"I imagine there was probably more than an apology back then," she spat. "He probably offered to get rid of me."

Carmel stared straight ahead.

"I don't know," she said.

Polly thought back to her mother's face: so perpetually weary, disappointed in the world. She tried to imagine what must have happened when Doreen had realized she was pregnant. Did she go to the doctor? Twenty years old, but so sheltered, still living at home; she must have been terrified.

Did she turn up at his work when she found out? Did she go around to his house, to be met by this gorgeous, immaculately groomed woman, and bottle it? Did she trail home afterward, tears running down her face, all her hopes and dreams for the future gone, exploded in one night's madness? One night Polly's so-called father professed to barely remember? A night that meant exactly what she had always suspected: nothing. Nothing at all. *She* meant nothing.

"No," she said suddenly, bile rising in her throat. "No. I can't do this. I can't."

And she turned around in the middle of the gleaming corridor and ran out against the flow of humanity pouring in; flew outside to the beautiful freezing winter's day.

Huckle had just gotten his cup of coffee, and was sitting feeding bits of a very poor croissant to Neil and enjoying the sunlight when he saw Polly, half blinded with tears, her red hair glinting, tearing down the hospital steps like a rushing wind, and stood up to catch her.

"Did you see him?" he said, and she shook her head mutely, dampening the shoulder of his jacket. He didn't mind.

"It's okay," he said, over and over again. "It's okay."

He didn't say anything else at all, just calmly helped her into the sidecar, tucked her in and stuck Neil under the cover with her, where he curled up and went to sleep on her lap, which helped as much as anything anyone could ever say. Then he drove them back carefully all the way to Cornwall, and Polly stared out at the glorious frosty winter day, watching the leaves drift across the road and wishing with all her heart that this had never happened, that she could undo it all, that she didn't have to remember the look of awkward, terrified kindness on Carmel's face.

Chapter Sixteen

Ooh, those are beautiful," said old Mrs. Larson a few days later. Polly was looking critically at her Christmas twists: little branches shaped like holly and made of raisin and cinnamon pastry, with a mincemeat filling. They were delicious; incredibly rich but very easy to make. She was going to make plenty for Reuben's family to keep them going, and a bunch more for the wretched Christmas fair that was coming up on Saturday, but for now she had gathered a little boxful together and was heading off to visit her mum. It had to be done.

She was going to take Kerensa with her; she'd be a good distraction. Well, normally she was a good distraction, talking nineteen to the dozen and cheering everybody up, though at the moment, of course, she was very turned in on herself and secretly googling things like "intra DNA tests" and crying about Jeremy Kyle. Reuben, in his usual busy, distracted state, either didn't notice or insisted everything was going to be tremendous and fine, which didn't help matters in the slightest.

Plus Kerensa was genuinely huge now, huffing around the place constantly uncomfortable.

They pulled up in front of Doreen's neat little council terrace, where Polly had grown up. The houses were a mixture of local authority and bought. You could always tell the bought, of course; they painted their front doors. Despite everything, it had been a happy place to grow up. Doreen hadn't minded Polly running in and out of the house; playing endless games of skipping at the neighbors' and watching *Top of the Pops* at her friends' on summer evenings; buying ice creams from the van and making toast. It was a happy place for Polly; it had taken a long time for her to realize it was a sad place for her mother, that she had had different hopes.

Doreen had been so proud of Polly for going to university—and so disappointed when she had downgraded her office job to work in a bakery, of all things. It didn't matter how much Polly explained that she was miles happier now, that she felt incredibly lucky to work in the lovely environment that she did, with the lovely people she knew. As far as Doreen was concerned, it was inexplicable; living in a lighthouse was a ridiculous idea, and all in all, given how much she had sacrificed to raise Polly all by herself, the fact that she would throw it all away on some cakes, an American without a proper job and a bird was a source of some sadness.

Polly sighed. Where she'd grown up didn't bring her down, but Doreen could.

"Let's get her drunk," said Kerensa, who had admired Polly's ring, then gotten slightly upset. Reuben bought her lots of jewelry, and currently she couldn't bear to wear any of it. "Seriously. Get her drunk. Then she'll talk."

"You just want to infect people with the stuff you can't do," said Polly.

Doreen very rarely drank. She didn't approve and thought that Polly and Kerensa's cheerful Pinot Grigio habit (when Kerensa wasn't pregnant) was a sign of weak character.

"Pretend it's fruit juice or spritzer or something. It's the only way." Kerensa looked sadly at the two bottles she'd insisted they buy. "I wish *I* could get drunk. Get drunk and think about something bloody else."

Polly patted her shoulder sympathetically.

"Listen," she said. "You don't know. Nobody knows. Don't worry about it. This baby will come out and everyone will love it and find things in it that look exactly like Reuben and you'll be overcome with love and everything will be totally fine and you'll be a family. Honestly. You have to think that."

"What if it comes out with one of those big dark eyebrows that meet in the middle?" said Kerensa. "Oh God. Oh God. What was I thinking? Seriously, if I ever have a stupid night of stupid pointless passion ever again— which I won't if I'm lucky enough to get away with this, which I don't deserve to, don't point it out, nobody is beating me up more than I'm beating myself up, believe me . . ."

"Yes?" said Polly.

"Well, just make sure it's with a short ginger guy with freckles," said Kerensa in despair.

"I'll keep a tight grip on you if we ever go to Scotland," said Polly as they stood in front of the immaculate door. "Okay, come on."

"What's the game plan?" said Kerensa.

"Now you ask me," said Polly. "I don't know. You just pour the wine and we'll take it from there."

"Nothing can go wrong," said Kerensa.

Doreen opened the door in her usual cautious way, as if worried about who would be there, even though they were expected.

"Did you bring that bird?" she said nervously. Polly had introduced Doreen to Neil once. It hadn't gone well. Doreen had asked Polly where he pooed and Polly had said oh he wears a nappy and Doreen had believed her and then looked anxious when she realized he didn't.

"No, Mum," said Polly, giving her a kiss on her dry cheek and handing over the box.

"What's this?"

"They're Christmas twists. I'm trying them out."

"Also, we have wine!" said Kerensa, waving the bottle. "Quick, Doreen, where are the glasses?"

Doreen was fond of Kerensa, if occasionally a bit intimidated.

"You look huge, Kerensa," she said bluntly as Kerensa sidled over to get glasses.

"Uh, yeah, thanks," said Kerensa shortly. She didn't like people pointing out how big her bump was. It just made her think even more that there was some six-foot hairy Brazilian in there. "It's mostly water retention."

"What did you do, swallow a swimming pool?" said Doreen. Polly and Kerensa exchanged glances. This wasn't like Doreen; she seemed very light-hearted.

"So, Pauline, how are things at the bakery?"

Polly resisted the temptation to roll her eyes. She

hated the name Pauline. It made her sound thirty years older than she was. Or rather, there was nothing wrong with the name; it just didn't suit her. She felt like Doreen and Pauline were contemporaries, not mother and daughter. She longed for the pretty names her friends had: Daisy and Lily and Rosie. Even Kerensa was old and local and traditional. Pauline just sounded gray and dutiful. Doreen's father, Polly's grandfather, had been called Paul. So it seemed they'd picked her name with the least effort imaginable.

Polly knew this wasn't really the case. She knew her mum loved her. Just that she found it difficult to show.

The mince pie bites were delicious, but it was Kerensa who was truly wicked, topping up Doreen's glass whenever she so much as looked away.

Doreen got up to bring "tea"—a reheated (but still frozen in the middle) shop-bought pie and some nasty plain salad with no dressing: large slices of droopy-looking tomato, over-thick cucumber and wilted lettuce that was all stalk. Kerensa looked at it in horror. Polly was used to it and didn't mind so much. There was a reason she'd rushed out to teach herself to bake as soon as she'd been old enough to turn on the oven.

Doreen, unaccustomed to drinking, loosened up after her second glass and got quite giggly by her third.

"Well, of course when *I* was pregnant," she said suddenly, and Polly stiffened. It wasn't a period of her life she ever spoke about. Kerensa squeezed Polly's knee in a kind of "I told you so" excited way.

"Yes?"

Doreen pursed her lips as if to stop herself talking.

"Well, things were different then."

"No, no, go on," said Kerensa, wielding the wine bottle. "Tell me. I want to know everything. Did you cry every day and feel like a heffalump?"

"Well, I was never as big as you," said Doreen.

"Yeah, all right, thanks."

"But yes," she said. "I cried every day. But it's different for you. You've got a happy family and lots of money and you're going to live happily ever after. It was just me and my Pauline, wasn't it, love?"

"And Nana and Gramps," said Polly awkwardly.

"Yes, yes. But you know," Doreen sighed, "I sat in that maternity ward—they used to keep you in for days then—and Nana and Gramps would visit, but my friends didn't, not really. Well, I didn't have a lot of friends really. Just a few people from school, and the women I knew at Dinnogs, and they disapproved, of course. Even though it was the 1980s, when you think things might have eased up a bit . . . no, not at Dinnogs. I think they're trapped in the fifties even now. Not that I would ever shop there again. Never. Not in a million years." She took another sip of wine, her face pink.

Polly looked around the room, immaculate from the net curtains to the identically matching floral three-piece suite. There on the mantelpiece was her Year 1 photo, one tooth missing, her hair a brighter red then before it had softened into strawberry blond, freckles cheerfully scattered across her face. She looked like Pippi Longstocking. And there on the wall was her degree certificate from the University of Southampton—Polly hadn't wanted it particularly, so here it was, displayed, even though her mother received so few visitors. And she knew that upstairs, her old bedroom was still just as it had always been, her bed made up just in case she ever wanted to come home.

It didn't matter that sometimes they couldn't communicate, that her mother had never, perhaps, been as naturally warm as she thought other families might be.

This was still home. It always had been.

Suddenly she didn't want to throw this bomb in here. Didn't want to disrupt her mother's careful, sheltered life any more than she had to. Yet she had to say something. Ever since Carmel's phone call, the only thing she'd been able to think about was the man dying in a hospital bed not too far from here. A man who was her biological father. Not her father in any meaningful sense, but a part of her nonetheless. And there was only one person on earth who could tell her the right thing to do.

Kerensa emptied yet more wine into Doreen's glass. She wouldn't have been this squiffy in years; she kept giggling and had gone very red in the face.

"Tell me what it's like," said Kerensa. "You know I don't have anyone. My mum says she can't remember, and Polly is absolutely no use at all."

"Oh, it was so long ago," said Doreen.

"It wasn't *that* long ago," said Polly.

"Tell us!" said Kerensa.

"Well . . ." said Doreen.

Kerensa, with some lack of grace, got carefully to her feet.

"I'll just wash up," she said, winking at Polly. "I'm still listening!"

"No, no, I'll do that," flapped Doreen, but without making any real effort to get up. Kerensa gave Polly a stern look and another hefty wink.

"Now," she hissed.

Polly refilled her own glass and leaned forward.

"Mum," she said.

"Doesn't Kerensa look blooming!" her mother was saying. "Oh, her mother is so lucky. How I'd have loved a grandchild. She's fallen right on her feet, hasn't she? Although I'd never have thought that little chap would have it in him!"

She giggled, then hiccuped. Polly realized she'd need to be quick, before her mother fell asleep at the table.

"Mum," she said. "Mum. I need to ask you about my dad."

She'd said it before, of course. But this time she wasn't going to be fobbed off.

Doreen rolled her eyes and poured herself another glass. There was a long silence.

"That rat bastard," she said finally.

Polly had never heard her mother swear in her life.

"Well?" she said. "Please. Can you tell me a little more? Please? It's important."

"Why?" said her mother. "Why now?"

Polly thought for a moment.

"Well, if Huckle and I are going to get married . . . then we might have a baby . . ."

"Oh please," said her mother. "You've been engaged for months and haven't even bothered to book a date or tell people what's happening. I don't think you can pin him down at all. He doesn't seem that fussed."

This wasn't the time to tell her it was Polly who had cold feet, and that this was why.

"Just tell me about Tony," she said. "What was he like?"

Her mother sighed, staring into her glass.

"I don't feel very well," she announced. This was a

common tactic. Polly was meant to drop the subject now and start asking after her mother's health. Doreen could discuss her health issues for several hours at a time. One time they'd been walking down the high street and Polly was sure she had seen her GP hiding inside a shoe shop.

"You're fine," said Polly. "You can go to bed in just a minute. But first, please . . . You owe me, Mum. I can't . . . I don't feel I can take the next step in my life without knowing. Without knowing more."

She felt bad lying like this. But she had to know.

Her mother blinked.

"Well," she said. Then she sighed again. "Your hair," she said, setting down her glass. "Your hair. That's exactly what his was like. And you know, lots of women, they don't like a sandy-haired man. I don't know why. I thought it was beautiful. Absolutely beautiful. It shone in the sunlight, and his freckles . . . they were like golden dots. I wanted to . . . I wanted to kiss them all."

She laughed, harshly and suddenly. "Listen to me." She shook her head. "Ridiculous."

"No it's not," said Polly. "Really it isn't."

"People think the eighties wasn't very long ago," said Doreen. "That things weren't that different. But I'll tell you, they were. Do you know, when Lady Diana Spencer got married, they sent her to see a doctor to see if she was a virgin or not. And they told people that; everybody knew. It was official. She went to see the official royal doctor and he said she was a virgin. In the eighties. SO."

Polly stayed silent, willing her mother just to carry on talking.

"I was on hats," said Doreen. "Well, hats and gloves really, but it was the hats I liked. At Dinnogs. For weddings, mainly, and Christmas felts in winter. Men wore more hats then. People wore more hats then. Central heating ruined everything."

This was obviously going off at a bit of a tangent, but Polly decided to ignore it and topped up her mother's glass again.

"So he used to come in . . . you'd always notice him. He was tall, like you. Thinner than you, though." She smiled. "He'd come in and look at the hats and chat to me . . . Well, he was a sales rep, he did a lot of business upstairs. Curtain material, that kind of thing. He'd always hover round the door. They put the pretty girls near the door, just to get the chaps in, you know." She blushed. "The young girls, anyway."

"You were lovely, Mum," said Polly loyally. In the very few photographs they had from that time, her mother had a Human League haircut and funny pointy shoulder pads.

"So he'd go upstairs, then he'd come down and talk about hats, and once . . ." She went an even brighter red. "Once he asked me to help him try on some leather gloves. He had . . . he had the most beautiful hands." She bit her lip. "It was the most romantic thing that had ever happened to me. The boys round my way, all farm boys . . . well, I wasn't interested, I really wasn't. I mean, he seemed so sophisticated. Well, he was twenty-three years old. Anyway, he asked me out and we went to a snug. That was the bit in a pub where women could go; they still had those in the eighties, you know."

"It seems a million years ago."

"It was! We smoked inside!"

Polly smiled. "Whoa."

"So we smoked Regal King Sizes, and I had half a cider and black and he drank a couple of pints, and he told me about life on the road and his car—he had a Ford Escort, he loved it."

Polly nodded.

"It was . . . it was the best night of my life. And he didn't try anything on, he really didn't. He gave me a lift home in his car. Then he came in the next week. And the next."

Suddenly Doreen's face sagged and she looked terribly sad.

"He just seemed so nice. I was twenty. I thought this was it. You met a boy you liked, he liked you, that was it, you got married, that was how it was then. None of this wandering about until you're in your thirties thinking you've got all the time in the world, then getting all panicky about it."

Polly ignored this.

"And he met my mum and dad, you know, it was all totally above board . . . they thought he was charming. And so handsome with that lovely hair. Of course you heard jokes about traveling salesmen, but I didn't think it would apply to Tony. More fool me."

There was a pause.

"I walked in to Dinnogs one morning, and it was so strange. As if I could feel something in the air. Lydia by the perfume station, she barely looked up, and normally you couldn't get five yards without her squirting something all over you. And Mrs. Bradley was standing there with a face like fizz. She had one of those monobosoms . . . you never see those any more, do you? I suppose she wore a corset. They're a dying breed . . ."

Polly held her breath. This was all new to her. She leaned forward ever so slightly, desperate not to startle her mother into clamming up again.

"And there she was." Doreen shook her head. "You know," she said, with a wondering tone, "you know, she was colored! Sorry, black. Sorry. I don't know what to say these days." She paused. "I wouldn't . . . I mean, I wouldn't have been surprised nowadays. But it was different then, it really was. I mean, we weren't in London, or Birmingham. This was the south-west of England. It was really white . . . I'm just making excuses now."

She breathed out again.

"She had a big belly on her. So. That was a lot to take in right then. And one in me, although I didn't know it, of course. That damn Ford Escort. Anyway. At first I didn't take her seriously, her standing there saying Tony's her husband and to leave him alone. I really didn't. She was screaming and shouting and I just got the security guard to ask her to leave."

She stared at the floor, bright red.

"Oh God, Polly. Oh God. I've never told anyone that. I never have. Things were different . . . Oh Polly."

The tears were coursing down her cheeks now, and Polly put her arm around her.

"It was just wrong that got wrong that got wrong. He did me wrong and I did her wrong, and then, well, you came along and I reckon we all did you wrong too."

Polly shook her head.

"You didn't. You didn't, I promise."

"I called him—no luck. No chance. There weren't mobile phones then, and I couldn't email him or Facebook. Then I tracked down his mam and dad; they were in the book."

She shook her head.

"They were pleased to see me. It had been quite the family scandal when he'd met . . . now what was her name . . ."

Polly was half crying and trying to comfort her mother and feeling awful and slightly drunk as well, otherwise she wouldn't for a moment have said what she said.

"Carmel," she supplied, without thinking.

Kerensa, who'd been shuffling unobtrusively in the kitchen, carefully listening in on absolutely everything, materialized like a bouncy ball in the middle of the floor.

"Coffee!" she bustled. "I think we all need some coffee! Doreen, you need a coffee machine in there. Man cannot survive on granules alone, especially when you're up the duff and only allowed one cup a day. It might as well be decent."

Doreen was staring at Polly in horror.

"You've seen her."

Polly swallowed, desperately wishing there was a way out of this, but not knowing what it was.

"She just . . . she rang me," she said. "I'm sorry. I didn't do anything. I just . . . I just wanted to know a bit more."

"So, what, are you friends?!" Doreen's eyes were wide with shock.

"No. She just . . . she said . . ."

Polly bit her lip with how much she didn't want to say what she was about to say.

"He's very ill. And he wanted to see me."

The color drained from Doreen's face. She was stone-cold sober now.

"And did you?"

"No," said Polly. "I wanted to talk to you first."

"So that's reasonable, isn't it?" said Kerensa. "That's the best thing to do in families, isn't it? Talk everything out?"

Polly shot her a look.

Doreen's hand was at her mouth.

"This is exactly why," she said, "I tried to keep this stuff away from you. All the horrible, bad stuff. I was just trying to protect you."

"But he paid money all those years!" protested Polly.

"Oh, I let you think that, of course. Let you think he cared. It was his parents. They'd rather have had me than her. That's all it was. Their guilt money." She practically spat.

Polly blinked, tears brimming at her eyes.

"So you walking in, dropping these bombs about reuniting with your father . . ."

"I wasn't! I'm not!"

"I haven't seen him since he got what he wanted and disappeared," said Doreen. "Didn't give a toss for the consequences. Not a toss. Knew where I lived. Didn't care."

She stood up.

"But well done for raking everything up again. Well done for reminding me of how I messed up. Ruined my life."

Polly jumped up and stepped toward her mother.

"Um, we should go, maybe?" said Kerensa.

"You should," said Doreen.

"Are you going to be all right?" said Polly, reaching out, but her mother turned away and wouldn't look at her.

"Nobody asked me that then," she said. "I don't know why you're bothering to ask now."

Chapter Seventeen

So," said Kerensa, after they'd driven some way in silence. It was getting late; the air was misting up and it was turning even colder. "That went well."

Polly winced through her sobs.

"Oh God," she said. "Oh God. Tell me that wasn't as awful as I think it was."

"Well, it could have gone worse."

"How? How could that have gone worse, Kerensa?"

"Um, a huge monster could have burst through the front window and wreaked bloody havoc everywhere. Zombie apocalypse? Nuclear bomb?"

There was a long silence.

"Oh Lord."

Polly checked her phone. She'd texted her apologies immediately but didn't expect to hear back, and she hadn't.

"Well, look on the bright side. She wasn't coming for Christmas anyway."

"Kerensa! How's that meant to cheer me up?"

"What do you want me to do?"

"I don't know."

Polly leaned her head against the cool glass of the window pane, a tear running down her face.

"Oh God, she really thought I'd been running around with my dad, playing happy families with Carmel."

They drove on in silence.

"Can I say something?" said Kerensa.

"Something more? More than you would usually just say?"

"Yeah."

"I can't imagine what it might be."

"No, listen, right. I don't want to diss your mum, but honestly, if you wanted to see your dad, and she'd point-blank refused to talk about him but spent a lot of time being miserable about it and putting the misery kind of on to you . . . I did ask permission to say this, by the way."

"Yeah, right, I get that," said Polly.

"Well. Honestly, I kind of think it's your business. It's your dad. He may have been an awful one . . . he may not have told his wife he even had another kid, although she obviously knew something was going on . . ."

"I bet it wasn't the first time," said Polly.

"Or the last," said Kerensa. "Traveling bloody salesmen! Ha! That's probably where they get their reputation."

Polly sighed.

"You see what I mean, though?" said Kerensa, as they pushed on through the harsh winter night. "You do know a little more now. But also, if you want to see him—if you want anything to do with him—well, it's up to you. You don't have to ask permission. Your mum . . . she needs to get over it."

"But she's so upset."

"I've known you a long time," said Kerensa. "And you know what? I don't think I've ever known your mum not upset about *something*. I think that's why you're so cheery all the time."

Polly was barely listening. She couldn't help thinking how happy her mother must have been when she got the job at Dinnogs; her mum, who'd left school without many qualifications; who'd been the pride of her family when she'd landed such a posh job.

She'd lost it of course when she'd gotten pregnant; Polly knew that much. They'd said it was because of cutbacks and that people were buying fewer hats, but Doreen had known the truth: even in the eighties, being an unmarried mother carried a certain stigma. She'd slunk home, defeated before she'd even begun. And Polly had been paying the price ever since.

"You remember Loraine Armstrong?" said Kerensa, apropos of nothing.

Polly nodded. Loraine's mum had been a young single mother too, and the pair had elicited snotty remarks and sidelong glances when they went clubbing together and to pubs, her mum often insisting to strangers after a couple of drinks that they looked more like sisters than mother and daughter. Doreen had always found them horrific.

"I reckon they had a better time than you guys did."

Polly reflected on it.

"I do too," she said finally. "Oh Lord. Take me home."

As they approached Mount Polbearne, Kerensa fell silent. Polly, roused from her own deep thoughts, glanced across at her.

"What's on your mind?"

Kerensa swallowed.

"Do you think that's what Reuben would be like? If . . . you know. If he found out."

"You still don't know for sure," said Polly. Kerensa stroked her huge bump, a sad look on her face. She could barely reach the steering wheel. She looked at Polly.

"Seriously. You don't know how badly I was ovulating that night. It was one of those times of the month where you'd fancy a tramp."

Polly nodded. They sat in silence.

"Because if he found out . . . I mean, I don't know what he'd do."

"You mean—God forbid—the baby would have to grow up like me?" said Polly.

"No!" said Kerensa. "That's not what I meant at all. And anyway," she added, "that would be a good thing."

Polly sighed crossly.

"It wouldn't be a good thing," she said eventually. "You're going to have to tough it out. You absolutely are."

Kerensa looked at her.

"What if it's born with a thick black moustache?"

"Like we said before, invent an Italian grandfather or something. I mean it. Sort it out. Do it."

"You can't tell Huckle. You can't."

Polly was still in two minds about it. It felt such a horrible dilemma. She wanted to tell him everything. But he was Reuben's best friend. His best man. The only reason Kerensa had met Reuben in the first place. Yet he was also Polly's other half, her fiancé. It was horrible. She didn't know how he'd react—she didn't know if he would even know himself. Could she risk it? Sometimes she thought that of course she could, it would be fine, but there was always a chance that it might not be. And then where would they all be?

Deep down she suspected it might be something only another woman would understand. A mistake on this level, something that would affect your whole life.

Huckle understood things. He was amazing. But could anybody understand this happening to their best friend?

"I haven't," she said.

"You can't, Pol. You can't. If I'm to have a shot at this, you absolutely can't."

Polly bit her lip and thought of her mother's hollow life. She agreed with Kerensa, but she felt entirely conflicted; entirely awful about it. About everything.

They rumbled across the causeway. The harbor lampposts were festooned with strings of plain white lights. Mount Polbearne didn't have much of a budget to compete with the fancier displays in the bigger towns, but the lights suited the cobbled streets, forming long dips and chains between the old-fashioned lampposts built to withstand the spray and wind. There were red bows on the lampposts too, and twinkling trees and candles in every window. The town looked extraordinarily lovely, filled with a deep peace; a lovely passing into the quietest season, of night and cozy beds and bright sharp stars glimmering overhead.

Kerensa drew up at the lighthouse door. The place was in darkness; Huckle must be sleeping. Polly kissed Kerensa gently on the cheek, then jumped down, wincing at the freezing air, as the Range Rover roared away.

The lighthouse was bitterly cold. She checked in on Neil underneath the kitchen table but didn't even stop to make a cup of tea. Huckle grunted, rather sleepily, as she moved her frozen feet toward his lovely warm body, so she rolled over, staring out of the window, where they still hadn't gotten around to putting curtains up. The stars looked white and pale against the freezing air; she was blowing out steam when she breathed out, the house was so cold. She couldn't warm up at all; couldn't even take warmth from Huckle. Instead she just lay there, desperately wiggling her toes, trying to see a way through.

She could only think of one: carry on as normal. Sometimes, if you pretended everything was normal, you had a chance of making it so. Keep buggering on, as the saying went. She couldn't think of anything else. Her mum would come around. They'd make it up. After all, she thought glumly, who else did they have but each other?

Work. Work would solve everything.

Chapter Eighteen

The next morning, Huckle was surprised and pleased to see Polly up and bustling about quite merrily, apart from a slight headache.

"Hey?" he said cautiously.

Polly turned round with her normal smile on her face.

"Hey," she said.

"You okay?"

"I'm fine," she said. "Cheese scone?"

"YES! God, I like living with you."

Polly popped a warm slice, covered in salty butter, into his mouth.

"Oh, heaven. So . . ."

She shook her head to indicate she didn't really want to talk about it.

"My family's bananas," she said. "And it's the village fair on Saturday. So . . ."

"All families are bananas," said Huckle.

"Exactly. They're all nuts. Nuts and bananas."

"An ice cream sundae."

"Precisely. So I've decided. There's no point in dwelling on it for years and years and years. They're screwed up, but it's not my fault, so I'm just going to get on with things and stop beating myself up about it. They did all the mad stuff, not me. I don't want anything to do with it. We are going to make a tremendous Christmas for Reuben, then pay off the puffin shelter so the puffins are safe, which will be more of a contribution to this earthly existence than I ever expected to make, then we are going to take the remainder of the money and go somewhere on holiday where they serve cocktails larger than my head—there's nothing larger than *your* head . . ."

"Thanks," said Huckle.

"And we're going to lie on the sand and make love and go swimming and get drunk and think about absolutely nothing at all. How does that sound to you?"

"That sounds awesome."

He came closer.

"Are you sure?"

"I am totally and utterly sure. Being unselfish is going to get me absolutely nowhere with Mum or with . . . with Tony. So I might as well be completely selfish."

"Is saving a puffin sanctuary and cooking for someone else's Christmas and running the town fair your definition of selfish?"

"Yes," said Polly. "Because it will make me feel good. Whereas none of the other stuff does. So I may as well stick to what I know will work."

"Okay," said Huckle. "Well, that sounds fine by me. I am going out to sell honey to lots of stupid beauticians to pay for this holiday of ours. You've inspired me."

"Good!" said Polly. "Take some of these mini cheese scones as bribes."

"I shall," said Huckle.

"Are you going to eat them all before you get to your first client?"

But whatever Huckle's answer was, it was lost in a sea of crumbs.

Chapter Nineteen

Polly put out the tray.

"Free samples!" she said cheerily, and the old ladies gathered around, cooing happily. She was trying pigs in blankets with honey—she had a good supplier for the honey, which helped—and more of the mini scones.

"Not you, Jayden," she said firmly to her second-in-command, who looked wounded and stroked the side of his moustache.

"But I need to test what I'm selling," he said.

"I thought you wanted to get in shape for You Know What."

Jayden colored instantly.

"Go on then. One."

Jayden grimaced. "That barely touches the sides. I think you're getting mean in your old age."

"Do you?" said Polly. Jayden was twenty-three, so of course he thought she was ancient for being over thirty.

"You'll be turning into Mrs. Manse . . ."

"Any more cheek from you," said Polly, whipping him lightly with a tea towel, "and you'll be scrubbing under the bread ovens for the next two weeks. Anyway, how are things going with Flora?"

"I'm just gearing up to it," said Jayden solemnly. "It's important to get these things right."

"It is," said Polly.

Patrick the vet came in, looking slightly harassed as usual. He liked Polly, although he disapproved mightily of her keeping a seabird as a pet. He'd long realized, though, that as in many other parts of his life, there wasn't actually that much he could do about it, so had learned to keep quiet.

"How's Neil?"

"He's good!" said Polly quickly. "Perfect BMI for a puffin, probably. Free sample?"

"Thank you. That wasn't why I came in, though."

"No?" said Polly.

Outside, it was absolutely freezing. The wind was blowing a gale sideways into the houses, whistling down the little alleyways that made up the bottom of Mount Polbearne; the houses became less frequent and the road steeper as you wound your way to the top, to the ruined church that stood there, ancient but magnificent.

No, today was a day for staying indoors with the fire on, watching the white-crested waves; or huddling somewhere cozy and warm, whatever the weather. Hence the excellent trade at the bakery.

Polly thought about Neil.

"He really is fine," she said. "I was quite cross with him, actually, taking losing the egg so well."

Patrick smiled. "Male chauvinist puff, huh?"

"I like to think, when he's staring out to sea, that he's feeling bad for his little egg," said Polly.

Patrick gave her a look.

"Instead of thinking about tasty fish?"

"Instead of thinking about tasty fish."

"You really shouldn't anthropomorphize animals," said Patrick. "Seriously, it doesn't do them any good. Neil won't remember that egg. Neither will Celeste. They're instinct-driven creatures."

As he said this, he helped himself to another sausage without even realizing he was doing it, but Polly didn't mention it.

"Do you think he might . . . find another girlfriend one day?"

"I don't know," said Patrick. "Puffins mate for life. They were just unlucky. Of course if you took him to the sanctuary . . ."

Polly gave him a look.

"I think we already know that's not happening."

"Well, quite. No, I think you're stuck with a bachelor puffin."

"Good," said Polly.

"You know they can live for twenty years?"

"Also good," said Polly.

Patrick shook his head. "Well then."

"Did you hear they might be shutting the sanctuary?"

"Really?" said Patrick. "Now that is a shame."

He looked at her closely.

"You can't adopt them all," he said.

"No," said Polly. "But I can do something."

He looked at the spread in front of him.

"What's all this in aid of, then?"

"Well, it's partly getting ready for the Christmas fair . . . and partly to welcome Reuben's parents."

"Oh," said Patrick. "Oh goodness. I wonder what they're like."

"Exactly how you'd think," said Polly. "And then some."

Chapter Twenty

The day of the Christmas fair dawned crisp and crackling. The village hall was absolutely heaving. People had come from miles around. Polly had been up for days on end making delicious gift baskets of gingerbread and clotted cream fudge and half a dozen small Christmas cakes that had been soaking in brandy for weeks now. Her stall was absolutely groaning, and, from the second the doors opened, totally mobbed. Selina was on her left-hand side with her lovely filigree jewelry that had taken hours upon hours of careful work.

"It's brilliant," said Samantha, bustling around the many little stalls. "This is going to raise so much money!"

"I'm getting all my Christmas shopping done!" said Mrs. Corning. "This is going to wrap it right up." Polly and Selina tried not to think about how much money they would have made if people had done their Christmas shopping directly from them.

Flora was helping on the bakery stall, having brought a huge tray of her fabulous religieuses. Polly was paying her for being there. Well. At least Flora was a student. And it was Christmas. She should get into the spirit more.

"How's Jayden?" she said cheerfully. Flora as usual simply shrugged.

"He's all right," she said.

"Polly, show this guy your ring," called Selina from the next table, and she leaned over obediently and showed off her beautiful seaweed engagement ring.

"Oh yes," said the man. "Something like that would be lovely."

Selina beamed. "Ooh, maybe this exposure thing works after all," she said, and Polly gave her a cross look.

"It is pretty," ventured Flora, and Polly let her examine it, feeling proud.

"It'll be you next," she said, remembering the conversation she had had with Jayden.

"Ha, no way," said Flora. "Don't think so."

Polly winced and pulled her hand back. Maybe she would have to have another word with Jayden.

"Have you seen Kerensa?" said Selina. "Only she's gone really weird on me. I haven't seen her for months."

"Hmm," said Polly, not quite trusting herself. "She's just been really exhausted with the pregnancy and everything, I think. I've hardly seen her either."

Selina gave her a penetrating look.

"When's the baby due again?"

Polly looked at Selina and decided that the best thing under the circumstances was to tell her a big fat lie.

"End of February," she said.

Mid-January was more like it. She could actually see Selina counting backward in her head.

"Oh, right," said Selina. "She's enormous."

Samantha was annoyingly tapping the mike at the front of the hall.

"Hello, everyone!" she said brightly. There was a large crowd milling around. "Now, thank you so much to everyone who's contributed to make the fair such a success . . ."

Selina and Polly swapped rueful looks.

"And now, I'd like to ask our town's resident baker . . . the woman who feeds us all those naughty treats . . ."

Polly stiffened. She didn't really like being referred to like some kind of drug dealer.

". . . to come forward and judge the baking competition! Jayden said it would be fine."

Samantha grinned widely at Polly, as if she had no doubt that there was nothing Polly would like better. Polly blinked. She had no recollection of Samantha asking her to do this, but it was entirely possible it had been mentioned in one of the many emails she had never looked at.

"Um?" she said.

"To judge the baking competition!" Samantha repeated encouragingly.

Polly reluctantly made her way to the front of the hall. On the long table behind the microphone was a vast array of home-baked goodies, and standing behind each plate was an apprehensive-looking villager.

Polly knew every single person there. Every single one was a customer. Or ex-customer, once this went the wrong way, she thought.

She started at one end of the table and tried each of the various pies, cakes, breads and tarts, although she could hardly taste them for nerves. There were old Mrs. Corning's rock buns . . . Muriel had made a date tart . . . and nine-year-old Sally Stephens, the vet's granddaughter, was standing proudly behind the most beautiful lemon meringue. All eyes followed Polly beadily as she moved from plate to plate.

"These are all wonderful," she stammered. "I really can't choose."

Samantha's face was stern.

"Well, you have to choose," she said. "I've donated first prize of a weekend at a spa."

Polly groaned internally. There were very few people in Mount Polbearne who wouldn't fancy one of those in the middle of winter.

She looked around once more at the eager faces. Then she picked up old Florrie's dull, dry biscuit.

"Um, this one," she said.

The elderly lady looked up with watery eyes.

"What?" she said in a quavering voice.

"You've won, love!" shouted Samantha cheerily.

"What?"

Polly had thought giving the prize to the neediest entrants was the best solution, but now she was feeling a bit unsure.

"You've won the baking competition! Congratulations, Florrie!"

Florrie blinked as someone from the local press took a photograph. Polly listened uneasily to the mutterings of the locals behind her. She'd probably lost about thirty percent of the goodwill toward her business in one fell swoop. This was going great.

"It's a SPA!" Samantha was now hollering in Florrie's ear.

"A what, love?"

Polly was thrilled when Bernard from the puffin sanctuary walked in the door, as it gave her an excuse to escape from the baking table.

"Hello!" she said, waving at him frantically and heading over. "Selina's over here!"

Selina shot her a look. Bernard looked anxious, as always.

"How are the puffins?" said Polly.

"Noisy," said Bernard. He glanced around. "This is a fund-raiser, is it?"

"For the village," said Polly.

"We should do one for the sanctuary," he said.

"Yes," said Polly reluctantly.

"Can I sign you up?"

"Probably," said Polly. "But don't worry. I'm still doing Reuben's Christmas to raise money for you guys. And I was thinking, Flora. In the summer, you might fancy going in and helping Bernie with the catering."

"Work on a bird farm?" said Flora, shuffling her feet.

"It's a job," said Polly.

"I can get a job anywhere," said Flora, and despite her sullen attitude, open-ended approach to timekeeping and total lack of initiative, you only had to taste her pastry to know that it was true; she could.

The one good thing about the stall, Polly supposed, was that they sold out early and could go. It took her a moment to compose herself enough to smile when she handed the money box over to Samantha, but she just about managed it.

Samantha, who lived in a big pile in London, as well as owning a second home in Mount Polbearne, just didn't have a handle on actual money, and that wasn't really her fault. So Polly smiled as widely as she could and said goodbye to everyone as she left.

"Aren't you coming to the pub?" said Selina. "Everyone else is going to the pub. You're coming, aren't you?" she said to Bernard, who looked confused, and then cheerful.

"I can't," said Polly, sighing. "I need to get practicing for Reuben's specialist bloody Christmas canapés. His parents arrive soon and I'm not sure I know what I'm doing."

"Well, say hi to Kerensa for me," said Selina, and Polly vowed to do absolutely no such thing.

Chapter Twenty-One

It was nearly Christmas Eve, and Polly was still hard at work. She had started playing Christmas carols in the shop now; she refused to do it earlier, partly because it made it sound like a coffee shop and encouraged everyone to stay for absolutely ages, and partly because she couldn't listen to "Mary's Boy Child" more than four hundred times per holiday season.

She hadn't heard from Kerensa, except a quick check to see if she was okay, which she insisted she was. She'd thrown herself into baking, trying out new types of gingerbread and mincemeat treats, and decorating—the bakery was overwhelmed with a little toy wooden village, with lights inside that she'd built up to look as much like Mount Polbearne as possible. The local children were absolutely obsessed with it and clustered around, having to be torn away by their parents, often with a sticky bun or pain au raisins in their mittened hands. It didn't occur to Polly until much later how much her model village inspired the children of their austere little tidal island. For years afterward they would come to look at it, and although as they grew older they could see how small and basic it actually was, they would be furious if she moved or changed the tiniest thing. Eventually, they brought their own children, and the little ones would still gaze and exclaim in awe while the bigger ones shook their heads, absolutely astonished that their parents could have grown up in such entertainment-free surroundings.

But that was in the future. Now she was in a decorating frenzy, as if trying to make the whole world welcoming and cozy.

Inside the lighthouse, she'd wrapped miles of tinsel around the balustrade, was planning a vast tree and had hurled fairy lights at almost anything that moved. She'd also stocked up on Icelandic-pattern cushions and blankets for the sofa, so they could hunker down and watch Scandinavian box-set dramas whilst wearing more or less authentic Scandinavian sweaters.

Huckle just let her get on with it, a smile playing around his lips. He knew it was displacement activity and hoped it would burn itself out. He knew she needed distraction.

"Sweetie," he said, late one night as they clung together in bed, bathed in the glow of eighty tiny penlights Polly had forgotten to switch off on her way upstairs, "you know, if you want to get rid of all that excess zeal . . . I mean, everything looks amazing, but I was just thinking you should channel it. I mean, we could . . . We could think about bringing the baby forward? Or even think about organizing a wedding? I mean, my parents were asking about it . . . Obviously they'll have a long way to come and . . ."

He could tell by the way she stiffened that he'd said the wrong thing.

"Well, I thought it was nice," he whispered gently in her ear. "My dad said . . . I mean, absolutely no offense to your mum or anything. And no offense to us, obviously, especially you, because you work your socks off . . ."

Huckle had tried working his socks off and had hated it. Ironically, since he'd started working in a very sock-free fashion, his easy charm and natural nice looks had made him just as successful as he had been in the corporate world, with none of the early-morning starts Polly had.

But even being successful in a home-made honey business is very much not one of the more financially lucrative ways to be a success. Fortunately, Huckle's wants were few; he had the same few well-made pieces of clothing in his wardrobe that only grew more faded and softer and thus rather more appealing with every passing year; he fixed up the motorbike himself if and when it needed it, and all the things he liked to do— walking, staying in, listening to unbelievably terrible MOR American rock music, drinking beer at the Red Lion, going to bed with Polly—were pretty inexpensive.

"Anyway, they have tons of money . . . God knows why, they don't deserve it. Polly, look. They've offered to pay for the wedding. Here. Apparently all their friends want to come to England, they think it's quaint. We could do anything you liked. Any way you wanted."

There was a long silence.

"You're not insulted, are you? I mean, I didn't say we'd definitely take the money or anything . . ."

Polly shook her head.

"Oh love. No. It's not the money. It really isn't—that's so nice of them. Incredibly nice of them. I'm not proud, I'm really not remotely proud."

"But . . ."

Polly shook her head.

"I can't . . . I just . . . Not now. Family stuff. I don't . . . I'm so busy. You know. I'm not . . . I'm so not ready . . ."

She meant to say, of course, *I'm not ready for marriage,* not *I'm not ready for you.*

But Huckle only heard one thing: that she didn't want to marry him.

"Okay," he said. It was hard to hurt Huckle's feelings; he was genuinely good-natured and rarely got upset over anything. But it was certainly possible.

"I'm sorry," said Polly. "But you know how it is . . . and I'm so busy . . ."

"Yeah, yeah, I know."

Polly thought about Carmel, spending years wondering if her husband was going to misbehave again. She thought of her mother, sitting alone in her kitchen eating soup night after night for the whole of the only life she was ever going to get.

She thought—briefly, glancingly—about the impossibly huge notion that she had half-brothers and -sisters out there in the world. Of course it had always been a possibility, but one she hadn't had to dwell on particularly. But now she knew for a fact that it was definitely, absolutely true, and more than that, that one of them must be round about her own age.

Well. She was in no position to think about families just now. Even building one with Huckle. Surely he could understand that? She just couldn't, and that was an end to it.

The wind whistled around the lighthouse, although inside, lit gently with fairy lights, it was cozy and warm, the remnants of the evening's fire dampened down but still gently heating the way up the house for once. The fire had been wonderful that night, and the entire building felt warm.

Yes, thought Polly, trying to stop making lists in her head, and snuggling down. He would understand. He totally would. Huckle understood everything.

But if life teaches us anything, it's that what we assume someone should know about us—even someone we really, really love; *especially* someone we really, really love—can be completely misunderstood or overlooked, or that the silence we think contains so much is simply unobserved. We believe—or we would like to believe—that the people we're closest to can tell what our intentions are, the same way your mother knows when you are small whether you've been stealing biscuits out of the biscuit jar by the fact you have chocolate smeared around your mouth.

But nobody is psychic. And for once, it was Polly who drifted off to sleep to the sound of the crashing waves, whilst Huckle lay staring into the darkness, feeling unusually thoughtful; unusually sleepless; very unusually alone.

Chapter Twenty-Two

He might have understood more if he'd been at Reuben's the next day, when Reuben's parents showed up, but he wasn't.

The mansion had been decorated from top to bottom. Polly couldn't help sighing, just a little. It was a bit silly, having money, given that there were only so many buns one could eat in a day; only so far she could pretend she could tell the difference between a cheap and an expensive bottle of wine; and how much she couldn't see the point of a highly expensive handbag (Polly's bags invariably became full of bits of tissue, odd pencils, half-used lipsticks and a light scattering of powdered yeast; she couldn't imagine the horror of doing that to something worth more than a small car).

But the difference between her little fairy lights and Reuben's professional decorating job was obviously substantial. The tree in the driveway, at the circular turn in front of the door, was three stories high. The theme was kind of diamonds and ice sculptures, which ought to be tacky but annoyingly looked utterly perfect against the metal frame and bright glass of the lovely modern house. Frost crackled on the ground outside and on the beautiful spotlit path that led down to Reuben's private beach. Polly took her tasting trays into the massive professional kitchen. Reuben was a good cook, but obviously he kept someone on hand to do all this kind of stuff. Kerensa was nowhere to be seen. She'd told everyone she was doing lots of pampering and baby massage stuff, but Polly knew for a fact that she didn't give a toss for anything like that, which meant she must instead simply be lying low.

Polly sighed. Did nobody get a happy ending? Did it simply not work? This should be the happiest time of her best friend's life—married to a bloke who, whilst nobody would describe him as "lovely," was fun and adored her and whom she adored back, and who suited her very well, expecting the birth of their first baby in their gorgeous mansion by the sea. It was like that girl who'd married the Prince of Monaco and had twins and always looked entirely furious about everything. Really, if Kerensa couldn't be happy, nobody could. And yet there she was, off with a Brazilian stripper. Well, briefly, but even so.

Polly sighed and dumped her two large trays of food, turning on the oven to heat everything up. She was officially catering just the Christmas party, Christmas Day and Boxing Day, but she'd agreed to put on a little taster session when Reuben's parents arrived, cold and presumably ravenous. She glanced around.

Marta, the maid, smiled at her politely, but they didn't speak. Polly made herself some coffee in Reuben's absurdly noisy and overcomplicated machine, which appeared to have enough technology to launch a Mars mission, then padded around the enormous room.

It was far bigger than what she had at the bakery to feed the entire town. As well as the industrial-sized ovens, there was a huge grill wok, and a pizza oven . . . you could run a fairly nice hotel from here. Which was, she supposed, what was happening.

The sun beamed in through the windows, adding to the warmth of the underfloor heating. As an American, Reuben liked his house boiling in the winter and freezing in the summer, and with the sun streaming in it was almost too warm. Polly wished she could stretch out on the floor like a cat and take a nap.

Suddenly she heard a noise, a loud flapping. It sounded ominous and weird. Marta didn't flinch, but Polly rushed out into the hall. As well as the vast tree filling the turret, she could see another, this one with carved wooden *Nutcracker* soldiers positioned all round it—in the sitting room, where a huge fire was crackling away despite the fact that the room was completely empty.

She opened the front door on to the sparkling driveway ahead and to her amazement saw a big black helicopter descending right in front of her. Of course she'd recognized the noise, but she hadn't seen a helicopter up close since . . . since they'd had that great storm a year or so ago. She put that out of her mind and smiled anxiously, realizing as she did so how much it made her feel even more like staff.

The helicopter made a tremendous noise as it teetered to a stop in a big H Polly hadn't even noticed in the driveway. Seriously, how did people get so much money? She knew Reuben did something with algorithms that drove big computer companies bananas, but she had no idea what an algorithm even was, though clearly it was something that allowed you to own a helicopter.

The blades finally came to a stop, and Reuben emerged, looking jolly as ever, taking off his headphones and jumping down. He waved heartily and Polly waved back obediently, still feeling like an indentured servant. Marta went forward and started collecting large amounts of heavy luggage, as Reuben helped down first his father, then his mother.

His father was so obviously future Reuben it was almost comical to see them together. He was bald, with only a hint of Reuben's ginger hair around the tops of his ears, and bushy pale eyebrows. The top of his head was covered with freckles. If you were a worse person than Polly, you might be tempted to connect some of them up and make a second face. His body was almost perfectly spherical, and he was wearing an extremely expensive-looking cashmere coat over an exquisitely tailored tweed suit—rather flamboyantly British—with a spotted handkerchief in the top pocket. His beautiful clothes did absolutely nothing to disguise the fact that he essentially looked like a snowman with tiny fat arms and legs sticking out the sides, or a cheerful baby.

Rhonda, Reuben's mother, was all hair. It was jet black, a color unusual in nature for a woman of her age, which was, of course, completely indeterminate, and she was wearing—no she wasn't. Yes she was. Fur. A full-length mink coat, completely without shame. She was short, too, and it actually looked a bit like a scene from *The Revenant*.

Well. Polly did not like fur and that was that, but also she could imagine how much Rhonda would care about whether she liked it or not: not a whit.

Rhonda had also managed to keep her false eyelashes on through an eight-hour flight and a helicopter transfer, which was pretty impressive when you thought about it. She had hugely made-up eyes that reminded Polly of Liza Minelli, and a large lipsticky smile. The lipstick was bleeding slightly.

"Hey!" She waved, and Polly stepped forward. Rhonda kissed her hard on both cheeks. "I remember you! You're the one that snuck out of Reuben's wedding to make out with that hunky groomsman!"

Polly smiled awkwardly.

"Ah," she said. "Yeah."

"Is he still on the scene? Doubt it. Ha, that's never the way to do it. You young ladies, you're always throwing yourselves about and—"

"Actually, we're engaged," Polly said quickly. Rhonda frowned, or would have done if her skin could actually have stretched in any direction at all.

"Well there you are, it just goes to show." She said it as if that was exactly what she'd thought all along. "Now where's that daughter-in-law of mine?"

If there was ever, Polly reflected, a woman who could deal with having Rhonda as a mother-in-law, it was probably Kerensa.

"She's . . . she's out and about," said Polly, awkwardly.

Rhonda sniffed loudly.

"Hear that, Merv? Out and about. Too busy to be here to greet her in-laws. And what's she even doing gallivanting about the place when she's carrying our only grandchild? Huh? Huh?"

"Ma," said Reuben in a conciliatory tone. "She's not gone far. And it's not your only grandchild. Hayley has two kids."

"Well, yes, *Hayley*," said Rhonda, in a tone of voice that said absolutely everything about who was the more important of her children. "I mean Finkel children.

Children that will be carrying on the family name. My adorable little Ruby-Woobie's children."

She wobbled Reuben's chubby cheeks, and to his credit, Reuben didn't try in the least to shake her off; he seemed to totally accept that his mother would want to do this to him, in public.

Marta vanished with the bags and Rhonda swept into the house, trailing an extraordinarily powerful perfume behind her.

"Oh Rubes," she said sadly. "I mean . . . You know." She was looking round at the stunning lobby, with its huge tree and massive modern balustrade. "I mean, it's so . . . it's just so sparse! Couldn't you have gone for something a little bit more fancy? Now in our town house," she said to Polly, "we commissioned panelling top to bottom. Gives it a real classy look, you know what I mean? Properly done. They had to use some wood you can't even get any more. Completely rare. I think we were the last people allowed to chop it down."

"Ha ha, yeah, she thinks that," said Merv. "She thinks we were allowed to knock it down. So adorably innocent."

He chuckled benevolently and wandered into the kitchen.

"Hey, what you got to eat in this hellhole?"

Reuben trailed after his parents with a look of pleased terror on his face.

"I mean, would it hurt you to put a bit of gold here and there, huh? Show the world you're on the way to making it."

"Round here most people think I *have* made it, Ma."

"Yeah, round here."

Polly deftly removed the trays of hot pastries from

the oven: the rugelach and the chocolate matzos just as they'd asked for, and her speciality—which she'd had to make about nine times before Reuben finally declared himself satisfied—knishes from the old country, i.e., Europe about three generations before.

Merv tried to grab a handful when they hadn't yet cooled down. He stared at his fingers like a puzzled bear.

"Da-ad," said Reuben, and Rhonda tutted and looked around.

"Where's the ice water?"

As it was December, Polly hadn't really considered iced water a necessity, but she rushed to Reuben's absurd industrial fridge and poured a glassful from the dispenser at the front.

"These are great," said Merv, stuffing the pastries into his mouth as fast as he could. "Of course, obviously I'm going to sue you for the burnt fingers . . . I'm kidding, I'm kidding. What are they anyway?"

Polly turned to Reuben. These were the special knishes she'd laboured over, refining a strange recipe she didn't know, sourcing ingredients that were incredibly hard to come by in rural Cornwall, and he didn't even know what he was eating?

Reuben didn't look remotely shame-faced.

"Hey, it's how *I* like them," he said. "And I'm paying."

Polly sniffed.

Rhonda cast an eye over the pastries.

"Not for me, thank you. You know I have to keep myself trim."

She waddled cheerfully over to the window and started tut-tutting about the state of Reuben's butler sink—"Seriously, it's so old-fashioned! You couldn't have got anything with nice taps? This looks like something the servants would use."

Reuben smiled affectionately, then sidled up to Polly.

"Where's Kerensa?" he said through gritted teeth. "I can't stand this. I can't do it without her and she's not answering her phone. What's up with her?"

Polly shrugged. "I don't know . . . pregnancy stuff?" she said hopefully, hoping the idea of it would be as weird to Reuben as these things often were. Thankfully it worked.

"Guh," said Reuben, shivering. "Yuk. I heard the term 'mucus plug' once and that was quite enough for me, thanks."

"Are you not going to be there?"

"Not a chance! As someone said, it's like watching your favorite pub burning down."

"Oh Reuben, you have to be there."

"I've booked the best ob/gyn in the country to be on standby, plus a doula and a maternity nurse, and we're going to get one of those Norland nannies that wear the uniform and refuse to have sex with me . . . I'm kidding, I'm kidding. About the sex, not the nanny."

"Is this what Kerensa wants?"

"It's the best," said Reuben mutinously. "Everybody knows it."

"Okay," said Polly.

Christmas was going to be fun, she thought. Just concentrate on the money. Think about the money. Get the work done. It would be fine.

"It's a shame you didn't pay more attention to the decorations," Rhonda was saying, looking around. "Disappointing you didn't feel you could make the effort."

"Okay, Ma," said Reuben, for the first time looking

shame-faced, like the naughty boy he must once have been. "Do you guys want a nap or something?"

"Are we in that same room?" said Rhonda. "Only, you know, it's so noisy."

"It's the waves, Mom."

"I'm just saying, they're incredibly noisy. Is there nothing you can do?"

"Yeah, Mom. I can go and stop the tide."

Polly was feeling increasingly awkward. Rhonda didn't want to eat, and Merv and Reuben had finished everything else, so they were all just standing around looking uncomfortable in that cavernous kitchen.

Where the hell was Kerensa? If she was here, she could say something funny, break the ice. Instead she was doing something Polly considered quite dangerous: she was making Reuben look bad. Reuben was used to getting what he wanted; being the center of attention. Standing him up in front of his parents was rude at best, potentially devastating at worst.

Polly glanced at Merv, who was dusting crumbs off his incredibly expensive coat. Looking up, he caught her eye.

"Yeah, come on, Rhonda," he said. "Let's take a snooze, let the kids get themselves sorted out, yeah?"

Rhonda sniffed.

"I won't sleep a goddam wink."

"You always say that when you're tired. Then off you go, snoring like a freight train."

"This is exactly why we're getting separate rooms. No, wings," said Rhonda, folding her arms.

There was the noise of the motorbike pulling up outside. Huckle had popped by to say hello. Polly had rarely been more pleased to see him.

"Huck!" she yelled cheerfully as he slouched in.

"Um, hey?" he said, taking in the room gradually. "Hi, Mrs. Finkel. Mr. Finkel."

"Merv, please. You're Huckle, right?"

Huckle nodded.

"You know, I never get to meet any of Reuben's friends."

"That's because he doesn't have any," said Huckle, smiling to show he was joking.

"I do! I have millions of friends! I have the best friends in the world and most of them are famous!" said Reuben.

"All right, Superman, I was only joking," said Huckle. "Hey, good to see you. How's Polly's amazing food?"

"Pretty good!" said Merv, patting his belly. "Good hire, Reuben."

"Actually I'm . . ."

But Polly decided not to pursue it.

"Thanks," she said. Huckle beamed and put his arm round her shoulders. Rhonda sniffed again.

"So where's—" Huck started. Polly kicked him sharply on the shin.

"Ow! What?"

"Nothing," said Polly. Huckle looked confused. Rhonda looked furious.

"She meant, don't ask about Reuben's wife, who didn't bother to turn up to greet us," she said.

"Oh," said Huckle, staring at Polly.

"Hello!" came a voice that echoed in the vast hallway, and Kerensa walked in—or rather, lumbered, because her bump was now absolutely enormous. Her roots were growing out and her face was bloated, the skin rough and spotty. Normally, Kerensa never looked anything other than perfect. Even Polly was shocked.

"Hey, Rhonda . . . Merv."

Merv patted her rather absent-mindedly, but Rhonda couldn't contain her shock.

"Oh. My. GAWD!!!!" she screamed theatrically. "Reuben, she's a whale! Look at you! I have never known a Finkel woman to blow up like that! Whatever's in there, it's bigger than Reuben!"

Kerensa attempted a wan smile, but she looked like she was about to burst into tears. Reuben scowled.

"She looks great, Ma."

Rhonda would have raised an eyebrow if they weren't already painted on halfway up her forehead.

Kerensa just stared at them all blearily, as if she hardly knew they were there. Her entire face was sagging, and there was fear in her eyes. She could just about handle being with Polly, but all the Finkels in a row was simply too much for her.

"I'm going for a nap," she said, dully, putting her expensive handbag down on the kitchen table. The gold clasps clattered horribly on the brushed concrete in the echoing room.

Chapter Twenty-Three

O kay," said Huckle, the second they got home. He looked riled. This was almost unheard of. He was the most unflappable of men, always. But now he stalked into the kitchen and put his hands heavily on the old scrubbed wooden table. Neil was nowhere to be seen. "What the hell was that?"

"What do you mean?" said Polly nervously.

"You and Kerensa. Swapping glances. Looking all nervous. It's patently obvious something's up. What the hell is it?"

"Um," said Polly. "I think she was just anxious about Rhonda and Merv . . . And you know, the baby coming. It's due in a month."

Huckle shook his head. "She can handle Rhonda and Merv. I've seen her do it before. That woman doesn't scare easily. No. It's something else." He looked at her. "And look at you! You're bright pink."

Polly cursed her fair skin, which always showed when she was blushing, and the fact that Huckle knew her so well. He was staring at her now, those bright blue eyes not lazy and kind but hard-edged.

"What the hell is going on?"

"Nothing!"

"She's hardly been around, and you've been all tight-lipped about everything. What *is* it, Polly?"

He made them both a cup of tea. Polly didn't say anything. Her brain was working frantically. She couldn't . . . but on the other hand, this was *Huckle*. Her other half. Her love. She had to . . . she couldn't keep secrets from him. No lies. No dishonesty. That wasn't what they were about, was never what they had been about. When she was with Chris, he had lied about how the firm was doing fine, how everything was great, how she shouldn't worry. And the next thing that happened, they went bust and lost everything.

She couldn't bear to look at Huckle's wonderful, open, puzzled face. He was so straight. He told her the truth—always. He'd told the truth about how cut up he'd been about his ex-fiancée, that he needed a good year to get over her—and Polly had let him go, had let him do everything he needed to do, until he was ready. They'd always been upfront with each other.

But this. This cut right through the heart of their friendships, of the world they had built together, of the happiness they shared.

Or maybe he'd understand. He was reasonable, right? Maybe he'd see it was just a silly mistake, just a misunderstanding. Or maybe she could wait . . .

He was staring at her, and she realized she'd been quiet for far too long. The game was up.

"Polly?" he said, and the light tone in his deep voice was gone, and there was no mistaking the deadly seriousness of what he was saying. "You have to tell me."

Polly closed her eyes. Thought about it. Wished herself anywhere else than where she was. Thought about what she owed her best friend. And thought about truth, which she certainly owed her fiancé. Thought about her own life.

And then she told him the truth about Kerensa.

Chapter Twenty-Four

She had never seen him like this before. Of course they'd had rows; they were human. The previous year, when he'd been working away in the States, had been incredibly difficult for both of them.

But before when they'd argued it had been about a thing—the right way to plumb a bathroom, or what was the point of going all the way to the cinema (thirty miles) if Polly was going to sleep through the entire movie every single time?

They had been differences of opinion. This wasn't like that. Not at all. Huckle's normally placidly handsome face looked bizarrely almost amusing as it ran the gamut of emotions—shock, astonishment, fury and then, finally, deep hurt. He didn't say anything for a while. Then he started to say something and didn't quite manage to get it out. He stuttered, and stopped. He turned away. Then he turned back again, and Polly felt her heart sink right to the floor.

"How . . . how long?" he managed to husk out eventually. "How long have you known?"

Polly swallowed hard.

"Since . . . well, a few weeks," she said quietly.

"A few weeks?" Huckle blinked. He looked like he was going to cry. "You knew about this and you didn't think to mention it to me? Ever? Not once?"

Polly shook her head.

"It wasn't . . . it wasn't really my business to tell."

"But Polly," said Huckle. "Polly, I'm . . . I'm meant to be . . . I'm meant to be your other half. Your . . . your soulmate if you like."

Polly couldn't bear him looking at her the way he was looking at her now: as if something he loved about her, or something he had thought about her, was somehow suddenly gone; as if she was not the person he thought she was. As if something precious and perfect they had had together had vanished. Tears sprang to her eyes.

"I mean . . . we're meant to tell each other stuff."

"But Kerensa swore me to secrecy!"

"Yes, to the rest of the world, not to me!"

"I couldn't," said Polly. "What if you'd told Reuben?"

"Well, I think he has a right to know, don't you? That he's going to be raising a baby that's got nothing to do with him. You don't think that's his business either?"

"But we don't know. Nobody knows. And we won't know until the baby's born."

Huckle shook his head.

"Reuben's my best friend, Polly! My best friend!"

"And Kerensa's mine," said Polly gently.

"No. This is . . . No. It's immoral. It's unethical. I can't take part in this, Polly. I can't . . . I can't have anything to do with it."

"Huckle, you know what Reuben's like! You know how awful he can be, how tricky! He drove her to distraction, he was never at home, kept treating her like a servant . . ."

"Does that make it okay?"

"No," said Polly. "No, it doesn't. I think she went out to let off some steam and things got slightly out of hand. These things happen."

Huckle nodded slowly.

"Do they? I mean . . . is that the kind of thing you might do?"

"No!" said Polly, scandalized. "Never in a million years!"

"But you think it's okay?"

"NO!" shouted Polly. "How can you think that?"

"Because a friend of yours did it and you covered it up."

"She made a mistake! She doesn't think it's remotely okay. Nobody thinks it's okay, Huckle. It was a terrible, horrible mistake."

"Putting on odd socks is a mistake," said Huckle bitterly. "Voting for the wrong candidate. But this: they've only been married a year!"

Polly nodded. "Don't . . . don't think she hasn't been beating herself up about it ever since. She loves Reuben. She really does. It was a slip. A silly slip that she'll never, ever forgive herself for."

"How can she live with herself?" said Huckle. "How?"

He looked at Polly as if she knew. Or as if he was asking how Polly could live with herself, keeping something so awful a secret.

"Are there . . . are there a lot of things you don't tell me?" said Huckle painfully.

"No!" said Polly. "No! The only reason I didn't tell you about this is because it isn't about me. It wasn't mine to tell. I wanted to, but she begged me, Huckle.

She begged. For precisely this reason. Because it's nobody else's business."

She suddenly found she was terrified. Everything
was falling apart.

"Are you going to tell him?" she asked in a small
voice.

Huckle pounded his fist on the kitchen table in frus-
tration.

"Goddammit," he said. "GODDAMMIT, Polly."

"I know," said Polly. "I know."

"What if he finds out later? What if the kid is clearly
not his? And then he comes asking us?"

"I don't know."

Huckle shook his head.

"I trusted you," he said. "I thought we had something
beautiful and real and kind of . . . kind of wonderful going on down here. In this beautiful place. With us. And
them, and everything we had . . . everything lovely:
friends, and family, and, well, everything I'd never been
able to find in my life before . . ."

He bit his lip.

"And now that's broken. It's ruined. It's shattered."

"No!" said Polly, running to the door. "No it isn't.
You're being completely unreasonable. This has nothing
to do with us."

"But all four of us were an 'us.' All four of us were
together. Were friends. Who trusted each other. Who
did things together. And now . . . three of us, what, have
to watch this weird baby grow up? And not tell the other
one? It's a conspiracy!"

Polly sighed.

"You can never put things back together how they
were," said Huckle glumly. "You can't pretend this
never happened. You can never unknow it."

"Where are you going?" said Polly, her heart beating rapidly in terror. "Where are you going? Are you going to Reuben's? Are you going to tell him?"

"No. Maybe. I don't know," said Huckle. "Just leave me alone."

She heard the motorbike start up and roar off. She glanced at the tidal chart, which she knew mostly by heart, but it was still useful. The causeway would be flooded this time of the evening. He had nowhere to go; he certainly couldn't get to Reuben's. He'd probably go to the Red Lion and have a pint, cool off. Well, he'd have to; it was a freezing evening and there was literally nowhere else to go. Unless he had a change of heart and walked back through the door . . .

She spent a long time staring at the door, waiting for him. Her tea went cold. Dinner was unmade. She picked up her phone, but as usual the signal was non-existent, so there was nothing to do except stare at it as if it really might get a message. She didn't want to text in case she said the wrong thing. She felt absolutely awful.

She went upstairs, but the rest of the house was freezing and it made her sad to see all the Christmas decorations, so she just turned round and came back down to the kitchen again, huddling beside the log burner.

Neil hopped over and perched on her shoulder, and she rubbed the back of his neck mournfully as she ran the argument through in her head again. Even in the depths of her despair she could see the patterns of her life that had always made her smooth things over for her mother, try and make everything all right. She'd tried to do the same for Kerensa, and it hadn't worked at all. You couldn't brush things under the carpet like that. Of course if she thought about it, it hadn't really worked for her mother either.

That habit she had of not facing up to things, of hoping for the best . . . Life wasn't butter icing. You couldn't just spread it over the cracks of the cake and make it look pretty and hope nobody would be any the wiser. It didn't work like that. Instead, the cracks got worse underneath, and then one day the wound was too deep to heal.

Polly burst into tears, horrible racking sobs, not pretty; the kind of snotty crying that hurts your throat and makes your nose bright red and that you just can't seem to stop. It didn't feel cathartic at all; it just went on and on and on. And every time she caught sight of the lighthouse lamp reflected in a window, she thought perhaps it was the headlamp on Huckle's motorbike, and that he was coming home, but it wasn't, and he didn't. And all the time she was wrestling with the worst question of all: should she tell Kerensa she had betrayed her confidence? Should she put the fear of God into her that Huckle was going to ruin her entire life, had the power to do so at any moment and that it was entirely possible he would? Which wouldn't just ruin her life; it would ruin Reuben's too, and quite possibly the life of the tiny child whose life hadn't even started yet, and Polly felt she knew a bit about that.

Chapter Twenty-Five

Polly dozed off, still crying, about two a.m., then woke again with a start. The fire was nearly out and the kitchen was terribly cold. She looked around, horrified. She was still completely alone. Where was he? What had happened? Was something wrong?

She glanced down at her phone, which, as usual with the odd fluctuations of the signal, had popped on at some point, gathered her messages and now was gone again. She sighed and scrolled through. There it was, just a simple text from him.

Staying at friend's.

Oh well, at least nothing had happened to him. For one horrible instant earlier, she had thought he might have decided to drive through the water-covered cause-way regardless of the consequences—she wouldn't put it past him. But he hadn't gone to Reuben's, because there were no missed calls or texts from Reuben or

Kerensa. Unless they'd all been caught in a massive bloody shootout, of course.

She shook her head, then wrapped herself in a blanket off the back of the sofa and headed up the stairs to bed. The bedroom was icy. Her feet simply couldn't get warm, no matter what she did, and she lay on her back staring at the ceiling, her eyes too dry for tears. What was going to happen now? It was nearly Christmas, and it looked like it was going to be an absolute disaster. Would Huckle even come? And if he did, would he be able to stop himself saying something? What if everyone had a few glasses of champagne and things got a bit heated? That happened at Christmas. That happened all the time.

She couldn't sleep now. She had to get up and prep for the bakery, then she'd promised to go over and do an afternoon tea for Reuben's business partners and his parents.

This was the problem with work, which also made it a solution, she supposed: that it was relentless, that it was always there, however you were feeling, whether or not you were ready for it. So even though she was exhausted, and desperately worried about Huckle, she had no choice but to get up and carry on.

She was kneading bread and mainlining coffee at the kitchen table, having turned on the radio loud to try and cheer herself up, desperately trying to shake herself out of this awful torpor. She'd worked so hard to create this life for herself, to make a success of it. But now it felt like it was creaking, beginning to crash around her ears. Neil came in because he liked the music on the radio, but even seeing his little face didn't cheer her up the way it normally would. It all felt so empty and futile, but what else could she do other than carry on?

Outside, Huckle was drawing up on the motorbike, slightly hungover after a night on Andy's sofa, having talked things through and realized that of course it wasn't his business, not really. He had no right to tell anyone anything. It was awful, of course it was, a terrible thing he would have to bear, watching his best friend raise another man's child. But it was what it was. He couldn't get upset with Polly about it; she hadn't done anything. And she must be utterly distraught after their fight. He shouldn't have stormed out like that. He would apologize and they would carry on, and he'd just avoid Kerensa.

Looking through the low, wide kitchen window, he could hear the music playing and could see Polly busying herself at the table, dancing away to the radio, getting on with doing what she always did; cheerfully carrying on with life as if nothing had happened. It stung him. He'd been in agony about this, and she'd been . . . well.

Huckle had fallen for Polly with an absolute certitude that this was a girl who knew her own mind, her own heart; that was what he loved about her. That she was ballsy; that she grabbed hold of life with both hands, went for what she wanted. It was wonderful.

But with that went something else. Huckle had twice given up a high-powered career, knowing it wasn't for him, that it didn't make him happy. He much preferred pottering about with his bees, looking after them, making something lovely by hand. He didn't care about status, things like that. It didn't mean anything to him, much to his parents' occasional despair when they reflected on his expensive education.

He wasn't a go-getter, he wasn't a workaholic; none of those things. And as he looked at Polly, the thought that was uppermost in his mind was: she doesn't need me. She has Neil, and the bakery—look at her. I'm in agony, in despair about this, and she's just carrying on as if nothing is happening. She'll always be okay.

He blinked, his heart full of sadness, and missed Polly looking up and seeing him, and how her heart leapt and she wanted to run to him and throw her arms around him and beg forgiveness; promise that she would never, ever do anything like that, not ever again, that they would share everything, but please, please, *please* don't tell Reuben.

Then she saw his face—so grave—and her own face fell too, as he walked in through the kitchen door.

"Hey," he said carefully.

"Hey," she said.

"You're back at it?"

"Yeah, it's Reuben's big party this evening, plus I've got some afternoon buns . . ."

Her voice trailed away.

"Where were you?"

There was a tremor in it. It was fear. Huckle heard it as an accusation.

"Out. I don't have to tell you everything, do I?"

He regretted the words as soon as they came out of his mouth. Polly just looked so sad.

"No," she said, and her eyes strayed back to her work surface and the flour dusted there. Neil stayed resolutely at Polly's side; he didn't even come to greet Huckle as he normally would.

"No," said Polly again. "I don't suppose you do."

She sighed.

"Well, I'd better get on."

Huckle had come back in the hope that . . . What? he thought. What was he hoping for? For Polly to fall at his feet, promising anything to make him stay? But that wasn't the girl he knew. That wasn't the girl he loved. Nothing like.

Yet to see her like this, so unfazed by everything that had happened, when he was faced with the utter horror of his friend possibly having to spend the rest of his life raising a child who wasn't his; who wouldn't look like him or have anything in common with him . . . It was just awful, and here she was, banging dough about like nothing had changed when everything had. Was this a female thing? Some secret conspiracy of girls against men? Huckle had always liked women, genuinely enjoyed their company. But this felt like a place he just couldn't go; he couldn't understand it, not at all.

He cleared his throat.

"I was thinking," he said. "There's this beauty convention, they've been asking me to pop in, do some display samples . . . maybe travel around a bit, visit a few buyers here and there."

"Traveling salesman," mumbled Polly quietly. This meant nothing to Huckle.

"So . . . I'm going to take off for a few days."

"But it's practically Christmas!"

"You're working, aren't you? You'll be busy," he said, raising his voice.

Polly blinked several times.

"Oh," she said. She didn't know what else to say. She didn't know what else there was to say.

"I'll get some things," said Huckle, staring at the floor.

Polly's heart was beating incredibly fast in her chest.

"You aren't coming to Kerensa and Reuben's?" she said.

Huckle shook his head. "Do you think that would be a good idea right now?"

"No," said Polly.

"Well then," said Huck. And he climbed the circular staircase to pack, and Polly watched him go.

Chapter Twenty-Six

Polly set off to Reuben's house in Nan the Van, doing her best to put everything out of her mind. Huckle would calm down, wouldn't he? Wouldn't he? It was a difference of opinion. Or rather, it wasn't a difference of opinion. They both knew Kerensa had made a terrible mistake. Where they differed was on what to do about it.

Polly wished he'd stated—utterly and categorically—that he wasn't going to tell Reuben. She should have got him to promise; to write it down and sign it or something.

Oh God. He was coming back, wasn't he? Of course he was. Of course. They'd fallen out, that was all. And he'd cool off and they'd sort it out and . . . well. Well. Things would happen. It would be okay.

But she didn't have time to dwell on it, as she picked Jayden up at the Little Beach Street Bakery. He was uncharacteristically quiet.

"What's up with you?" she said.

"So anyway," said Jayden, looking awkward and staring at his knees. Polly shot him a sidelong glance.

"What?" she said, realizing she'd been so caught up in her own problems, she'd hardly spoken to Jayden at all. He went even pinker.

"So I was thinking about what you said."

Polly cast her mind back.

"About asking Flora to marry you?"

"Yeah. And you said I probably shouldn't do it because she's a student and everything and I'm only twenty-three."

"Yes," said Polly, remembering her brief conversation with Flora at the Christmas fair as she expertly maneuvered Nan the Van across the causeway.

"Yeah, well, I thought about it and I've decided I'm going to totally ignore your advice."

Polly looked at him.

"Oh good!" she said sarcastically. "Well, everybody else does."

"So. I'm going to ask her."

Polly bit her lip. Flora was so nonchalant, it was hard to tell how this was going to go. And she was only twenty-one. Twenty-one! At that age Polly could barely find her keys, never mind get married.

Mind you, things didn't seem to have changed that much twelve years later.

"Well," said Polly, resigning herself to picking up the pieces later, "that's great news. No, it is. I'm really pleased."

Jayden smiled.

"Well, she hasn't said yes yet."

"I'm sure she will," said Polly, not in the least bit sure. "And it will be lovely. How are you planning to ask her?"

"What do you mean?"

"Well, are you going to do a romantic gesture? Wrap it up or hide it or something?"

"Wrap what up?"

"The ring, Jayden!" She looked at him. Honestly, she really wasn't sure he was ready for marriage.

"Oh yeah," said Jayden. "My mum says she's got one somewhere I can have."

Jayden's mother only had one son amongst many girls in the family and had possibly, in Polly's view, occasionally been a little overindulgent. She hoped Flora knew that Jayden's mum still squeezed toothpaste on to his brush for him in the morning and left it loaded in the bathroom.

"Are you sure Flora will like that? She wouldn't want a ring of her own?"

"A ring's a ring, right?" said Jayden, looking confused.

Polly took a very deep breath.

"I mean, you've only got some seaweedy stuff," he added, looking even more confused.

"Yes," said Polly. "But it's very special to . . ." She was suddenly aware that she was about to cry, and swallowed it down hard.

"What's up, boss?" said Jayden.

Polly breathed out.

"Nothing," she said, hitting the A road over to Reuben's house. It was the most glorious morning; good walking weather, and there were plenty of hikers out along the beautiful trails. Polly was suddenly very conscious of her horrible lack of sleep. "Whatever you think will be best . . ."

"Do you think I should do something special?" said Jayden. "I was just going to ask her. But there's still time to go to the jeweler's."

"Is there really a rush?"

Jayden thought about it.

"Well, it is Christmas," he said.

He looked up as they turned in to the incredibly impressive drive toward Reuben's house.

"Wow," he said. "Wow. Is this all his?"

"It is."

"It's amazing," he said. "I've never seen a house like it. It's incredible. Wow. This would . . ." He trailed off. "It's weird that some people are rich like this and some aren't," he added. "You'd think they'd spread it around more."

"Then they wouldn't be rich, I suppose," said Polly. "But yes, I don't understand it either."

"He must be so happy," said Jayden, as they crunched over the gravel toward the house. "He must be, like, the happiest guy in the world."

Chapter Twenty-Seven

The happiest man in the world was marching up and down by the front door, shouting at someone on his mobile phone.

Polly didn't even bother pausing at the main entrance. She was happier around the back anyway. Marta was there and could help her out.

There were a lot of people turning up for Reuben's party: colleagues of Reuben's, as well as many of his friends and acquaintances (like many incredibly rich people, Reuben had the knack of attracting large crowds of people he didn't know particularly well). As she parked the van, Polly heard a massive roar start up next to her and popped her head out of the door. A huge machine was there, making fake snow.

"Seriously," she said, "that has to be the least environmentally friendly thing I have ever seen."

"No," said Reuben, wandering round the side of the house, still shouting on his phone but pausing to put his hand on Polly's shoulder. He had, she never forgot, so few real friends. And what kind of a real friend was she being to him right now anyway? "No, that'll be the full outdoor fires I've got coming later to heat you up from all the fake snow."

"REUBS!"

"What? It's going to be an awesome party!"

He pointed over to where the tennis court usually was. In its place was a bar made of ice.

"Is that what I think it is?" said Polly. "Oh my goodness, really?"

"Really," said Reuben. "Don't try the vodka luge until everyone's finished being served, okay?"

"Duh," said Polly. "But still. I mean. Incredible."

"Thank you," said Reuben. "Have you seen Kerensa?"

Have you seen Kerensa? was becoming quite the refrain.

"I'm not sure she isn't too big to be in a party mood," said Polly.

"Well tough," said Reuben, jutting out his bottom lip and looking about six years old. "She used to be fun and also not a whale."

"Reuben, she's about a million months pregnant. Nobody's expected to be fun at this stage."

"I thought she'd be one of those really cute bouncy pregnant women," said Reuben mournfully, as someone carted what appeared to be blocks for an igloo across the garden. "Not one of the gigantic elephant ones."

"I don't think anyone chooses how they get to be when they're pregnant," said Polly. "I think it just happens and then you hope for the best."

"I've been hoping for the best for months," said Reuben.

Another person walked past with an ice sculpture of a bear. Polly glanced at it, then looked back to Reuben, slightly horrified.

"How big is this party?"

"Who knows? Who cares? I've got a planner. Listen. I wanted to talk to Huckle, but he's gone AWOL too. It's not like Huckle to actually do some work."

"Excuse me," said Polly crossly. "He works a lot actually."

"Yeah yeah, here are some bees, look at the bees, buzz buzz buzz. That's not work, is it."

"He's actually doing a lot of sales . . ."

"Yeah, okay, whatever. But you know my wife, Polly. Tell me, is this normal? Huh? Is it normal for a pregnant woman to go batshit bananas and all weird and bizarre all the time?"

"Some women eat coal," pointed out Polly.

"Yeah, but my wife isn't some women," said Reuben, still pouting. "I mean, my wife is totally the greatest, right? So. What's going on here? What's up? I think I have the best wife, but she's schlubbing around like Schlubby McSchlubberson. On holiday."

"Listen, Kanye West," said Polly, angry suddenly, even though she knew Reuben had a point. Actually, this made her angrier. "It's her body. It's her pregnancy. It's not all about you."

"Yeah it is!" said Reuben. "This is my son! It is totally so about me!"

"It's about both of you."

"Well, yeah, I realize that. But at the moment I'm not even in this picture. And man, normally I'm all over like everything."

A bunch of surfy-looking guys, all ripped and handsome, wandered over and high-fived Reuben. As usual Reuben looked like he didn't have the faintest idea who any of them were, and tiredly returned the high-fives whilst totally ignoring the surfers' effusive greetings.

"It should be about me a little bit, right? Not just somebody mumbling past me and being tired all the time and ignoring me and disappearing on secret missi—"

Reuben closed his mouth as if he'd said something he shouldn't.

"What secret missions?" said Polly.

"Well, I don't know, do I?" said Reuben crossly. "If I did, they wouldn't be secret. It's ridiculous, she's never here."

He sighed, and looked as deflated as Polly had ever seen him, all the bounce draining out of him even as the enormous DJ rig started sound-checking right behind him, the colored lights bouncing off the fake snow.

"All right?" said Father Christmas—the most Father Christmassy Father Christmas Polly had ever seen, with a full white beard, a proper fat belly, kind creased eyes, the works. He was leading a real—no, surely not. But yes, it certainly smelled real—reindeer.

"Yeah, whatever, Santa," said Reuben, and the round man wandered off.

"Look," said Polly. "Honestly. When the baby comes, everything will be different. I'm sure it will. It's just hard, pregnancy."

"Good different?" said Reuben. "What if it gets worse?"

"I don't know," said Polly. "But I'm sure it'll be fine."

She wasn't in the least bit sure. But Reuben seemed a little cheered.

"Okay," he said.

"Just the blues of being, like, fifteen stone," said Polly.

"Yeah," said Reuben. "I can relate. Totally. I'm sure that's what it is too. Yeah. Thanks, Polly. You're a real pal."

Polly felt awful.

Reuben turned round, his freckled face brightening up.

"Okay, everyone! Who's ready to PARRRR-TAAAAAYYYYYY?!"

"Yeah!" came back a plethora of voices from the people setting up. Everything was in position now, and guests were starting to arrive; they were nearly ready to begin.

"Not you, Polly," reminded Reuben. "You're working."

"I KNOW, you putz," groaned Polly, and she headed back into the kitchen with some relief, as the speakers cranked up, and "It's CHRRRIIIIIISSSSTTTT-MAAAS" came rolling over the incredibly expensive stereo, and the doors were opened and the guests started to pour in and the party began.

Chapter Twenty-Eight

Polly rushed around with the other caterers, who were making great vats of mulled wine, even though the vodka luge was clearly much more popular, and huge winter stews that scented the air with cranberries and what Polly suspected was reindeer, though that hardly mattered, since none of the skinny-looking model girls—how did Reuben even know these people?—would eat a morsel. They were all too busy downing drinks and smoking on the pristine fake snow that now carpeted the stunning lawns at the back of the house, which was completely festooned with fairy lights of all colors.

It was beautiful, incredibly beautiful, and she felt a great sadness suddenly. Reuben threw wonderful parties. She shouldn't be here, slaving away over pastry, while Huckle and Kerensa were God knows where (Reuben himself was in the middle of a great crowd of people taking selfies, then studying them thoughtfully, deleting the pics they didn't like. This appeared to be what constituted socializing now). If it had been the four of them together, she thought wistfully, they'd have been having so much fun.

There was a cotton candy stand, with snow-white candyfloss being twirled. The models seemed to quite like that; it weighed even less than they did. And there was a big queue to sit on Santa's lap in his grotto, which was manned by rather foxy-looking elves. The DJ had stopped so that an incredibly cool retro swing band could play; they were doing ironic Christmas hits, with three girls in big circle skirts and bright red lipstick singing backing vocals, and people had started dancing. Huckle was a terrible dancer. It was strange; in bed, or on a surfboard, or in a beehive, he was completely graceful and natural and totally at ease, but ask him to move to a beat and he couldn't do it at all. By contrast, Reuben had taken classes and she always found it a true pleasure to dance with him, as he pushed and pulled her around on the dance floor whilst Kerensa watched and laughed at her technique. But that wouldn't be happening either.

Polly sighed, handing round more exquisite canapés filled with hot spiced-wine-flavored pâté. She had somehow managed, she noticed, to overcome the food aversion of Reuben's guests; they were scarfing them down. Well, at least one thing was going right. She refilled her tray in the kitchen as staff bustled about trying to keep up with the demand for champagne and mince-pie martinis. The hubbub of the room, the high-pitched squeals and laughter, was growing louder; the party was in absolutely full swing and going with a bang.

Suddenly the mike cut out and the band clattered to a halt. Polly thought Reuben was getting up to make a speech, which was just like him, but she didn't hear people applauding. She glanced around. Where the hell was Kerensa? This entire party was going on without her. Reuben must be fuming.

She moved forward to get a closer look and saw, to her horror, that it was Jayden who had climbed onto the stage. He looked fatter than ever in a shirt that was clearly too small for him, and his face was red and sweaty with nerves. He'd even shaved off his cute moustache, which made him look slightly featureless and awkward. The crowd of incredibly trendy London fashion and art types looked at him coolly. The room had gone very quiet, and Polly was suddenly intensely nervous for him.

He took the mike from the rather displeased-looking singer, and it immediately howled with feedback.

"Um, hello?" he boomed into it, far too loudly, holding it close to his mouth. The audience recoiled a little, and it was clear that his hand was trembling.

With a shock, Polly realized what he was about to do. Oh no. This was not the time or the place for a big proposal. This wasn't the crowd. She could see that Jayden would think that this incredibly posh do, awash with champagne, was quite the spectacular opportunity, but she couldn't imagine how quiet, shy Flora would react. She hadn't even known Flora was coming. If she had, she'd have gotten her to help.

"Um, Flora? I just want to . . . Flora, are you there?" Jayden obviously couldn't see a thing and was blinking carefully.

"Who are you?" said one wag cheekily, and the crowd laughed.

Polly glanced about. She spotted Flora, pale and rigid, cringing against the wall of the huge room. She

wanted to go to her, but there was a thicket of people between them, all of them staring at Jayden, who
looked incredibly uncomfortable and awkward now, up
there in front of everyone, like a dream gone horribly
wrong.

"Flora! Could you come up here, please?"

Flora was frantically shaking her head, but when it
became apparent who she was, the crowd, hungry for
what was going on, parted to make way for her. She
slunk through, head down, her long carpet of hair covering her face.

Polly could not think of a worse place to get a proposal. She thought back, her heart aching, to Huckle
asking, so quietly and gently that she hadn't quite understood to begin with what he meant, and then the gradual
dawning realization that he meant everything, and she
wanted to cry. She fingered the seaweed ring; twisted it
round and round on her hand, vowing to do whatever it
took to get them back together.

Flora also looked like she was about to cry. She was
helped awkwardly onto the stage, where she stood with
her head bowed. Jayden, who was perspiring freely now,
turned to face her and, with great clumsiness, got down
on one knee.

"Rip!" shouted someone in the crowd, and Polly suddenly wanted to machine-gun them all. She was cross
with Jayden, too; she'd told him not to do this, that it
was too soon and Flora wouldn't like it, and here he
was now, making an idiot out of himself. Some horribly scrawny model girl let out a high-pitched fake laugh
of disbelief, and Polly only stopped herself sticking
her with a fork by thinking about how many times the
model girl would probably get divorced in the future.
She sighed bad-temperedly.

"Flora, would you make me the happiest man in the world . . . ?"

There was silence in the room—an unpleasant silence, Polly could sense, as the huge gang of cool kids waited to laugh at the awkward chubby fellow with the shaking hands. She wondered if she'd lose Jayden, if the humiliation might make him give up or leave town altogether. And losing Flora for the holiday season would be a huge blow. The girl was a little divvy and distracted, but she had a natural gift for baking that Polly could only dream of. Ugh. This was going so wrong.

But to Polly's amazement, Flora simply shrugged her shoulders.

"Yeah, whatevs," she said, in a voice so low it was practically a whisper.

Polly blinked. What? The crowd stared too.

"YES!" shouted Jayden, raising both hands in the air, revealing very damp patches under his arms. "Yes!"

He turned round to kiss Flora, but she'd already bolted from the stage. Jayden air-punched one more time, then jumped down after her.

"Hang on!" he shouted. "I've got a ring!"

The band tittered politely.

"How charming," said the singer into the mike, and Polly wanted to slap him. Then they struck up with "I'm in the Mood for Love."

As Polly went to find the happy couple to congratulate them—nobody else seemed to be—she walked slap-bang into Reuben.

"Your friends are all horrible," she blurted.

"Yeah?" said Reuben, who was brandishing a gigantic cigar without actually smoking it. "Well at least they're *here*."

He had, Polly thought, a point.

She found Flora—looking furiously embarrassed—and a beaming Jayden by the downstairs cloakroom. Flora was putting on her coat.

"Um, congratulations, you two!" said Polly. Jayden gave her a not entirely friendly look.

"Yeah, well, you're the one who told me not to."

"Well, obviously I was wrong," said Polly, trying to be breezy.

"You weren't wrong," growled Flora. "I was black affronted up there."

"Oh, my sweet pea," sighed Jayden. "I love you so much."

"I'm going home," said Flora.

"I'll come with you to talk you around," said Jayden eagerly, and looked at Polly.

"Sure, you can go," she said wearily. She'd stay and clear up. It was fine. She had nothing more pressing to do.

Chapter Twenty-Nine

Polly went outside. The sky was low and it was utterly freezing. She walked forward a little, just pleased to be out of the crush and the pressure and the noise inside, even though the party was starting to wind down. Even models and actresses had mums somewhere who needed them home for Christmas morning, she reflected. Sleek black cars were pulling up to the doorway; people were clutching the goody bags Santa had given everyone. Thankfully, there were other people to help clean up, and she might leave a lot of it to them; Polly felt utterly exhausted.

She wandered across the busy driveway and around to the side of the house, with its path down to the private beach. It was so beautiful there, so calm and peaceful as the noise from the house receded and she could hear the heavy black waves pounding on the beach. She sighed. Christmas Eve. And this year had started out so promisingly . . .

"Hey."

She turned around. Kerensa was walking along

wrapped in a huge blanket, wearing a shapeless pair of black pregnancy trousers and a huge oversized hoody that did nothing to minimize her enormous bump.

"There you are!" said Polly. "Everyone's been worried sick! Reuben didn't even do one of his speeches!"

"Well, thank heavens for small mercies," said Kerensa. Polly went closer. Kerensa was shivering with the cold.

"Come inside," said Polly. "You'll freeze. It's not good for you to be out here like this."

"Are all those people gone?" said Kerensa. "I just feel like I can't face it. That they'll all stare and judge me and . . . Oh God, I don't know what's happened to me. I don't know."

Polly grabbed her friend's arm.

"You're punishing yourself," she said. "And you don't even know if you have to."

"Oh, I have to," said Kerensa.

Polly took her hand. It was icy cold.

"Come on," she said firmly. "Inside. We'll go through the tradesmen's entrance. None of that lot will think to look there."

"Thanks for opening up," said the tall blond man, sitting in the chilly puffin café.

"It's all right," said Bernard. "I didn't know where else to go either."

They glanced around.

"You know, if your girlfriend can help," said Bernard, "it will make all the difference to us. All of it."

Huckle nodded. He stared out of the window; there

was a hint of snow in the heavy clouds above. It looked like it might unleash itself at any moment.

"I mean, she'll be a total hero," said Bernard.

"Yeah, yeah, I know. She's a total hero. She helps everyone. Yeah, that's great. Thanks."

"Are things all right between you two?"

Huckle picked up his beer and put it down again.

"Ah, well. You know. Life gets complicated."

"You don't need to tell me," said Bernard. "I've got two million puffins to rehouse."

They clinked glasses miserably.

"Happy Christmas," said Bernard. "Who knows where we'll be next year?"

"Surely it can't be worse than this," said Huckle. Outside the puffins flew and danced in the sky. They all seemed to be having a great time.

"I've got some frozen chips in the freezer," said Bernard. "Want me to stick some on?"

"Sure," said Huckle, sighing. He glanced at his phone. No messages.

But he didn't need to speak to her; he knew exactly what she'd be doing: bustling through the kitchen, her cheeks pink from the heat of the stove, a tendril of that lovely pale hair cascading down her face, sleeves rolled up, checking that everything was coming out on time, arranging delicious morsels on plates, yelling at Jayden, ticking over, completely immersed, completely sure of herself. But never, ever too tired or busy not to look up at him in total delight every time he walked through the door.

He missed it so much it felt like a physical pain.

He thought back over the last evening. It had been strange and awful all at once. He drank some more beer.

Even his parents had been out of reach, which wasn't like them. He sighed again.

"Something up?" said Bernard, coming back with the chips. Huckle wasn't hungry, but he took one listlessly. It was soggy. Bernard really, really needed someone to help with his catering.

"Nothing."

"Seriously? Because, you know. It's late. And you're here."

"Yeah," said Huckle.

"You know," said Bernard, "anyone who wants to save a puffin sanctuary . . . I think they're a pretty good bet."

Huckle smiled ruefully.

"She just . . . I mean, she just doesn't want to get married, I don't think."

"Hmmm," said Bernard. "Maybe she's more like that fox Selina. Cunning. Treating you mean and reeling you in like a swordfish."

"A swordfish?" said Huckle. "Anyway, she's not like that."

"Hmmm," said Bernard again.

There was a pause.

"Bernard, could I ask you something?"

And he never told Polly afterward that it had been Bernard, of all people, the puffin man, who'd confirmed what she'd been telling him all along: that it was absolutely none of his fucking business.

"You go back. Tail between your legs. And you smile and be really, really nice to the puffling. Baby. I mean baby."

He paused.

"And that minxy girlfriend of yours . . . I'd close that deal, if it's making you this crazy."

"Hmmm," said Huckle. "That's one point of view. Or maybe . . . maybe she just doesn't want to marry *me*. Maybe that's it. Maybe I should cut my losses now."

Bernard shrugged as if he didn't care either way, which he didn't.

"Anyway, how are you?" said Huckle, changing the subject, because it was making him so sad.

"Not bad," said Bernard. "I own a failing puffin sanctuary and I'm in love with a beautiful jewelry designer who doesn't know I'm alive."

They chinked beers again, Huckle deep in thought.

"Merry Christmas," he said.

"And to you."

Chapter Thirty

By the time Polly and Kerensa got back inside, everyone had left. There were still some people dismantling the stage, but otherwise it was as if the hundreds of beautiful people had appeared and dematerialized in a dream; everything had been swept up and put away and returned to how it was, and the magic of the house had gone.

Kerensa stood staring out of the window like a bird in a cage desperate to be free.

The promised snow had not come down after all. It was bleak outside; not clear and cold but gray and solid, as if the clouds were blanketing the world, making everything heavy and sad.

Polly stood at her shoulder and gazed out too. There was little to see, just the occasional glimpse of a lighthouse. There was a ship a long way out to sea, a tanker, on its way to Plymouth perhaps, from who knew where—Sri Lanka? China? Italy? What was it carrying? The men who crewed her would be missing their families tonight. Missing their loved ones. She raised her rapidly chilling cup of tea to them as the great blinking lights passed by.

The shadows under Kerensa's eyes were more pronounced than ever.

"What happened to Huckle?"

Polly shook her head.

"Never mind. Difference of opinion."

"Tell me," said Kerensa. "Tell me what's happened. Is it to do with me? Please tell me."

"It's fine," said Polly, more harshly than she'd meant to. "We're fine. He thinks I'm working too much."

"Well, tomorrow's going to be fun," said Kerensa. "When you're working again."

"You can't have Christmas without a gigantic fight," said Polly. "Isn't that the law?"

"Oh God, and my lot are coming too," said Kerensa. "You know what my mum's going to be like with Rhonda."

"They're very similar personalities," said Polly without thinking. "I mean . . . I don't mean that. I really don't."

"And what about your mum?"

Polly sighed. "Oh God. I texted her to say I'd come over after lunch."

"And?"

"She didn't say yes. And she didn't say no either. It's been quite the silent treatment. She's relentless."

"She's all right," said Kerensa.

"Well, I wish she'd tell me. I'm going over anyway, though I don't think she really wants me to come. And I'll be driving, so no booze. Yeah. And possibly no Huckle. Will be brilliant. I'm looking forward to sitting in total silence and watching *EastEnders*."

Kerensa nodded.

"That sounds better than here."

Polly thought self-pityingly of the plan she and Huckle had had originally—lying in bed in the light-house, drinking champagne. Why couldn't she have just done that? Why had everything gotten so mad and out of control? Why had she ended up saying yes to every-thing except the one thing she really wanted to do? Yes to everybody else, and no to them.

"Oh God," she said. "Next Christmas will be better, won't it? Won't it?"

Kerensa didn't say anything for a while.

"But Polly, what if . . . what if . . ."

Polly didn't say anything. She simply moved toward Kerensa and gave her a huge hug. She couldn't quite get her arms around her, but they stood there together, two friends in the dark.

Polly suddenly became conscious that she was stand-ing in something. Had she spilled some of the leftover milk as she was taking it to the fridge? What had hap-pened to the cup of tea she'd been continuously remak-ing and forgetting to drink for the last seven hours? She cast around, then glanced at the floor.

"Oh," she said. Kerensa hadn't realized.

"Um," Polly said. Kerensa still had her eyes closed and was leaning in, enjoying the hug.

"Kez," she said. "I don't want to alarm you. But I *think* . . . I think your waters might have broken."

Kerensa's eyes snapped open.

"What?" she said, and looked down. "Oh Lord," she said. "Oh Lord. But it's WEEKS away."

Polly sat Kerensa down on an expensive leather arm-chair. She thought briefly about the consequences of this, but put them out of her mind. Kerensa's eyes were wide open and she was breathing heavily. Polly found a cloth.

"OMG, what happens now?" she said.

"I don't know!" said Kerensa. She looked up at Polly. "I didn't go to any of the antenatal classes."

"What do you mean?" said Polly. "That's where you were all those times you were out of the house! That and shopping for the baby."

Kerensa shook her head.

"I couldn't," she said. "I went to one and it was all so vomitous, all those carey-sharey husbands, everyone showing off and pretending they were more in love than anyone else and that their birth was going to be the best. I couldn't do it. Reuben wouldn't come anyway, and I couldn't handle everyone else with their perfect lives. Couldn't handle it at all."

"So what were you doing?" said Polly, grabbing the phone handset.

For a moment, Kerensa half smiled.

"Doesn't matter," she said. "Not now, anyway."

Polly shot her a suspicious look, but this wasn't the time.

"So, who do I phone?"

"Actually," said Kerensa, "I feel okay. I don't . . . Polly, it's weeks to my due date. It must just be a mistake."

"I don't think burst waters are a mistake. So that's all fine," said Polly, trying to stay calm. "You get to skip the boring hanging-about bit."

There was a pause. Then Kerensa gasped as she thought of something.

"It means the baby's got too big," she said, her eyes filling with tears. "It's a gigantic big Brazilian stripper baby."

"Stop it," said Polly. "There's nothing to be done about it now. Nothing. The baby is coming. Will I get Reuben?"

Kerensa blinked. Then suddenly her breathing hitched, and she bent over quickly.

"Ohhhhh!" she said, and her entire body tensed for what felt like a very long time to both of them. She was silent for a moment, then straightened up a little. She looked at Polly. "I think . . . I think that might have been one," she said.

"I agree," said Polly. "I'd better get Reuben."

"As soon as he arrives, everything's going to go bananas," said Kerensa, her breathing slowing gradually.

In the quiet unlit kitchen, surrounded by the scent of Polly's bread that she'd put in so it would be fresh for breakfast, it was oddly peaceful and timeless. Both of them briefly wished they could just stay there for a little while longer. The Christmas tree glimmered and glistened in the hallway. The world stopped; breathed, waiting for Christmas morning. Waiting, Polly supposed, for a baby . . .

Kerensa reached out her hand and Polly squeezed it.

"You know," said Polly, "everything is going to be all right."

"Is it?" said Kerensa. Her face was full of fear.

"Yes," said Polly. "I'm here. It will be fine. Things end up fine."

"Do they?" said Kerensa.

"Yes," said Polly. "That's the promise of Christmas. Believe it."

They squeezed hands again. Then Kerensa lurched over once more.

"Okay," said Polly. "You're going to have to time your contractions."

"How come you know this stuff?" grumbled Kerensa.

"I watch *Call the Midwife*," said Polly. "Your husband is going to come back from t'pit and not want to see it."

"Yes, well, I wish," said Kerensa.

Polly made sure she was sitting comfortably.

"Okay," she said. "I'm going. I'm going to get him, okay?"

They shared a look.

"Everything changes now," said Kerensa.

"Everything always does," said Polly.

She kissed Kerensa lightly on the head, then turned and left the silent, fragrant kitchen as the great boat out on the horizon finally disappeared.

Chapter Thirty-One

Privately Polly couldn't believe it was in the least bit good for a new baby to be surrounded by so much fuss and fluster. Reuben had to be instantly persuaded out of calling for a helicopter, on the grounds that the baby was still probably a day or so away and that it would be the single most dangerous part of the entire birth.

Rhonda was running around—after emerging with a suspiciously full face of makeup for the time of day—trying to make everything about her and announcing what it had been like when Reuben was born (a feat of extraordinary pain and endurance that nearly killed her; she had lost eleven pints of blood, not something that anyone felt was particularly useful to say at the time). Reuben had of course instantly ignored/forgotten the fact that he'd been annoyed with Kerensa at the party. Normally this was the most infuriating thing about him. But that night Kerensa was profoundly grateful for it as he stood in the middle of the kitchen barking orders and waking up his incredibly expensive gynaecologist, who tried to explain that he probably wouldn't be needed for quite a while, seeing as Kerensa's contractions were still a good fifteen minutes apart and, so far, not terribly debilitating, so perhaps they should call him in the . . .

Reuben gave this extremely short shrift and sent the helicopter for him instead.

In an instant, a fleet of black cars had arrived at the door. Kerensa had at least packed a bag, but Reuben had packed two suitcases, and the entire boot of the car was soon filled.

"Come," said Kerensa to Polly.

"Are you sure?" said Polly. Kerensa looked around at the others. "Yes," she said. "Will you get my mum first?"

It was agreed that Polly would pick up Kerensa's mum and meet them at the hospital.

"Wait!" shouted Reuben as she left. "Don't take that deathtrap van, you'll kill everyone."

And he hurled her the keys to Kerensa's Range Rover.

Polly drove like the wind down completely deserted roads, revelling in the smooth automatic car that didn't let in drafts. She had to phone Huckle. It was her first instinct in everything: phone him, tell him.

But she hadn't told him everything, had she? And if she told him about this, well, it would hurl them straight back into that incredibly knotty problem.

Reuben would call him. Of course he would. Reuben would call him and then . . . well. Then they'd see.

Kerensa's mum, Jackie, was standing on the kerb, her own suitcase completely packed, the joy and nerves and excitement plain to see on her face, all mixed in together.

"Baby Express?" said Polly cheerfully, leaning out of the window.

"This is totally the best Christmas present ever," said Jackie, and Polly was suddenly so pleased and relieved to be with someone who was a hundred percent straightforwardly delighted about everything that was going on that she too relaxed and enjoyed the drive to the hospital, through little towns with jolly pubs where revelers had celebrated Christmas Eve; where old school friends, long scattered, came back together just for the night; students came home; everyone was at home to be with their families for Christmas, just as it should be, even though tomorrow there would be disappointments: batteries that didn't work, unsuitable gifts, arguments about politics, dry turkey, and too much drink taken, who's looking after Granny, ancient unearthed sibling rivalries replayed around the table and overexcited children vomiting and crying.

But all of those were for tomorrow. Tonight there was a lovely sense of anticipation, almost nicer, as lights on in houses and cottages showed children bouncing up and down on beds and mothers trying to get them settled; people pulling mysterious shapes out of garages, marching with holly and wrapping paper; fairy lights flickering; the cars they passed piled high with bundles.

Polly remembered the old story about how at midnight on Christmas Eve all the animals fell silent in memory of the waiting baby and the creatures in the stall at Bethlehem and the sheep on the hillsides. When she'd been little, she'd always wanted to stay up till midnight to see if next door's Pomeranian would stop its usual yapping.

Had her mother told her that story? she wondered. Was that where it had come from?

They sped on through the night toward Plymouth. Polly glanced at Jackie.

"Are you all right?" she asked gently.

Jackie half smiled.

"It's so strange," she said. "It only feels like yesterday that Kez was a baby. My baby. Having a baby. Well. Her dad wasn't half so calm as you, driving me to the hospital. Mind you, she wasn't for hanging about, that one. Always in a rush. Nearly had her in the parking lot."

Jackie smiled.

"She was . . . she was the sunniest child, Polly. The light of our lives, truly, even when the boys came along. There's something special about your first child, there really is. Always."

Polly just nodded.

"And recently . . . I don't know. I've been worried about her. It's like the spark has gone out of her. Have you noticed? Do you feel that?"

Polly shrugged. "I think . . . I think maybe she's had a tough pregnancy."

"Maybe," frowned Jackie. "She's certainly looked enormous."

"I wouldn't say that to her."

"Ha! No!"

Jackie glanced at her phone.

"Nothing. She knows we're on the way, doesn't she?"

"She does," said Polly. "Also she'll be surrounded by everybody fussing. They probably won't let her do much. There's probably a special way of having babies rich people do, where it doesn't hurt and there isn't any mess or anything."

"Hmm," said Jackie.

Polly thought of a poem: all the way to the hospital, the lights were green as peppermints, the roads finally emptying out. It was time now; everyone, it seemed, was where they had to be, home for Christmas, whatever home meant for them, whether it was with friends, or loved ones, or working in a shelter. It was time. It was ready. The bright stars of the world were holding their breath.

Chapter Thirty-Two

On the private wing, there was bustle and fuss and soft flattering lighting and a rather bored-looking consultant still wearing his tweed jacket and clearly waiting for something to happen.

Rhonda was yelling into her phone at Reuben's siblings back in the U.S., while Merv was strolling up and down the corridors with his hands behind his back. Reuben was shouting about how awesome Kerensa was and how she was going to have this baby entirely naturally without any drugs, and there was some muted response from Kerensa that seemed to disagree with this theory entirely, and all in all it felt like there were a lot more people in the room than was entirely necessary, including lots of staff, and then of course Jackie burst in too, so then there were tears and hugs and Rhonda stepped back somewhat coolly, it had to be said, and Polly stood by the sidelines.

She caught Kerensa's eye, but Kerensa seemed to be somewhere else altogether; off in another land, where pain and something very strange and new were happening, and Polly didn't think it was entirely right that they should all be there for something so very special, and certainly not her, so she squeezed Kerensa's hand, whispered, "You'll do it, my darling," then kissed her on her damp forehead and quietly retreated, stealing down the hospital corridors.

They were deserted, just a man in the corner cleaning with one of those big double-wheeled mops. Polly had no doubt he wanted to get home to his family for Christmas too.

She took out her phone and looked at the screen. Nothing. What was wrong with Huckle? Where was he? This was Christmas. What did it mean? Were they finished? Was it over? Surely not. She called, but there was no answer. Of course in Cornwall this didn't always mean very much. She sighed, and sent him a text.

Happy Christmas. Please can we . . .

She deleted the last bit. Maybe let everything go calm for a little while. Just a while.

Then she dialled another number.

"Hello, Mum. Yes, I know it's late but the causeway's closed and . . ."

They sat up with cups of tea, her mother having made it quite clear that there would never be any more booze with the two of them in the room. She'd also looked very sadly at the Range Rover and murmured that she'd always hoped Polly would have had a nice car of her own, but Polly had chosen to ignore that.

"I remember the night you were born," Doreen said

quietly, as they sat, the omnipresent television on, playing carols from Trafalgar Square. There was a small
plastic tree, with fake presents underneath it, that made
Polly sadder than she could bear to think. She brought
in all her gifts she'd been thankfully too lazy to remove
from the car, even though she knew that a Marks and
Sparks dressing gown, a new scarf and a nail voucher
her mother would never use were hardly the stuff
dreams were made of. Likewise the basket she could
see with her name on it. When she was a teenager she'd
loved the Body Shop, and Doreen had helpfully never
deviated from it since.

"Tell me," said Polly, staring into the gas fire and
wishing Neil were there.

"Well. Your grandad . . . of course it was too much
for him. I mean, they'd been very supportive and everything, even though I'd lost my job, couldn't be on the
shop floor, not really, not with that bump sticking out
and all the men coming in to buy hats for their wives . . .
It sounds a thousand years ago, but it wasn't really."

Polly smiled.

"And your grandma, God rest her soul, I mean, she
never learned to drive. So we took a cab, an old Cortina,
stank of fags. I couldn't bear the smell. When we got to
the hospital, she checked me in but then left me. She had
to get back, or she felt she should, or Dad needed his tea
or . . . well. I don't know why. I never did really. Maybe
she was worried she'd bump into one of her friends or
something. They were supportive, they were, truly. We
lived with them for a few years, until this house came
up. And they never told me off. I mean some girls, they
got thrown out. Some got sent away, you know. The
Catholic girls, the things that happened to them were
unbelievable. And recent, too."

She took a long sip of her tea.

"So. Anyway. I had to . . . I had to do it all by myself. All alone. They weren't very interested, the nurses. They were too busy chatting to the nervous husbands and the doctors. They hadn't much time for a little scrubber like me. When it hurt, one of them said to me, well, you should have thought about that, shouldn't you?" Her eyes filled with tears.

"I'm sorry," said Polly.

"Not your fault," said her mother.

"Was it awful?"

Her mother looked at her.

"Well, yes," she said. "Until . . . until I saw you."

They fell silent. The swell of the carols on the television grew louder. They were singing the Coventry Carol. It was beautiful.

"I didn't even get to hold you for very long . . . they used to whisk babies off in those days. You know it was even suggested that I give you up. That was perfectly common, perfectly normal."

"Did you consider it?" said Polly, feeling daring even for asking. Her mother frowned.

"Of course not," she said. "Of course not. I mean, no disrespect to women who felt they had to, none at all. But no. No, I couldn't. And I had my parents, even if they weren't . . . It took my dad a little while to come round to you . . ."

Polly stiffened. She had the fondest memories of her kind, reticent, pipe-smoking grandpa.

". . . five whole seconds, I seem to remember." She smiled to herself. "You were born with that hair," she said. "You looked so very like your father, straightaway. But I loved you . . . I loved you fiercely. Everything else in my life had gone so wrong, was so awful. You . . .

you were so right. Maybe that's why I've fussed over you . . . worried about you too much."

"No you haven't," said Polly uncomfortably.

Her mother shrugged.

"You were . . . you are . . ."

The rest of the sentence hung there in the overheated room. Now the singers were bawling out, "Hail, thou ever blessed morn! Hail, redemption's happy dawn! Sing to all Jerusalem! Christ is born in Bethlehem," as the clock ticked over, and it was practically dawn on Christmas morning.

"I'm sorry. I just always wanted you to be safe, and happy," said Doreen. "By having a bit of money and a bit of freedom and some security. I mean, every parent wants that. And I never had that for you."

Polly nodded.

"So when you dash off buying lighthouses and giving up sensible careers and demanding that I come down and appreciate the sea air and wander about in the country and things . . . I do get scared. I do. I'm sorry."

"I understand," said Polly.

"But don't disappoint that lovely boy," said her mum. "Don't let me or anybody else stop you from that. Ever. I'm telling you now. Forget what happened to me. You marry him and have babies and live on fresh air if you have to. Be happy. I was never brave enough to be, never brave enough to step out there. But you could be. You can, Polly. Please, please, do it for me."

Polly nodded, and tried not to sigh.

"Okay," she said.

They got up to go to bed.

At the door, Doreen stopped.

"Did you see . . . did you see your father in the end?" she asked.

Polly shook her head.

"No, Mum," she said. "You're my family."

Doreen swallowed hard.

"I've been too proud," she said. "I know that. It's hard . . . It's been such a long time. But if you wanted to . . . well. I can't see it would make much difference now."

Polly nodded.

"Okay," she said. "Thanks. And happy Christmas."

They embraced, and Polly winced a little at how thin her mother was, and vowed that next year she would get her down to Mount Polbearne more and insist, despite her protestations, that she sit outside the bakery with a cup of tea in her hand, and no telly, and instead enjoy the sunshine and get to say hello to the passers-by, and if she didn't want to live her own life, necessarily, then she ought to share more of Polly's. And that would be her Christmas gift.

Chapter Thirty-Three

Polly slept better than she had in weeks, back in her childhood single bed, with the posters of Leonardo Di-Caprio and Kevin from the Backstreet Boys on the walls. Reuben had texted to say they were all staying at the Exeter ground. It was something about being back there, back home, and something about not having to get up and work the next day for highly demanding American guests and also something about the fact that it didn't seem to matter how late she might lie awake wondering about Huckle, it wasn't going to make a blind bit of difference, so there wasn't really any point.

Plus, she was beyond exhausted.

She woke to, amazingly, the scent of bacon and eggs frying. Was her mother actually cooking? This was unheard of. She checked her phone. Nothing except a quick text from Reuben saying that nothing much was going on, this was super boring and rubbish, please could she make some doughnuts and bring them to the hospital, and make enough for the nurses too, please, and tell

Huckle to call him because he hadn't heard from him at all.

Polly was just starting to worry seriously about Huckle when he called.

"Where are you?" she said crossly, when in fact she had woken up rested, happy to be reconciled with her mum and all prepared to be sweet to him and make it up.

"Plymouth," said Huckle.

"Plymouth? Why?"

She was suddenly filled with panic that he was waiting for a train to London to catch a flight back to the U.S. He couldn't be. Surely. No. No he wouldn't, would he?

"Why? Are you flying home?"

"What? What are you talking about? No!"

There was a long pause, then, "Polly . . . Polly, I thought I had a home."

"So did I," said Polly miserably.

"No . . . I'm just. Polly, you understand, don't you? I feel awful about all of this. Awful for Kerensa, awful for Reuben. I'm just . . . I'm just away working for a little while so I don't come and put my foot in it, or say something awful, or just get upset . . . so we don't fight. Do you understand?"

"Not really. What are you doing?"

"I told you, I'm working."

"It's Christmas Day. How can you be working?"

"It's a city," said Huckle. "It's a totally normal day for loads of people here. You've been out of the loop for too long. I have a meeting with a Jewish beauty consortium."

"Okay," said Polly.

"Also, I thought you were working today?"

"Apparently so," said Polly, glancing at the phone, which was lighting up with more orders and messages.

"Wish me luck with my mum's oven. I don't think it's been used since the Royal Wedding. The first one."

"You're at your mum's?"

"Yes," said Polly. "The baby's coming, and I don't want to risk the tides."

"The *baby's* coming?"

"Look at your messages!"

"Yeah, well . . . But you're still working."

"Reuben wants catering," said Polly.

There was a pause.

"I can't get down," said Huckle.

"Well, I don't think it's imminent. I think first babies take ages."

There was a silence.

"Okay," said Huckle finally. "Well, I can tell you're busy."

Don't let me be busy, Polly tried to silently beam to him. *Come back. Whisk me out of this. Make everything lovely and fun again.*

"I guess you're busy too," she said.

"Oh, you'd better believe it," said Huckle.

There was another long pause.

"How's Neil?"

"Not here," confessed Polly.

"You left him alone on Christmas Day?" said Huckle.

"I know, I know. I'll make it up to him. Can puffins eat chocolate?"

Chapter Thirty-Four

The triumphant text message had arrived before Polly had a chance to heat up the fryer for the doughnuts. She offered to take her mother, who'd declined, but nicely, and said she'd see her in a few days.

Polly walked down the hospital corridor, all nerves. The swanky private wing was, she was slightly aggrieved to note, nicer than most places she'd ever lived in. Oh well. Even so, the Christmas decorations seemed a little forced. Someone had made a gigantic star out of cardboard bedpans. It was kind of revolting and charming at the same time. The nurses were wearing Santa hats, as were several of the patients, which looked rather sad.

She found the right room without too much trouble, partly because it was covered in hundreds of absurdly gigantic blue helium balloons, and a line of muffin baskets that stretched out the door. Americans, Polly remembered, liked to celebrate this kind of thing.

She took a deep breath, and knocked gently.

Inside, it was chaos. Kerensa was sitting up in bed looking exhausted and anxious but tender and strange all at the same time. Reuben was jabbering into his mobile by the window.

"Yeah! Yeah! He's perfect! He's awesome! Seriously, I'm telling you, you wouldn't get a better child than this. We're seriously considering getting him a special tutor, because I'm telling you now, this kid is smart. I mean, better than smart, I mean super smart . . ."

"How are you," mouthed Polly, as she gingerly tried to embrace Kerensa without accidentally whacking the baby on the head with her handbag.

Kerensa smiled tiredly.

"Well, that was interesting," she said.

"By interesting do you mean heartily disgusting?" asked Polly.

"It's really, really disgusting," said Kerensa. "I don't know why anyone does it. Honestly. It's rubbish."

Her voice went a bit wobbly and Polly thought she was about to cry, so then, of course, they both did start to cry.

Finally Polly plucked up the courage to look down.

He was just . . . he was just a baby. Dark fronds of hair on his head, eyes tightly shut, looking like an astronaut who'd just landed from another world and taken his suit off but still carried the faint aura of other-worldliness and stardust.

Polly blinked.

"He's beautiful, Kerensa."

"I know!" said Kerensa, snuffling.

Reuben was still hollering into the phone and wasn't paying them any attention. Polly took Kerensa's hand and squeezed it very tightly. Then she offered the baby a finger, and he grabbed on to it without opening his eyes.

"That's amazing," she said, feeling his tiny grip. His little mouth worked, looking for something.

"Oh don't be hungry," said Kerensa. "I tell you, breastfeeding is also disgusting. And impossible."

"Keep at it," said Polly.

"Oh, I will," said Kerensa. "He's obviously loving it. Plus Reuben says it gives you a bunch of IQ points, and we're already raising the greatest genius the world has ever known, obviously."

Polly smiled.

"Hey, Polls!" said Reuben, finishing his call. "Meet my awesome son, huh! Awesome son, going to take on the world, blah blah blah."

His face went uncharacteristically soft for a moment and he lowered the phone that was usually superglued to his fingers. He moved away from the window and stared deep into the baby's face. Polly found she was holding her breath. He put his hand on the baby's head.

"Huh, dark hair," he said. "Normally the Finkels have, you know . . ." He indicated his own ginger locks.

"That's just cowl hair," said Kerensa incredibly fast. "It'll come out. It's not his real hair."

"No, no, it's cool, I like dark hair," said Reuben, gazing at the baby. "He's beautiful, isn't he, Polly? Don't you think he's the most beautiful baby there's ever been? And super smart. He totally aced his Apgar test. First exam he ever had, and he aced it."

Polly blinked.

"Yes," she said. "What are you calling him?"

Kerensa and Reuben exchanged glances.

"Ah," said Kerensa.

"What?" said Reuben. "Herschel's a great family name."

"Herschel," said Kerensa. "Herschel Finkel."

"Ohh," said Polly, putting a polite expression on her face. "That sounds nice."

"Hershy? Hersch? Herscho?" said Kerensa. "What's wrong with Lowin?"

"That's lovely," said Polly.

"Yeah, right," said Reuben. "Way to get him bullied at school."

"Oh and Herschel Finkel isn't?"

"Nothing wrong with it," said Reuben stoutly.

"We'll get around to sorting out the name," said Kerensa.

Just then Rhonda and Merv burst into the room with huge shopping bags full of clothes and, absurdly, lots and lots of toys, which, given that the baby was at the moment not much more than a floppy fish, was a bit hard to understand.

"Here he is! The most beautiful boy in the world! Aren't you! Aren't you, my gorgeous? You're going to be a true Finkel, aren't you? You come to your bubbe!" And the new grandmother bent her teased, backcombed head and covered the tiny face in kisses, leaving bright pink lipstick traces wherever she went.

Polly noticed that Kerensa was trying hard not to cry; she was obviously exhausted, and the weariness made her lovely face droop. Rhonda looked at her.

"Are you feeling depressed?" she asked in what she obviously regarded as a low whisper and thus was only audible to the next four rooms down the corridor. "Because you know you can watch for that."

"I'm fine," said Kerensa. "Just tired." She crossly wiped away a tear.

"There there," said Rhonda, stroking her cheek. "Don't you worry. Any help you need, any doctors you need, anything you need, we'll sort it for you. You're our family now. You are my daughter now too, huh? So. Anything we can do we will do for you, for you are the mother of the most beautiful Finkel man ever known."

Kerensa couldn't speak but nodded quietly. Rhonda got up and indicated to Merv.

"Come on!" she hollered. "Leave them alone! They clearly need a bit of peace and quiet."

This felt a bit rich, seeing as how Merv had just been staring quietly at the baby and beaming with happiness, but he started moving toward the door anyway.

"We'll be back soon," he said.

"We will!" said Rhonda. "Oh, I can't bear to leave him! My first grandchild!" She gave him one last lipstick kiss. "That beautiful boy," she added. "That beautiful, beautiful boy. My grandson!"

Her mascara started to leak a little.

"I know," she said to Kerensa, "I know that to you this little bundle is everything. But can I say that to us too . . . to us it feels exactly the same. That we are carrying on, that our family is carrying on into the future, and it is the most wonderful feeling on earth."

Merv passed her a large handkerchief, and she blew her nose noisily.

"So you look after yourself, huh? Because you have done a wonderful thing for us. A wonderful, wonderful thing. Now, Reuben, you show us where this restaurant is. We have to eat, yes? Everybody has to eat. We'll come back soon. Give your wife some rest and stop taking photographs. You'll damage my perfect grandson's little eyes, I'm sure it's dangerous . . ."

She kissed the baby and Kerensa once more, then, still talking, bustled her husband and son noisily out into the corridor.

The room was very quiet after they'd all left, just the gentle bleeping of a machine here or there in the distance. There were so many flowers, it looked like a greenhouse. Polly went to the window and gazed out at the garden outside.

"It's weird," Kerensa said, her voice completely flat. "There's all those people just walking about out there, getting on with their daily business, without the faintest idea that everything in here is just . . . well, glorious and awful all at once."

"I wonder how many people looking out of these windows feel that," said Polly, her heart heavy. She turned round. "Oh KEZ," she wailed.

"Why are *you* so sad?" said Kerensa. "You're not the one sitting here with a dark-haired baby."

Polly burst into tears.

"What? What's this about?"

"It's Huckle," said Polly.

"What?" said Kerensa, looking alarmed. "Why isn't he here? What's happened to him? I thought he'd be the first to come and see Reuben's baby. I thought you wouldn't be able to keep him away."

She stared at Polly as the truth dawned on her.

"You didn't . . ."

"I had to," said Polly. "He knew something was up. He knew there was something I wasn't telling him. It was tearing us apart."

Kerensa blinked.

"So now what? Where is he? Calling Reuben?"

"I don't think so," said Polly. "I think he's wrestling

with his conscience. Also, I think he might be breaking up with me."

"He can't be," Kerensa said. "He can't be. Not you two. Not Polly and Huckle. Who'd get custody of Neil?"

"Me," said Polly quickly. "But that's not the point."

Kerensa shook her head.

"Oh God," she said. "Oh God oh God oh God. Everything . . . everything so horribly, horribly ruined. Everything so messed up. Because I made one stupid mistake. One stupid, stupid thing."

Polly blinked. "It's always the women who pay. We always do. It's been this way forever."

"I'm not some Victorian parlourmaid," said Kerensa.

"You might as well be," said Polly bitterly. "You're a fallen woman. We're always left holding the baby. Suffering the consequences." She thought about her mum.

Kerensa looked down at the sleeping infant.

"I love him," she said. "I love him so much. I can't tell you. As soon as I met him, as soon as they handed him to me, I just thought, I know you. I know you. Everything about you. Everything you are. And I love it all. I think all of it is perfect, and splendid, and I always will. But I'm going to have to pay for that."

"Not necessarily," said Polly. "He might not say anything."

"But he might," said Kerensa. "Maybe not now. Maybe one day. In the future. When something happens. When something goes wrong."

Polly shook her head. "I'll beg him. I'll deny it. I'll . . . I'll stand up in a court of law and swear against it."

"It doesn't matter," said Kerensa. "Because already every piece of happiness I have from my boy here . . . every word Rhonda says . . . it cuts me like a knife. Stabs me through and through. And I think it always will."

"One in ten," said Polly. "One in ten men are raising children that aren't theirs. That's what they say,
isn't it?"

"It can't be true, though," said Kerensa. "It can't be.
Surely. That can't be right."

"We'll never know," said Polly. "Nobody will ever
know. That's the point."

She placed a hand on Kerensa's shoulder and ran
a finger down the baby's cheek. His skin was so soft,
so pure and new. He was perfect. None of this gigantic mess was his fault. She swore then, silently, that he
would never, ever feel that it was.

She looked at Kerensa.

"I'm godmother," she said fiercely.

Kerensa nodded. "How are you going to reject the
devil and all his works though?" she said. "We basically
are the devil and all his works."

They looked at the perfect little face once more.

"You're not going to mess this up," whispered Polly.
"Neither am I. And neither is Huckle. He'll come round.
We'll sort it. We will." She smiled. "Friends. Not just
there for the nice things in life. Although this, I will tell
you, is a very, very nice thing."

Kerensa nodded and swallowed hard.

"Yeah," she said.

"Yeah," said Polly.

There was nothing more to say. Polly didn't want to
go, but she had to. She gave them one last hug.

"I hate leaving you alone."

"Reuben will be back in a second," said Kerensa.
"Don't worry, I'm sure he'll manage to keep both sides
of the conversation going, as usual."

"He's happy," said Polly. "Your mum has headed off
to contact everyone she's ever known. Rhonda and Merv

are happy. The baby is gorgeous. Everyone is happy. Our job is to keep it that way, don't you think? Who knows? Maybe then we get to be happy too."

She thought of Huckle's haunted, handsome face. Was it possible? Could it ever be? How careless life was.

Chapter Thirty-Five

Polly left the private wing profoundly and utterly choked and yet strangely happy at the same time—meeting the new baby had brought about in her some odd deep joy she hadn't anticipated; something pure and lovely and wonderful. She'd expected to be worried when he arrived—as worried as Kerensa felt—but in fact he was so gorgeous she could feel nothing but hope. Surely everyone could love a baby enough. Even if Reuben found out? Even if the kid was taller than him and could grow more facial hair by the age of nine? He wouldn't desert his family, would he?

Except Polly herself had had a father who hadn't wanted her. Who hadn't wanted to know her. It was possible. Was it ever possible?

As she reached the main entrance, deep in thought, she nearly collided with the woman who was standing stock still in the middle of the hallway, staring at her.

"Sorry," she mumbled, but to her surprise, the woman put up a hand to stop her.

"Polly," she said.

Polly focused, dragged herself away from her musings, and was brought up short in shock.

"Carmel," she said, her mouth moving but making barely any sound.

Carmel was equally startled, but her face was joyful and full of excitement.

"Polly! You came!"

There was a silence. Polly swallowed hard.

"Well . . ." she said. Carmel's expression was so radiant, Polly hated to disappoint her. But she couldn't . . . she just couldn't . . .

She should have realized that this might happen, but it just hadn't crossed her mind—the hospital was vast, and the private maternity wing was tucked away in a pleasant building overlooking the gardens at the back. But of course, nothing was impossible.

"No," she said. "I'm here seeing somebody else."

Carmel's face fell.

"Oh," she said. "Oh, I'm sorry. I thought . . . I thought . . ."

"I never had a dad," said Polly. "I never had one."

Carmel nodded. "I realize that. Completely and utterly. I do. I was wrong to contact you and I want to apologize."

"Thanks," said Polly.

"I shouldn't have dropped a bomb in your life like that. It was wrong of me . . . I was distraught. Everything was so awful and I was thinking of him and what he was begging me to do, and not about you."

Polly nodded. "I understand that," she said. She couldn't help it, she liked Carmel.

There was a pause, and Polly moved to walk away.

"But," said Carmel. "Perhaps you could see it as a

favor . . . a favor to a stranger. Something you might do for anyone. For a dying man. I know he's nothing to you. I think if I'd let him, you might have been a lot to him. It's me you have to forgive," she went on. "I had children of my own. I couldn't risk . . . couldn't risk my own family. Couldn't. I told him if he ever went near your mother, if he risked our family again for somebody else, then I couldn't be held responsible for my actions."

She blinked.

"I hope one day you'll understand what I did. I would have fought tooth and nail for my children to have a full-time father. I'm sorry about how that's made you feel. I'm not sorry for keeping my family together."

Her eyes flashed as she said it. And Polly thought how she didn't blame Carmel for fighting for her family. She wished her own mother had been better equipped to fight for hers. But that was what it was.

"Okay," she said.

"Okay what?" said Carmel. "Okay with what I did, or okay you'll come and see him?"

Polly thought for a long time. She thought of Kerensa's innocent little baby, and how he deserved access to anybody who might ever love him. She wished Huckle was here. She wished she could somehow speak to her mum about it, but she'd already asked so much.

She felt very, very lonely.

"Are . . . are any of your children there?" she asked.

Carmel shook her head.

"No," she said. "They're coming this afternoon."

Polly nodded. She would go in, say hello, say good-bye and that would be it. She would have done her duty, fulfilled the last request of a dying man. It was the right thing to do. Then she would call Huckle and tell him to go and see the baby, no matter what was going on between the two of them. And then she would . . . well. She didn't know. Get back to work, she supposed.

"Yeah, all right then," she said.

The men's oncology ward wasn't anything like as nice as the private maternity wing. It was gray, and there was a lot of coughing, and so much sadness.

The Christmas decorations looked even more miserable here than elsewhere. Men gray around the gills sat with tracheotomy holes in their throats. Bored children rolled around eating sweets and complaining. Here and there curtains were drawn around the beds, with who knew what mysterious events happening inside. There was a strong smell of Dettol and spilled tea and something else Polly didn't want to experience too intimately.

She glanced around, unwilling to let her eyes rest on any faces. Her heart was beating strongly, too strongly. She felt her hands trembling and tucked them into the pockets of her jeans.

Right at the end of the ward there was a bed underneath a window—it was the nicest, quietest spot on the six-bed ward, and instinctively Polly knew there was a reason why you got it.

The figure lying on the bed was asleep; long, very thin. Even though his hair was mostly gray, she could see quite clearly the sandy streak in it. She wished she'd taken a minute to run a comb through her own hair, although she was at least wearing makeup; if you didn't wear a full face of slap at all times, Rhonda asked you if you were sick, or had given up.

She halted, nervous and unsure. Carmel leaned over the bed.

"Tony," she whispered. "Tony dear."

There was such tenderness in her voice—a lifetime's worth, Polly reflected.

The figure on the bed—you could see his hip bones through the thin sheets; it was extremely hot on the ward—stirred slightly. There was a drip above his head, presumably morphine. Polly hoped he wasn't in pain. That whatever was eating him from the inside was being tended to carefully and effectively; that he wouldn't be made to linger on in any way.

But she didn't feel anything beyond that. She didn't feel the need to throw herself on the bed and shout "Daddy! My daddy!" She barely knew how daddies worked. Instead she stood there, her hands plunged into her pockets, trying to compose herself; trying to make her face into the right kind of expression: concerned without being fake or weird. Her mouth twisted a little, and she bit the inside of her cheek.

"Tony," said Carmel again, and he blinked and slowly opened his eyes.

They were the exact same shade of blue-green as Polly's own.

Polly shuffled a little closer, into his field of vision. Carmel gently picked up a pair of horn-rimmed glasses from the bedside table and fitted them round his pale, narrow head. He stared at Polly as if he were looking at a total stranger.

"Is it the nurse?"

His voice was a little quavery, but she could hear him well enough.

"No," said Carmel, holding his hand. "No, Tony. This is Polly."

There was a long silence.

"Polly?" came the voice finally. It cracked a little.

"Yes," said Carmel.

Tony drew a long breath. It took him a while; he wheezed slowly, in and out. It sounded absolutely horrible.

"Polly. Pauline?"

Polly nodded.

"Hello," she said. She didn't know what to call him, so she didn't call him anything.

Those blue-green eyes blinked again. It was absurd. Of course, what else could a baby be made up of but the information from both its parents—a toe shape here, an eyebrow there? That was all there was. She thought once again of Kerensa's baby, then shook the image out of her mind. This wasn't the time.

"Nice to meet you," she added, her own voice trembling.

Tony's veiny hand, with its protruding drip, waved feebly in the air in her direction. Polly, rather reluctantly, moved forward and put her own hand out. He grabbed it with slightly surprising force and she felt him squeeze. She glanced down and almost couldn't stifle her shock: the same square nails; the same very long forefinger. She had her father's hands.

"It's uncanny," said Carmel. "Sorry. It's why I couldn't stop staring at you. Sorry."

Polly looked at her.

"Well," Carmel went on. "It's just how it is, but none of your . . . none of your siblings look quite as much like him."

Polly couldn't do anything other than nod.

"I'm so sorry," said Tony, his voice croaky. "I . . . It was . . ."

"It's all right," said Polly. "I understand."

And as she said it, she felt a weight fall off her; something she had barely realized had been heavy on her her entire life. As she looked at the wasted figure of the man in the bed, she realized he wasn't the perfect father figure she'd been dreaming of, that she'd wanted so very badly. Neither was he the bad bogeyman of her mother's imagination, the implacable enemy to be hated forever. He was just a man who had made a mistake, exactly like the one Kerensa had made, more or less, and then had to live with it for the rest of his life.

It was just there, nothing you could change or prevent. Once upon a time, perhaps, it could have been made better, but not now. And that was okay. Well, it wasn't, but it had to be. Because it was all there was.

"Are you . . . are you having a good life?" croaked Tony.

Polly nodded. "Yes," she said. She thought about Huckle and suppressed the thought that things might be unraveling at pace. "Yes, I am having a good life. It wasn't always. Then I found out what I really wanted to do . . ."

"You're the girl that makes bread, aren't you? I saw you in the paper."

"I am the girl who makes bread," agreed Polly.

"You should teach her to cook then, she's always been rubbish," he said, grinning a slightly ghastly grin in Carmel's direction.

"Shut up, you," said Carmel, and Polly could see again the massive weight of affection that had obviously survived everything life could throw at it, still more or less shining brightly. Would she ever have that?

She tried to smile at him.

"Yes," she said. "I love what I do. It took me a while

to get there, and I'm massively overworked and exhausted all the time and I don't make any money and
all that stuff, but I'm happier than I've ever been in my
entire life."

Tony nodded. "Good," he said. "That's really good,
isn't it, Carmel?"

Carmel smiled. "She must have had a wonderful
mother," she said softly, and all three of them fell silent
for a moment.

"Is she . . . Do you want to meet the others?" said
Tony hopefully, as if he knew already that he was asking too much.

"No," said Polly. "No. I don't think so. I have my life
and they have theirs, and I wouldn't want to complicate
matters. Complicate everyone's lives."

"It was me who did that," said Tony.

Polly took her hand back and stepped away from
the bed.

"It was nice to meet you," she said softly. "But I'm
going to go now."

"Aye," said Tony. "Aye, yeah, that's all right. Of
course."

He looked at her, and his eyes were glistening with
tears.

"Do you forgive me?"

Polly nodded. "Of course," she said.

"Thank you. Do you have little ones?"

"No."

"Oh well. I know this will sound wrong, but . . .
you should, you know. It's . . . Having a family . . . I
shouldn't be telling you this, but . . . it's wonderful. It's
a wonderful thing. A family of your own."

Polly felt this was going too far.

"Goodbye," she said.

Carmel jumped up. Her eyes were full of tears.

"Sorry about that," she said, walking her to the ward door.

"It's all right," said Polly stiffly. "He was being honest. He chose you. And that's all right. He's lucky to have you."

Carmel bit her lip.

"Thank you," she said. "Thank you for doing this for him. I know you didn't want to. It means . . . It means so much."

And instinctively she threw her arms around Polly, who stood, a tad reluctantly, then found herself hugging her back.

"Okay. Goodbye now," said Polly. This would have to do. She turned.

At the end of the corridor, she heard a yell. It was Carmel, calling her name. She turned back.

"Sorry!" said Carmel. "Sorry. Sorry to bother you, sorry to keep bothering you, I really am. But: can I ask you for one last thing? Sorry. I know it's too much. But it is Christmas . . ."

Polly blinked and stood still, not saying anything.

"Could I . . . could I possibly have a photograph of the two of you together?"

Polly nodded. "Of course," she said.

Their first-ever photo. The first father-and-daughter photograph Polly had ever had.

She sat down on the bed feeling weird and awkward, with a stupid lump in her throat she couldn't dispel, and took her father's wizened hand fully in her own, grasped it, fingers interlaced, for the first and the very last time, and squeezed it, and he squeezed back as if they could connect with each other just here, just this one time, and then the photo was taken and it was time to go.

"Any time you need me," said Carmel, "come and find me. Here's my number. Anything. Any questions. Come and find me."

And Polly turned and walked slowly out of the hospital, into the parking lot, where the first snow of the season was starting to fall; blanketing the ugly hospital buildings, covering the pain and sadness, turning the world fresh and white and new again, starting over with a clean slate.

Chapter Thirty-Six

Polly had picked up Nan the Van—which Reuben had kindly got a flunky to bring over when she'd explained she only had one mode of transport, and Nan was it. She drove slowly away from the hospital, the world changed in front of her eyes. The gently falling flakes turned into a flurry, then began to fall steadily, silently, covering the ground. The light was fading from the afternoon and Polly tried not to worry about how she would manage the causeway. She would get home somehow, back home to her puffin and her lighthouse and her oven, and she could figure everything else out later. Or maybe sooner.

Because the thing was, she guessed, you always thought you had time—time to fix the relationships that had broken down; to do all the things you thought you'd get around to; to finish everything, tie it up with a neat bow and that was it.

But life wasn't like that at all. Things festered for years. Things that ought to be gotten over never were. Bitterness became a defining characteristic of people's lives. And she could see it happening. It had happened to her mother. It might happen to Kerensa and that little baby. And she understood why, at the end, her father had tried to make sure that it didn't happen to him.

She wasn't going to go through the same thing. She and Huckle had been so happy together. Could they get it back? Could they make it right?

She turned on the radio, which was playing jaunty Christmas music intercut with ominous snow warnings and suggestions that you not travel unless it was absolutely necessary. Polly ignored these. The A road was fine, the trails of the many cars in front of her making it easy to follow. She was not looking forward to the turn-off, though. The snow hadn't been forecast, so the gritters wouldn't have had a chance to get out. The problem was, unless she found a hotel before the turnoff—which she didn't have the money for—there was absolutely nothing between there and Mount Polbearne. If she did turn off, she was stuffed.

Her thoughts drifted to Huckle. What was he doing? What on earth was he thinking? Whatever else happened, she had to get home.

As the exit loomed, several things happened very quickly.

Lost in her thoughts, Polly had to indicate in a fluster. A huge truck behind her honked menacingly, which startled her, just as her telephone rang. As the van twisted toward the exit ramp, a tiny rabbit flashed out from the undergrowth and straight across her path; she caught a glimpse of the little pawprints in the fresh snow. Nan struggled to get purchase on the road, failed, lurched forward and headed straight down the hill toward the road at the bottom, which was thankfully empty, shooting straight across it and coming to rest, rocking menacingly, in the snowdrift that had already started to build on the opposite verge, just out of reach of the oncoming traffic.

Polly didn't realize she was screaming, nor that she had somehow in her panic pressed the answer button on her phone.

"It's all right, it's all right, it's all right!" she heard a desperate voice saying on the other end of the line. "It's all right! It's going to be—"

"GAAAAA!"

"Polly! Polly! Are you there? What is it? What is it?"

Polly desperately tried to catch her breath, but it came in tearing sobs. The voice became more alarmed.

"Polly? Polly, what is it? What's happened?"

Finally she found the breath to speak, a great ripped-out gasp.

"Hu . . . Huckle?"

"Yes. What happened? What's the matter? It wasn't because of me, was it? You haven't done anything stupid? Please tell me you're okay!"

Polly blinked and looked around. Nan the Van appeared to be slowly sinking sideways into the snowdrift.

"Nan . . . the van came off the road," she whispered. "We're off the road. We're . . . I don't know where . . ."

"Oh my God," said Huckle. "Oh God. Are you all right? I told you to check the tires."

"You told me to check the tires?!" exclaimed Polly. "I just nearly died in a horrible accident and you're making sure that I know it was my own fault?"

"No, no. Sorry. I'm sorry. You gave me such a fright . . . At first I thought you'd heard the news and were just upset about it—God knows we're all upset, so it could have been that, could have been anything . . . Jesus. Are you all right?"

"I think so," said Polly, trying to breathe out through

her nose like she'd read somewhere, even though it felt weird. "I think I might be slightly stuck." She paused, trying to think straight. "Where are you?"

"Didn't you get the news?"

"The news that you're back?"

"No, the news from the hospital."

"What news? What's happening?"

"It's the baby," said Huckle.

Polly didn't say anything.

"What?" she said finally. "What? What's happened with the baby? You didn't . . ."

"Of course not," said Huckle crossly. "No. No. The doctor came and looked at the baby . . . I was just leaving, and calling to find out if you knew. Apparently there's something wrong with it."

Chapter Thirty-Seven

It was as if a bell were tolling deep inside Polly's soul. Everything else fell away; all the little petty things, all the worries and concerns and jealousies and getting-bys, they all left, immediately, to be replaced by her deepest, darkest fears.

"Oh my God," she said. "Are you coming? It's filthy out here."

The snow was falling more heavily than ever.

"Of course."

"What's wrong with him?"

"I don't know. I think Kerensa was trying to get you. She sounded hysterical."

Polly blinked. Oh God.

"Are you really stuck?" said Huckle.

"Yes," said Polly. "And there's nobody on the road. Nobody on the road at all."

"Well, you'll need me then, won't you? To pull you out."

"Can the motorbike do that?" said Polly sceptically.

"EXCUSE ME," said Huckle. "Don't diss the bike when you're upside down in a ditch."

Polly turned up the heating, but it didn't make a lot of difference.

"Hurry up," she said, meaning it. "Hurry up. I need you, Huckle."

Over an hour later, Polly was still sitting stock still, too scared to try and get out of the van, even as she could feel the snow piling up around her; too petrified with fear. She had tried to call Kerensa but couldn't get through, and Reuben's number just went to voicemail.

But the baby had been perfect. Utterly perfect. She'd seen him; held him. Everything had been fine.

She thought again. Babies could have fits; or the doctors could have done all those tests and come back with something awful. Cystic fibrosis or spina bifida or any of those terrible, terrible things that haunted parents' worst nightmares.

She was trapped in a cycle of desperate fear, huddling deeper and deeper into her coat, wondering where on earth Huckle was—it shouldn't be taking him this long. There was only one exit to Mount Polbearne. Had he tried to get that bloody motorbike over the causeway? Had he just skidded off into the water, lost to the sea, like so many boats around the ragged Cornish coastline, so many men beneath the waves in high winds and weather?

A fragment of an old song about a shipwreck came to her, "And many was the fine feather beds floating on the foam / And many was the little lords' sons who never did come home."

Where was he? Where was *she*? The road was quiet: the occasional passing lights of a traveler trundled on through the darkening afternoon and the whirling flakes, but they didn't stop.

She huddled deeper in her seat. Perhaps everything was over now, everything was done, and there was nothing to do but stay here. Everything had gone wrong and she'd lost the only thing she'd ever wanted and . . .

TAP TAP TAP!

Polly realized she was sinking into a stupor; that she was half asleep. She didn't know where the noise was coming from.

TAP TAP TAP!

She glanced around blearily. Something or someone was tapping on the window. Was it a tree? Where was she?

She leaned over and wound down the window. There, hovering outside, beating his little wings frantically, was Neil. He *eep*ed furiously at her.

"Neil!" said Polly, feeling a stupid smile spread across her face. Why did she feel so weird?

"Polly!" came a voice, and charging up behind Neil was a headlamp, and behind *that* was Huckle's face. Polly stared at him woozily.

"I thought you were dead," she said, smiling at him in a funny way.

Huckle wrenched open the van door and pulled her out, shoving her unceremoniously on to the ground. The shock of the cold air felt like someone had poured a bucket of cold water over her head. She coughed and choked on the freezing snow bank.

"Oh my God!" Huckle was saying. "The stink in there! There's some gas feeding back; you must have bumped something when you came to rest. Oh my God,

Polly! You could have poisoned yourself! You can't . . .
I can't believe . . . It's a deathtrap, that van! Everyone's
been telling you that!"

Polly shook her head.

"Didn't you feel weird? Woozy?"

"Yes," said Polly, frowning. "It felt nice."

"Oh God," said Huckle, pulling her to him, then letting her go again as she suddenly had to turn away and
vomit into the snow. He handed her some water.

"Jesus, Polly." He was almost as white as she was.
"JESUS. Shit. When did everything go so wrong?"

Polly shook her head. "I don't know," she said tear-
fully. "I don't know. I wish I did so I could go back and
fix it."

"You didn't do anything," said Huckle, holding her.
"It's not your fault, my darling. It's not your fault. Oh
my God, you're shivering."

Huckle flagged down a car, finally, and a very kind
lady called Maggie let Polly sit in it whilst he rigged up
the motorbike to pull Nan the Van out of the snowdrift.
He parked her up carefully by the side of the road, with
all the windows open, then thanked the woman.

"Where are you going?" she asked.

"We have to get to the hospital in Plymouth," Huckle
explained.

"In that thing?" she said, indicating the motorbike.
She was a teacher, of the very nicest sort, and had a way
of telling you what to do without beating around the
bush. "Don't be ridiculous. Get in the car. I'll take you."

"It's a Mini," said Huckle. "I'm not sure it'll do much
better than—"

"Get in," she said.

Neil flew in and sat on Polly's lap. Maggie stared at
him for a bit.

"Ah," said Huckle.

"Is he going to poo in the car?" she asked, as they took to the cleared, gritted A road.

"Can't promise he won't," said Huckle, grinning apologetically, and luckily, it turned out that Maggie had a soft spot for smiling young men.

Chapter Thirty-Eight

Polly wanted to run straight to the private wing, but Huckle stopped and made her drink a strong coffee from the vending machine. Then he looked into her eyes.

"Are you okay?"

"Apart from the nine weird things that have happened today," said Polly. She gave herself a quick internal check. "I think I am," she said. She looked up at him. "Oh my, I must be the most bedraggled mess."

"If you're thinking *that*, you must be on the mend," said Huckle.

"That's obviously a yes, then," said Polly, feeling her damp hair in dismay.

Huckle took her in his arms.

"Oh Polly Waterford," he said. "You are lovely to me in every way."

"I just threw up," said Polly.

"Yeah, okay, forget about that bit," said Huckle. "Because I don't think you're hearing what I'm trying to say to you."

"That you aren't going to leave me any more because of not telling you about Kerensa?"

Huckle shook his head.

"I wasn't ever going to leave you," he said. "It's just . . . you know. I've been cheated on in the past, and it was so hard. It hurt so much. And I thought I knew you so well, and I panicked. But you can't . . . you can't ever know another person. Not through and through. People have their reasons for things. And you can choose to love them for who they are, and, well, that's the deal. That's how it is. I understand why you did what you did. I'd rather you hadn't . . . No. I wish the entire thing hadn't happened."

Polly nodded.

"But I can live with it. I can."

She laid her head on his shoulder and let out an enormous juddering sigh.

"I love you so much," she said.

"We're going to have to love each other," said Huckle soberly. "Because we have to be there for Reuben and Kerensa. When they need us. Which I think starts now."

Holding hands, and dreading what they were about to discover, they moved toward the lift, both of them trying not to dwell on the worst. That beautiful, innocent little baby. That something could be wrong with him, that something could have happened . . . it was horrifying. So unfair. So wrong, that a baby could be born to pain.

The lift took forever to arrive. Up in the private wing, the great displays of winter flowers in the corridors seemed to mock them, as did the balloons and gift baskets outside Kerensa's door.

Polly and Huckle glanced at one another, squeezed hands tightly, and knocked.

Inside the room, things were eerily quiet. In fact, given that the room contained Reuben, Kerensa, Jackie, Merv, Rhonda and a brand-new baby, things were utterly, bizarrely quiet.

"Hey," whispered Polly. "We came as soon as we could."

"Any trouble getting here?" asked Merv, who was staring out at the heavy snowfall still coming down over the garden.

"Neh," said Polly, deciding that now was not the time to explain. She turned toward the bed. The baby was lying peacefully asleep in his bassinet. Kerensa, white-faced, didn't meet her eyes.

Reuben was pacing up and down.

"Well," he said to Polly and Huckle. "Now you know."

Polly went cold.

"Yup, now it's out. Now I'm going to be a laughingstock all over the world. Oh good. People laughing at Reuben Finkel. It doesn't matter how much money I have or how well I do, I just can't get away from it, can I, Pa?"

He spat the last part bitterly.

"C'mon now, Reuben," said Merv, but Reuben shook him off.

"It's your fault," he said.

"It's nobody's fault," said Merv. "Seriously, son."

Polly was frozen to the spot. This wasn't going to be nice.

"All I wanted was for my son to be perfect. Is that too much to ask?"

Polly stared desperately at Kerensa. This couldn't be all about Reuben, surely. He couldn't just go on and on like this. There was a baby to think of. A mother to think of.

And then Kerensa did the most surprising thing.

She winked at Polly.

At first Polly thought—she was still feeling a little bleary—that she might have imagined it. But no. It was definitely there.

And was that a little color stealing back into Kerensa's face?

Huckle grasped the nettle.

"Reuben, what's up? What's wrong with little Herschel?"

"Um," said Kerensa. "Actually I think you'll find that's not his name."

Huckle ignored her and stepped forward. "What is it, bro?"

Reuben looked up at him.

"I can't believe it," he said. "Seriously, dude. I can't believe it."

"What?"

A nurse bustled in.

"Oh look at you all," she said. "Listen, there's lots that can be done, okay?"

"Can you . . . show them?" said Reuben.

"Reuben," said Merv. "Is this necessary?"

"Yeah," said Reuben. "Yeah, it is."

Polly's teeth were chattering. Actually chattering out loud.

The nurse shrugged and picked up the baby like he was a little football. To Polly's eyes she handled him quite roughly, but then she herself was hardly versed in picking up brand-new infants. She'd have to assume the woman knew what she was doing.

She unwrapped his swaddling, then his fresh organic cotton babygro. The baby didn't like that at all and started bawling lustily. His hair really was very dark.

His nappy looked ridiculously large on the tiny form. Polly had never seen such a new baby naked; she hadn't realized they were like tadpoles really, all head, with kind of little flippery arms and legs.

"Okay," said the nurse. "Well, here it is."

Polly was gripping Huckle's hand so hard it was going white. They peered over.

Right across the baby's tiny bottom was a bright streak of red; a huge strawberry mark that made him look as if he'd been spanked.

Polly's hand shot to her mouth, and for just a second she was unutterably terrified that she might laugh.

"A *birthmark*?" said Huckle, astonished. "You called us out here because you're worried about a birthmark?"

"Yeah," said Reuben. "Not just any old birthmark, though. A huge, ass-obliterating satellite of a birthmark! Just like I had and my dad has. Thanks, Pa!"

"You should have told Kerensa!" said Merv, his hand drifting behind his back. "I told Rhonda!"

"No, Ma found it!" said Reuben. "They couldn't get rid of them in those days." He turned to Kerensa, whose hand was also over her mouth. "Aw, honey, I'm so sorry. I had mine lasered off when I got my legal emancipation. So I'm not a fricking lizard skin like Pops. You've been awesome about this," he added tenderly.

Kerensa couldn't do anything except wave her free

hand about. She was half smiling, half crying, as was Polly.

"It's nothing!" scolded the nurse. "You have to stop getting your knickers in a twist about it. He's a lovely healthy baby."

"Why didn't it show up on the scan?" asked Huckle, probably more crossly than he intended.

"Well it wouldn't. Plus he's a very wriggly baby," said the nurse. "I wonder who he gets that from."

Reuben stopped fidgeting with his phone long enough to look up.

"Huh?" he said. "Yeah, whatever."

The nurse expertly rebuttoned the baby into his babygro and swaddled him so tightly he couldn't move. Polly thought he would hate it, but in fact the little body relaxed and turned into a parcel, and the nurse handed him straight back to Kerensa, who took him cheerfully and snuggled him right up the front of her nightie, as if she was a kangaroo and he her joey.

They didn't say anything in the lift. They didn't say anything to each other in the long hallway, quiet now with as many beds as possible empty so people could be with their families for Christmas; plus it was late, after the normal visiting hours that applied to the rest of the hospital. This was just them.

They didn't say anything until they finally reached the end of the corridor and the automatic doors opened silently into the whirling wonderland beyond, the flakes illuminated by the lurid orange of the hospital's external lights but the ugly parking lot and the squat buildings hidden by the beautiful soft white. The trees beyond were lit dimly by the glow from the city and had transformed into a Narnian wood, and without a word to one another they ran toward it.

Once safely inside, both of them screamed, "YESSSS!" at the top of their lungs, then grabbed one another and whirled each other round and round in the snow until they were pink-cheeked and sparkling-eyed with delight, and bursting with happiness. Huckle crushed Polly to him and she laughed, and Neil fluttered down from a tree he'd been exploring and watched them jump up and down with joy, then joined in.

At last the cold drove them back inside, both of them beaming. They went to the lobby to call a cab.

"Where are we going?" said Polly.

"Aha!" said Huckle.

"What?"

"You'll see," he said. "Stay here, I'm going to make a call."

Polly waited, her heart completely full. Oh, the mind-bending, world-crushing relief. She took out her nearly-dead phone and texted Kerensa. She didn't know what to say, so in the end she just put five hearts and loads of kisses, then some more hearts and a very small emoticon of the closest thing she could find. That was going to have to do.

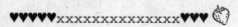

She glanced up and back into the main body of the hospital, wondering where Huckle had gone.

And that was when she saw them. A large group of people walking along the corridor, quietly, slowly. They had their arms around one another, as if they were consoling each other. One, a woman around Polly's age, was weeping, and a man was holding her close. There were a couple of children, walking solemnly, as if they knew something bad was happening but weren't quite clear as to what it was. Someone was carrying a very small child, fast asleep, nuzzled against his mother's neck.

And bringing up the rear, weeping copiously and supported by two older men—her brothers, by the look of them—was Carmel.

Polly shrank back, hidden by the vending machine, watching the sad parade of people walk past.

They looked—well, they looked normal. Nice. Mixed race, married to black and white, just a totally average, supportive, well-dressed family.

She turned away, in case Carmel saw her face, but Carmel was bowed over and blinded by tears.

Tony must have died, thought Polly. This was it. The father she had never had was no more. The kind of father he must have been, she supposed, she could see in the utterly distraught faces of the men and women passing by.

She stood stock still and watched, feeling incredibly sad and strange, as the party made its way out into the freezing night.

"Okay!" said Huckle, bouncing round the corner. "Madam, your carriage awaits. Hey hey!"

A cab had pulled up outside.

"Where are we going?" said Polly, glancing around the parking lot, but the family had dispersed.

"Just get in," said Huckle, winking at the driver. Neil followed close behind.

Polly desperately needed to talk to him about her father, but she didn't get a chance, as Huckle was bouncing up and down in his seat and talking about how amazing it was, and how great things were, and weren't they lucky, and surely Kerensa would never, ever do anything like that again, and how now they would all appreciate every moment . . .

Polly looked at him.

"Yes," she said quietly. "Yes. I want to appreciate every moment."

Just at that moment the car swung off the deserted road and through the massive gates of an enormous stately home.

"Where are we?" said Polly suspiciously.

Huckle smiled.

"Ah," he said. "Hang it. Sometimes you have to do these things. It's too dangerous to go home. This is the nearest hotel to the hospital."

"Yes, but it's . . ."

The gravel drive seemed a mile long. The trees were bent over with the weight of snow. A white winter moon shone through the clouds.

"It totally is."

"We can't afford this!"

"Sssh," said Huckle.

"And I'm wearing a pinafore!"

"Yeah, yeah, you are."

Polly sat up in alarm. "What's up?"

"I called them and explained the situation," said Huckle. "It's either this or a night sheltering in Accident and Emergency pretending we've got broken wrists."

A liveried man rushed out to open the taxi door, and they were ushered through a grand entrance into the most ridiculous stately home. There were precious antiques and oil paintings everywhere, and the wallpaper was made out of some sort of material. It was stunning. Polly looked round and fiddled nervously with her pinafore buttons.

"Now, Mr. Freeman." The receptionist came forward smiling. "We heard all about you being caught in the storm. We know about your clothes situation, so if you need anything, just let us know and we'll see what we can do. Also, we've taken the liberty of upgrading you to a suite."

Polly turned on Huckle.

"What is this?"

"Nothing!" said Huckle. "I just said we'd had some fabulous news and could they look after us."

"Pets are welcome here, aren't they?"

Neil pretended to be lifting his foot to examine his claws and not eating the tinsel. "Um," said the receptionist who was very nice and absolutely desperate to get home. "Sure! Also," she confided, "we had a massive group coming tonight and they've all had to call off because of the weather. So you are definitely in luck. Enjoy."

She glanced back at Huckle.

"I like your boyfriend's accent," she said.

"So do I," said Polly.

The room was absolutely immense, with a four-poster bed in the middle of it. Polly nearly cried with happiness when she saw it. There was an enormous claw-footed bath in the bathroom, which had a heated floor and two incredibly fluffy robes hanging up, with slippers.

"Oh my God," said Polly. Huckle grinned. He knew

how much she absolutely loved a bath, and while she turned on the taps and filled it full of foam from a selection of expensive smellies, he went and poured them both very large gin and tonics from the minibar.

As Polly wallowed blissfully in the endless superhot water, sipping her G&T, Huckle knelt down beside the bath.

"You know," he said, "I don't like doing it very often. But being a workaholic like you sometimes really pays dividends."

"Your meeting went well?"

He frowned. "Better than well. I always work better when I'm miserable. It's so weird."

"What happened?"

"I've sold the new range to a whole chain of beauticians. Fresh honeycomb wax, all local, all organic."

Polly looked at him in astonishment.

"Seriously?"

"Seriously. Common or garden wax is no longer good enough for the tender mimsies of the southwest."

"So you're paying for this place with pubes?"

Huckle grinned. "Is it worth it?"

Polly beamed. "Oh my God, yes! You clever thing! Yes!"

"Just don't ask me to work like that every week. It's exhausting!"

After she'd soaked for long enough, but before she passed out from utter fatigue, they got into bed and ordered far too much from room service, then she told him everything that had happened with her father, and he, in his perfect, gentle Huckle way, simply listened; properly listened to everything she had to say, in the way she'd missed so very much.

When she was finished, he didn't ask how she was

feeling or say anything stupid about closure. He just said, "Oh." And "That sounds hard."

And Polly nodded, and thought about the odd counterbalance of weights in the universe—how bad things could happen, and sometimes wonderful, wonderful things could happen, but you weren't always fated to be in the heart of the story; sometimes it simply wasn't about you; you didn't always get all the answers.

And some days, when you were lying in a four-poster bed, with the person you loved more than anything else in the world asking if you would like more club sandwich, and should you curl up and watch a film together, and saying that you might have to stay tomorrow too because everything and everyone would be snowed in . . .

Well. Sometimes that was all right in itself. Sometimes that was more than enough. Sometimes it was everything.

Chapter Thirty-Nine

Polly woke on Boxing Day feeling happy and sad at the same time and didn't know why, then she blinked and realized.

Outside, the beautiful grounds of the hotel were completely covered in a thick blanket of snow. Amazingly, someone had come in the night and taken away her clothes, and returned them laundered and folded up in tissue paper. This was, she thought, as nuts as all the extraordinary things that had happened over the last couple of days.

They ate a ridiculously huge breakfast, then went for a wander around the grounds, kicking up snow with their feet. Polly had spoken to Jayden, who was still trying to talk Flora around, and now she was fretting about the old ladies, who might not be able to get down the treacherous cobbled pathways to the bakery or Muriel's little supermarket. She would need to go back soon, to make deliveries to her elderly customers, who relied on her. There were always plenty of emergency supplies on Mount Polbearne, because of its often sticky winters, but it was good just to have a quick check in on everyone, make sure they were all all right.

"Hush," said Huckle. "It's Boxing Day. Everyone in Britain has far more in their house than they can possibly eat in a million years. Everyone will be fine for a few hours. Please. Trust me. Relax."

So they walked in the beautiful, sunny, snowy grounds, talking of this and that: of Huckle's new business line, how he was going to have to outsource production even more, beyond Dave, his regular bee man, and how it ought to work; and of what Kerensa and Reuben would call the baby—Huckle was fairly sure Herschel would win, and Polly accused him of only liking it because it sounded like Huckle.

Then there was a pause as they walked, and Polly said, "I am so sorry," and Huckle said, "Me too."

Then Polly said, "Will that do?" and Huckle thought, just for a brief moment, about bringing up how the hotel might be a nice place to get married one of these days, but decided they'd been through enough for now. He was so relieved that they were back, that they were Polly and Huckle again, that he was determined never to rock the boat about anything, not even when Neil had made pancake-butter footprints across the posh restaurant table and the maître d' had pulled a face that Polly had patently ignored. No. Not even then.

He tugged her braids under the big woollen hat.

"Of course."

And they squeezed hands again, and thought they had had a very narrow escape after all.

After a while Huckle said, "Do you think you might go to the funeral?"

Polly blinked.

"No," she said. "I met him. I kind of understand—I

do understand. The stuff people do in their twenties . . . they're not grown up really. And in the end . . . Well. He learned his lesson, didn't he? He went back and raised his family and he obviously really loved them and was a wonderful father. I was his mistake, but that wasn't my fault. My mum could maybe have dealt with it slightly differently, but it was a great love affair for her, and it wasn't for him. And that's nobody's fault either; sometimes these things just don't shake down. But no," she said. "I don't think I need to hear lots of people stand up and say what a great guy he was, you know?"

Huckle nodded. "Of course."

They walked on in silence.

"What about his children?" he asked.

Polly thought back with a pang to the close-knit-looking group of smartly dressed people. How nice it must be, when things were really tough, to have people to lean on like that. She'd never known what it was like to have brothers and sisters. Huckle's brother was a bit of a rogue, but he was family. She would have liked something like that.

"Mmm," she said. "They all . . . I'm sure they all have their own lives. I'm the last thing they need to complicate matters."

"Yes, well, wait till they discover you make the world's most awesome bread. You'll be welcomed with open arms," said Huckle cheerfully.

Polly shook her head. "God, no. What if they think I'm there to cause trouble, or to get at his will?"

"Do you think there's any money?"

Polly shrugged. "Dunno. Don't care." She frowned. "I wonder if my mum will keep brooding."

"Maybe she'll have to get a job," said Huckle.

"Huck!"

"What? There's nothing wrong with her. Do her good to get out of the house a bit."

"She's fragile," said Polly.

"Maybe she's like that because everyone's been tip-toeing around her for so long."

"She looked after her own parents very well."

"That's true," allowed Huckle. "She should look after other people's. For money."

"Hmm," said Polly.

They'd made a full circle of the grounds and were back at the grand entrance. Polly was looking longingly at the posh indoor spa arrangement.

"I'd love a swim."

And as if by magic, a swimsuit in her size was found, and they went and swam under an indoor waterfall and bathed in clouds of puffy steam in the steam room and giggled in the jacuzzi, and despite the fact that they spent less than twelve hours at the beautiful country house hotel, it was one of the nicest holidays Polly had ever had in her life.

Chapter Forty

The snow was settling in, possibly for a long stay, but the sun was out, the roads were clear and there was hardly any traffic—people were obviously staying in, settling down for the lovely hazy days between Christmas and New Year with chocolate and liqueurs and a general sense of having nowhere to go and nothing to do except a jigsaw and some audio books.

Polly and Huckle took a cab to Nan the Van, which was still parked safely by the side of the road. When Polly turned the key in the ignition, amazingly the engine roared into life first time, and she climbed behind the wheel while Huck went to start the motorbike. Before they headed off, Polly called Kerensa, who announced cheerfully that she was coming home with Lowin, whereupon Reuben yelled, "Herschel!" in the background and a squabble commenced, which sounded exactly like Kerensa and Reuben getting back to normal.

"Are you sure you should be coming home so soon?" said Polly.

"Oh yes," said Kerensa, a sparkle in her voice. "I know most people are meant to feel a bit tired and washed out after childbirth. But I feel oddly good."

"Because my baby is awesome," came the voice in the background. "Totally the most awesome."

Polly smiled down the phone.

"My godson too," she said.

And still the snow came down.

Polly started making batches of bread every morning and delivering it to the elderly of the village, and eventually, when people kept catching her on her rounds, to just about everybody else as well. She'd given Jayden some time off—he rather looked like he needed it—and when she finished in the bakery, she headed back to the lighthouse, where they kept the stove running day and night for once, keeping the sitting room at the top of the house warm and cozy, and heating the bedroom too.

And when the day's work was done—for Huckle had a lot to do too, with the business taking off—they ate buns and crackers and cheese and drank champagne and lazed in bed, watching films and looking at the snow coming down and listening to reports recommending that people not travel unless it was absolutely necessary, and smugly chinked their glasses together because they didn't want to travel at all.

Reuben and Kerensa were, if the hourly photographs were anything to go by, completely immersed in a baby-moon of gigantic proportions, cuddling and cooing and sending loved-up pictures of their three hands or feet, or of them all snuggled up in a bed the size of Polly's mother's front room, beaming mightily and joyously,

Reuben fully back to his bouncy King of the World persona, the baby looking more like him every day.

Kerensa looked exquisite; a large, soft, beaming earth mother, the drawn look gone from her eyes. It helped that the baby was a perfect eater and sleeper—according to his father—and that they had absolutely oodles of help around the place, but regardless, she was a changed person; back to the fun, confident, wonderful best friend Polly had always known, and she was entirely thrilled for her.

Polly phoned her mum every day—which she didn't normally do—and somehow, because they'd had to throw everything up in the air, because they'd had to talk about things that nobody had ever wanted to talk about, she finally felt she understood a huge great tranche of her life that had formerly been a mystery to her. And because she understood this, it was as if things had become lighter, easier between them; as if her mother was no longer holding up massive barriers, desperately trying to control what Polly knew and how she felt.

She thought of her dad from time to time, with a slight air of melancholy. But it was what it was. Nobody had a life untouched by sadness, not in the real world. And for now, looking at Huckle playing ping-pong football with Neil in front of the fire, his long body stretched out, his shaggy hair glinting golden in the firelight, she felt that in so many areas of her life, she was so blessed that she couldn't complain. Lots of people didn't have what she had. And she had so very much.

She knew that at some point next year they would get married, but that would be next year. She could think about the organizing and the costs and everything then. It would be lovely. Fine. Small. Just what they wanted. She didn't need to get superstitious about it any more, terrified about it, or just worried in general because she'd never known how it was meant to go. It would just be her and Huckle. She wasn't desperately looking forward to it, but it would be fine. It really would. Marriage, babies; whatever came next. She was ready for it all.

She came and lay next to Huckle and helped him blow the ping-pong ball about, which drove Neil bananas. He'd *eep* and hop and get so cross they'd stop playing, whereupon he'd flutter down and push the ball straight toward them until they agreed to play with him again.

She cuddled up against Huckle's warm body on the rug, relishing the incredibly unusual feeling of having nothing—absolutely nothing, apart from the morning run—planned for the rest of the week. It was too snowy to go out; there was no need to take any exercise, or organize or arrange anything. It was just hours of clear nothingness ahead, with little more to do than make love, watch films, eat Quality Street and drink fizz. That would do.

Chapter Forty-One

Early on New Year's Eve, after Polly had done her rounds and was crawling back into bed, the phone rang deep in the bowels of the lighthouse.

"Kill them," said Huckle. "Whoever it is. Seriously. I'm not answering the phone."

They let it ring out. It went on for ages and ages. Huckle groaned.

"No," he said. "No. Everything is exactly how I wanted it."

Polly checked her phone, but as usual she couldn't get a signal.

"It will be a sales call," she said. "Don't worry. I've spoken to Mum today. Let's just ignore them and they'll go away."

The ringing stopped as she smiled sleepily and cuddled up to Huckle even more closely. "See," she said.

"You have magic powers," said Huckle, leaning in to kiss her. The phone started again. It sounded oddly more insistent than before.

"Go away!" said Huckle.

Polly made a groaning noise. "Oh God, I'd better answer it."

"If it's Reuben or Kerensa, can you tell them we're out of their ridiculous lives now? Please?"

"Why am I going downstairs anyway?" said Polly, wincing as the freezing air on the stairwell hit her.

"Because you'll enjoy it so much more when you come back into the warm," said Huckle. "I'll build us a nest."

Polly smiled and inched her way downstairs to pick up the heavy black Bakelite phone.

"Polly!"

"No," said Polly.

"What do you mean, no?" said Reuben, offended.

"Whatever it is," said Polly, "I'm not doing it. I'm kind of on holiday, which also includes feeding everyone in town. So. No."

"Maybe I'm not calling you to get you to do anything for me."

"Okay, so what is it?" said Polly.

"Ah," said Reuben.

"NO!" said Polly. "Absolutely not. No. I'm not doing it."

There was a pause.

"Polls . . ."

"No!"

"Because the thing is," said Reuben, "you know I agreed to pay for you to cater Christmas? Well actually, technically speaking, Christmas morning and that box day thing you have after Christmas . . ."

"Christmas morning when you were at the hospital because your wife was giving birth and I was driving your mother-in-law?"

"Yeah," said Reuben. "You see, you weren't technically there."

"That wasn't my fault!" said Polly. "That was your baby decided to come early!"

"Yeah, nevertheless . . ." said Reuben.

"NO!"

"Because, you know, that puffin sanctuary is looking mighty hard up . . ."

It was absolutely freezing downstairs in the little office. Ice patterns had formed on the windows. Huckle had cleared the path down the stone steps to the harbor every morning, but the snow was still piling up. It was unusual for quite so much to lie on the island; normally the wind and the salt in the air cleared it quickly. But this year they were totally inundated.

Polly thought with some sadness about the *Back to the Future* triple bill they'd had scheduled for that afternoon. And then she thought of all the puffins that would be absolutely decimated if left to their own devices in Cornish waters. She sighed.

"What do you need?"

"I've got all the ingredients here," said Reuben. "Just come over. Say hi to everyone. Herschel is dying to see you."

"Is that how it's going to go?" said Polly. "You're going to use the baby to guilt me every time you want a sandwich until the end of time?"

"He is your only godson."

Huckle crept down behind her with the duvet pulled around him.

"Work?" he said crossly.

"Bring Huckle," said Reuben authoritatively down the phone.

"No!" said Huckle, but it was too late. Reuben had already hung up.

"Oh for heaven's sake," said Polly. "Seriously. I don't think being friends with those two is remotely good for us. And I don't even know if we can get there."

Huckle glanced out of the window.

"I don't think that's going to be an issue," he said.

A tiny dot in the sky grew larger and larger and eventually came into focus, the noise growing louder and louder.

"He sent the *helicopter*?" said Polly. "This is utterly ridiculous. Honestly. For a few pastries!"

"The best pastries," said Huckle, and Polly rolled her eyes.

The helicopter touched down carefully on the harbor front, which Polly was sure was entirely illegal. The snow had stopped, and it was a bright, freezing, crunchy day; a beautiful day in fact. Which didn't change the fact that she didn't want to be out in it at all.

The pilot beckoned to them to hurry up, and Polly pulled on a coat and grabbed her bag. Neil hopped up to the helicopter to have a look at it—he obviously thought it was a really big puffin—and Polly let him come inside. Huckle looked grumpy, then followed her out of the house.

"This is annoying," he said. "Because obviously Reuben is being a total pain in the arse, but I've always really wanted to go in a helicopter."

"Me too," said Polly. They grinned at each other as the pilot gave them both a set of headphones and strapped them in, then off they went.

They held hands as the helicopter lurched sideways and they circled the lighthouse once; it was odd to see it veer away below them at an angle that felt quite close to being in the sea, which was beating up against the rocks with white-crested waves. There were very few fishing boats out today; even the men were taking a little time off to reconnect with their families at Christmas.

Mount Polbearne from above, under its mantle of snow, looked like a postcard, the little rambling cottages and streets jammed up against each other, tumbling over one another, all the way down the cobbles to the busy harbor, and Polly snapped some pictures on her phone.

She could see Muriel's shop, still resolutely open when the rest of the world was taking a break. She saw Patrick out walking one of the stray dogs he seemed to collect around him at all times—he couldn't bear to let an animal go to the pound or anywhere it might be put down, so often had the most motley collection of fleabags around his heels. She saw two of the toddlers of the town, done up like little Michelin men in their winter zip-up outfits, tumbling and playing with stones on the beach, whilst their parents clutched their arms tightly around themselves and—from the look of it—shot evil glances at the door of the Little Beach Street Bakery for being shut when they clearly needed hot chocolate now more than ever.

Then the helicopter turned and flew over the sea—Mount Polbearne was a proper island this morning, cut off completely, its own little world, and Polly felt, as she often did, a little pang for leaving it, even if it was only for the day.

"I've had worse commutes," she told Huckle, who smiled back, enjoying the trip as much as she was.

They flew over the mainland of Cornwall, its rocky crags giving way to fertile fields, now all laid out in white stripes and white hedges; tangles of woodland as old as the legends of the land King Arthur once strode through silent under their blanket of snow; creatures deep in the undergrowth below. An owl searching for field mice glanced up at them as they passed above. The few cars on the roads looked like toys; horses turned out loose in their fields started a little at the noise of the helicopter, which made Polly feel guilty.

Away from the coastal towns, it felt like the beautiful county was spread out below for them alone; almost no people, just the soft, silent countryside they had both taken so much to their hearts, and Huckle squeezed her hand tightly, and she returned it, as the sound of a church bell reached them through the roar, and then the northern tip of the county came into view on the horizon and the helicopter turned toward the great house on the top of the cliff, Reuben's mansion, with its huge H painted on the ground. Reuben, Kerensa and the baby were out front, waving furiously.

"Okay, ready to go," said Polly as they landed and thanked the pilot. Neil hopped around with a confused look on his face. Probably slightly noisier flying than he'd been used to.

Reuben and Kerensa looked utterly delighted; Kerensa far better than any woman who'd given birth less than a week ago had the right to. Baby Herschel-Lowin was sleeping happily in his father's arms. Rhonda and Merv also came out to greet them. This felt odd; Polly had expected to be hustled into the kitchen to start getting on with things.

"What's up?" she said.

Everyone was beaming at them in a slightly peculiar way, especially Kerensa. She and Reuben exchanged glances. Reuben's staff were also lined up out front in a weird, presidential visit kind of a way.

"So anyway," said Kerensa, "I was trying to . . . we

were trying to find a way to say thank you. For your support. For everything you've done for us over the years. To give you a Christmas present."

"I should say now," said Reuben, "that this was mostly a way for Kerensa to keep shopping when she was all miserable about being pregnant."

"Shut up," said Kerensa, beaming happily at him.

"What's going on?" said Polly, feeling nervous.

Kerensa came up and took both their hands.

"Look," she said. "You absolutely don't have to do this if you don't want to."

"Do what?" said Polly with suspicion. Kerensa beamed and pulled her inside.

The house had once again been totally transformed. White orchids and lilies lined the entrance hall, their heavy scent hanging amongst the smell of cranberries and oranges that had filled the house throughout the Christmas season. There were runs of flowers up and down the circular banister. And ahead were rows of white seats with bows on the back, laid out in front of the huge conservatory . . .

There was a long silence.

"Oh," said Polly, in deep shock. It couldn't be. They couldn't possibly mean . . .

Kerensa looked at her.

"Because you see," she said, so excited she could barely get the words out. "Well. I wanted to thank you. For. You know. Everything. And so did lots of other people. And I know you were busy and didn't want fuss and don't like buying stuff and don't have any money . . ."

"Thanks," said Polly.

"And so I thought . . . when everything was really tough . . . I thought, why don't we do it for you! Then you'll be all married and you can just get on with your lives."

"I can't get married!" said Polly. "I need to lose half a stone and get everything arranged and grow my nails and . . ." She petered out.

"Of course you don't have to," said Kerensa, looking slightly concerned. "I mean, there's a few people coming, but we can just have like a New Year's party."

"What do you mean, a few people?" said Polly, feeling panicky.

"Well. Obviously all our old crowd from school . . . and your college crowd . . . and your mum . . . and . . . Well, I wasn't sure who to ask from the village, so I just invited everyone."

"Everyone?"

"Well, yeah."

"You invited every single person in the entire village?"

"They won't all come," said Kerensa uncertainly.

"They will," said Polly. "Oh my God. Oh. No. Kerensa . . . I mean . . . I mean, it's a fun idea and . . . I mean, I don't know how you could possibly want to do this a week after having a baby . . ."

"Because I have the most awesome wife and baby in the world," said Reuben smugly. "They can do anything."

"Yeah, right," said Polly. "But this is just . . . it's just . . ."

Caterers arrived with a massive ice swan. They all stopped and watched it pass.

"Can't you marry Jayden and Flora instead? They're definitely up for it."

Kerensa's face fell.

"Oh," she said. "I'm so sorry. I thought . . . I thought it would be an amazing idea. I thought you guys would be absolutely delighted. You know, to not have to worry about the stress and the cost and everything."

"Stop talking about how skint we are," said Polly. "Look, I'm sorry, Kerensa, I know you meant well, but I didn't . . . I mean, we wouldn't ever want a big thing . . ."

She paused.

"Are Huckle's parents here?"

Kerensa didn't say anything. Polly swore. Then she turned to look at Huckle.

"This is awkward, eh?" she whispered. "Shall we just tell them thanks, and maybe sneak out? Or stay for a bit, possibly . . ."

Huckle looked at her, straight into her eyes.

"Or," he said quietly, "we could just do it."

"You knew about this?"

"No," he said. "But, you know. We're here now."

"I'm wearing dungarees! And thermal pants."

"Ah," said Kerensa. "I might be able to help you with that."

"And, you know, WAXING, and my eyebrows need plucking and my hair is a mess and . . ."

Huckle blinked.

"I think you look beautiful," he said.

And suddenly, for Polly, it felt like all the anxieties, all the frustrations and worries of keeping the bakery running and the lighthouse warm and her friends happy and dealing with her own deep-buried issues . . . it suddenly felt as if everything, every one of those was lifted from her shoulders, everything was taken away and the world seemed a brighter place, as the sun glinted off the snow outside and the huge fire crackled merrily in the grate, and all her fears about marriage, about that step, and what it meant, and what it had meant for her family, seemed to vanish as she looked at the handsome, open, guileless face of the man she absolutely adored . . .

And everything else fell away.

"And I would like to marry you," he said.

"Are you *sure* you weren't in on this?" said Polly suspiciously.

"I promise I wasn't." He shook his head. "Although my parents did mention they'd suddenly changed their plans."

"So you had a hint?"

"Come on!" said Kerensa. "Come with me! I have lots of stuff to show you, all of which you can fit into but I can't because my tits have exploded into milk-filled HHs and I still appear to look eight months pregnant despite the fact that the baby is officially out and not in any more."

And she spirited Polly, whose head was in a whirl, upstairs to her room.

Chapter Forty-Two

Polly walked into the room.

"What the hell? What is this?"

Kerensa beamed with happiness.

"I know!" she said.

The dressing room annexe, normally full of Kerensa's ridiculous collection of shoes and bags that Reuben insisted on buying her, had been completely transformed into a white boudoir. And in every available space a different style of wedding dress was hanging—strapless; lacy; a ridiculous princess number over the door.

"What . . . what is this?" Polly blinked.

"Choose one."

And there, at a little table at the side, looking slightly concerned but sipping from a flute of champagne nonetheless, was Polly's mum.

"Mum?" said Polly.

Doreen stood up and they embraced.

"You knew about this?"

Her mother, who was all done up in a fuchsia suit that

had last seen use in about 1987—and still fit—smiled and nodded.

"You have a very good friend in Kerensa."

"What did you . . . I mean, are we really getting married, or is it a fake one?"

"We posted the banns for you," said Kerensa. "They've been up in the church for six weeks."

"Why did nobody tell us?"

"We swore everyone to secrecy and threatened them with not being invited. We knew there was absolutely no way you two heathens would be setting foot inside a church anyway. You have to go to the registrar in a couple of days, but apart from that, it's the real thing, baby."

Polly shook her head.

"And *this* is what you were doing all that time?"

Kerensa shrugged. "You know how miserable I was. I hated thinking about the baby; hated thinking about how I'd ruined my life. And I was worried, you know. Worried about you."

"YOU were worried about ME?" said Polly.

"Yes! You had this fabulous guy standing right there and you were all like, oh, I'm too stressed out to get married, oh, I'm not ready, blah blah blah."

"But he always knew I loved him," said Polly.

"He's a bloke!" said Kerensa. "Blokes don't know ANYTHING unless you spell it out in foot-high letters and stick it in front of their noses. All he'd have been thinking is 'Polly no marry Huckle. Huckle so sad. So so sad. Huckle go marry twenty-year-old.' "

"No he wasn't," said Polly.

" 'Huckle so sad and lonely!' "

"She's right, you know," said Doreen, and it was to

Polly's great credit that she didn't immediately turn around and say what on earth would you know about it?

Kerensa beamed.

"My mum's here too, saying I should have done it like this instead of dressing up like Princess Leia, and it's actually even more annoying because she has a point."

"How did you get here, Mum?" said Polly.

"That nice young American boy sent a car for me," said Doreen. "He's looked after me so well! Such a lovely chap."

"Reuben?"

"He's a darling," said Doreen.

"He is," said Kerensa, looking fondly at the crib in the corner where she'd laid Herschel-Lowin.

Polly looked around.

"And you promise me Huckle knew nothing about this?"

"Nope," said Kerensa. "Reuben thought he'd pitch a fit and insist that you needed a chance to do it your way. Whereas we've decided that it's just time for the two of you."

"Seriously?"

"You're so busy, you'd never have gotten around to it."

Kerensa knelt down.

"You're not cross, are you?"

Polly looked around again. Planning her own wedding wasn't at all the kind of thing she'd dreamed of as a child. Everything she'd dreamed of—running her own business, being independent, baking things people wanted to buy—those things she'd done. But in this big, mad, beautiful house . . .

"Who else is coming?" she asked weakly.

"Everyone," said Kerensa, with a wicked glint in her eye, and sure enough, there were already fleets of cars crunching up the drive toward the house, and laughing, shouting people disgorging from them.

"Oh Lord," said Polly.

There was a woman lingering by the door carrying a huge box of what was clearly makeup. Polly turned to her.

"Okay," she said. "Whatever it is you do—do it all. Twice. Then add some more for luck."

Kerensa poured them all glasses of champagne.

"Don't look at me like that," she said. "I have a breast pump."

"I really don't deserve this," said Polly. "I don't deserve any of this. Not really."

Kerensa blinked. "You've been the best friend in the world," she said hoarsely. "Anyway, choose a dress, the rest are going back. Reuben hired the entire shop. Plus you'll need an hour for Anita to paint your nails and stick extra hair in."

"What do you mean, extra hair?"

"All the brides these days have extra hair," said Kerensa. "Well, they have lots extra in some places and lots less in other places. We can do that too."

Polly thought of how often Huckle had said he liked her strawberry-blond hair natural and curly rather than how she normally did it, ironed flat and sprayed down.

"Actually," she said. "I think I'll just leave it like it is."

"But it's all curly."

"Maybe curly is all right."

"My God, your children are going to have, like, the world's curliest hair."

Polly smiled to think of it.

"Well," she said. "Maybe I've made my peace with that."

She started trying on the dresses, having a giggle at

the really massive princess one—she couldn't help it; it looked stiff and strange and not like her at all, and was profoundly uncomfortable to wear.

"No," she said. "Definitely not."

"It's okay," said Kerensa. "I've taken lots of nice pictures of you in it anyway, so if you want to you can substitute that frock in the wedding pictures later. Reuben can do all the computer stuff."

"Hmm," said Polly. And then she saw it. It was just behind the cupboard, and wasn't at all like the rest of the showy diamanté numbers. In fact it was rather plain: a simple vintage dress with a boat-neck lace top and a deep V at the waist. If anything, it was slightly medieval. It didn't have petticoats or hoops or sparkles or ruffles or bows. Neither did it cut her off as the strapless numbers did, making her look like the top half of her was cavorting about naked. This dress was subtle, sweet, understated . . .

She slipped the cool silk underskirt over her head. It flowed down her body and fitted immediately, perfectly, as if it had been made for her. It shimmered as she moved; it wasn't too tight or too puffy; not too fussy and not too plain. The tiny glinting vintage sequins caught the light in a subtle way; the pale ivory color set off her red hair perfectly. She looked in the mirror and barely recognized herself.

"Oh," Doreen said quietly. "Oh. That's exactly what I'd have chosen. For you," she added quickly, looking up and wiping her eyes. "I mean for you, of course. That's what I would have chosen for you."

Polly came over and hugged her mother for a long time and they had a small cry together. Then Anita, the hair and makeup girl, unpacked her box and started work.

Polly could see more cars arriving.

"Oh my Lord," she said. "I'm quite nervous now."

She turned to Kerensa. "What music are we having?"

"Just the normal stuff," said Kerensa quickly. "Don't worry about it."

Polly blinked.

"Oh my God, what about rings?"

"We've borrowed a couple for you," said Kerensa. "They have to go back and then you can choose your own."

Polly shook her head.

"No, it's all right," she said. "I think we have a better idea." And she sent a quick text to Huckle.

After half an hour of painting and polishing and primping—at one point there were three people working on her at once—Kerensa gave Polly some fresh underwear and declared her ready.

"I still think I should have had more notice and I wouldn't have eaten all that toast and leftover canapés over Christmas."

"Shut up," said Kerensa. "You look beautiful."

And she did. Exquisitely beautiful and perfect and gorgeous in the pale winter sunlight that reflected off the snow and streamed in through the huge windows overlooking the bay. Polly blinked as she watched the activity on the drive. Old Mrs. Corning was being helped out of a large car by Pat the vet. Everyone was here.

"How?" she said. "Seriously? Everyone's known about this for weeks?"

"Yup," said Kerensa smugly.

Polly shook her head, bemused.

"This is mad."

"I think it's the funnest thing to happen to Mount

Polbearne for ages." Kerensa peered out of the window. "Oh wow."

"What?" said Polly. She glanced out. It was Huckle's mum and dad, looking cheery and bemused, and with them was Huckle's very troublesome brother DuBose.

"Whoa," said Polly. "You really did get everyone."

"Just lock up the jewelry," said Kerensa. "Oh! I almost forgot. I have a present for you."

"On top of what?" said Polly. "Oh my God, Kerensa, this is totally mad already."

"Sssh," said Kerensa. "Doing this has been about the only nice time I've had this year." She looked adoringly at the baby in the cot. "Worth it, though."

She brought out a velvet jewelry case and handed it to Polly, who opened it. Inside was a delicate necklace on a platinum chain, with a tiny row of puffins, each with a little diamond. You couldn't even tell what they were unless you got close; otherwise it just looked like a lovely piece of filigree.

"Oh my God," said Polly.

"Hah!" said Kerensa. "I knew you'd like it."

"I love it!" said Polly, her eyes filling with tears. "Oh my God, I don't know what I did to deserve this."

"Everything," said Kerensa. "Come here. I told them to use the waterproof mascara."

The two girls held one another tightly.

"I'm going to do this," said Polly disbelievingly. "I'm actually going to do this."

"Unless you reckon anyone better's going to come along," said Kerensa, and they both burst out laughing.

Doreen stood up cautiously, still a little nervous. Polly noticed that she had had her nails done and was even wearing a tiny bit of makeup. She had made the most massive effort. Polly blinked.

"This is . . ." Doreen swallowed hard. "This is all I ever wanted for you. No. I wanted whatever you wanted for you," she said with some difficulty. "And I should have been better at letting you see . . . letting you know that whatever you wanted was fine. And . . . I should have . . ."

"Mum," said Polly. "Forget about that. Forget about everything. It's fine. It's all fine. Please."

And they embraced too, just as a very trendy photographer in cowboy boots and a bald spot came in and started taking shots of them with an unnecessarily complex-looking camera.

"Reportage," hissed Kerensa. "Nothing cheesy."

"Yes, because this isn't at all cheesy," wept Polly. The photographer ignored them completely and kept snapping away.

"Hang on," said Polly. "What about music? And readings? And all that stuff?"

"Well, you told me all that," said Kerensa.

"What do you mean? No I didn't. How?"

"When we were at school," said Kerensa. "Remember? I made plans then. We wrote it all down in an exercise book. You helped."

Polly went white.

"You didn't . . ."

"What?" said Kerensa innocently. " 'I Want It That Way' is a perfectly good song to walk down the aisle to. I did actually speak to their management, so they're on their way . . ."

"YOU DIDN'T?"

Kerensa grinned. "I didn't."

"Oh," said Polly, mostly relieved and a teensy-tiny bit disappointed.

"Ha! I knew it! You totally look disappointed!"

Polly shook her head.

"Trust me, I am so round the bend with shock and terror, disappointment is the furthest thing from my mind."

"Don't worry," said Kerensa, squeezing her hand. "We've gone very trad."

She glanced at her watch. It was coming up to two o'clock.

"Okay," she said. "You know, I think it's nearly time."

"Oh my God," said Polly. "Oh my God. I'm not ready. I'm not ready. Where's Neil?"

"He's with Huckle," said Kerensa. "The groomsmen stick together. Don't worry. And you're never ready. Oh, and Huckle's fraternity brothers are here too. I'm amazed you didn't hear them before now. Reuben wouldn't let them stay in the house; we had to put them up in a hotel."

"Because they're frat boys?"

"And he wanted to be one and they wouldn't let him. He says he's working on a disease to eradicate them all."

Polly shook her head.

"This is mad."

"I had a lot of displacement energy," said Kerensa grimly.

Marta came in, beaming and giggling, and exclaimed at Polly's transformation. Polly hugged her too.

"Mr. Finkel says it's time," Marta said. "He says come on, and bring the baby with you."

Kerensa nodded. She hopped into the bathroom and shimmied into a pale silk slouchy dress that immediately eliminated all the lumps and bumps and made her look like she hadn't had a baby at all. In fact she looked stunningly lovely, all her spark, her mojo right back.

"Chief bridesmaid," she announced.

Outside the door was a tiny gaggle of children from the village, as well as Reuben's youngest sister. They were an orgy of cream and flowers and giggles and gorgeousness, and as Polly emerged, they burst into spontaneous applause.

"Hello, you lot!" she said cheerfully. She crept forward and peered over the balcony.

Kerensa hadn't been lying. Everybody was there. Absolutely everyone. The entire gang from school, and her college friends—obviously word had gotten out—all done up in their wedding best. Polly hated to think what would have happened if she'd said no. The logistics of everything were mind-boggling. She glanced down the big staircase, her heart beating terribly fast.

"Are you ready?" said Kerensa.

"Yes! No! Oh my God," said Polly. She stepped back. "Actually," she said. "Mum. It is totally up to you to say no, honestly. Completely. But I was . . ."

She was so confused and emotional, she could barely get the words out.

"I just wondered if maybe . . ."

"Anything," said Doreen.

"I thought I might . . . maybe we could call Carmel? Just . . . I mean, there's . . . I mean, I have a whole bunch of half-brothers and -sisters out there who I don't know or anything, and well, I mean. If I was. If I wanted to get to know them. Maybe. One day. Well."

"You want to invite them?"

"Maybe just Carmel," said Polly. "To start with. But if I was . . . if I was ever to get to know them, this might not be a bad way of beginning it."

They looked at each other.

"On it," said Kerensa, pulling out Polly's phone from the handbag she'd spirited it into.

"Hang on," said Polly, raising her hand.

Doreen stared at the floor for a moment, then looked up again with something resolute about her eyes.

"Yes," she said. "Yes. If there is a family out there for you, Polly . . . more of a family, I mean. Yes. It's so far in the past now . . . Yes. It's fine."

Polly nodded. "Thanks."

"I'm texting right now," said Kerensa.

They hung on with bated breath. Then Kerensa looked up.

"They'll be here in time for the afternoon tea," she said.

"No way," said Polly.

There was a sound of scuffling and some impatient throat-clearing from behind them.

"Right," said Kerensa.

"Right," said Polly. And Doreen put out her arm to walk her down the aisle.

Chapter Forty-Three

Polly stood for just a second at the top of the stairs, looking dazedly at the whole of the life they had built together spread out before her. People were bunched around the staircase, smiling, beaming at her, dressed up in hats and wobbly on high heels, and oh my goodness, it was incredible to Polly that they'd all managed to keep it a secret.

And then a path was made, with a red carpet running down it, running through the throng of giggling delighted people, and she saw, just for a second, Huckle's broad back, in a black jacket. Neil was perched on his shoulder, wearing a bow tie, obviously caught up in the solemnity of the moment. Reuben, a head shorter, was standing next to him. Polly just stood for a second, a thrill going through her as suddenly, gradually, the crowd became aware of her, and Reuben glanced around and nudged Huckle, who turned too, both of them with white Cornish heather in their buttonholes, and Polly's heart leapt, and the same swing band as before—but now looking not at all so snotty—started playing a song it took Polly a moment to recognize.

Huckle spotted her, and his face lit up in a way she would never forget for as long as she lived.

And he gave her the biggest wink as she started down the stairs in the pretty low-heeled shoes she'd picked out, biting her lip, desperately hoping she wouldn't stumble, a bevy of bridesmaids around her, one throwing rose petals that were spilling out all around the long skirt of her dress and the new shoes that she hadn't had a chance to practise walking in, and it was quite useful, in fact, that she had to concentrate so hard on not falling down the stairs that she didn't really have a moment to start crying or get terribly anxious about it.

But then suddenly the fact that everyone was there, the way the entire world appeared to have known about her big day before she did; the fact that she had had absolutely no idea about what was planned or how she was going to react . . . suddenly all of that melted away. Because Huckle was holding her gaze with his strong blue eyes. And Neil was hopping on his shoulder in his bow tie, and in his claws he held two entwined rings of fresh seaweed from the low tide on the shore.

The song continued. *"It must be love! Love! Love!"*

The rest was more or less a blur, although Polly had heard lots of people say that about their wedding day. She remembered amazing food; and Mattie the vicar doing the traditional vows with a huge beaming smile; and loads and loads of champagne; and constantly being surprised by people she hadn't seen for too long, buried as she had been in work and her own problems.

She remembered Reuben's speech, which had somehow turned into a massive tribute to how brilliant he was, and she remembered Huckle's because he simply stood up and said, "This is love and I am in it" and sat down again, and she remembered his face when his mum and dad came up to embrace them; and she remembered Merv dancing with Doreen, and Jayden saying to Flora, "We could get married like this" and her face being absolutely horrified, and Bernard throwing himself on her and thanking her for saving the sanctuary, which meant Reuben had clearly paid her invoice before she'd even sent it, and she'd made a mental note that turning the puffin café into something would have to be her summer project, but before she could start discussing it with him, Huckle had pulled her away, and Selina, looking absolutely foxy in red satin, had slipped in and grabbed Bernard's elbow.

And she remembered, later, Carmel turning up, looking very nervous—alone, but with her camera— and she'd hugged her, and Carmel had toasted her, just once, smiling a smile with heartbreak behind it, before they were both whirled into the massive hora that had started.

And then, late at night, the cars started to arrive, including a huge limo for Polly and Huckle and Neil, and they cuddled up in the back seat, giggling occasionally, kissing often, shaking their heads at the madness and the joy of it all, and when they reached the causeway across to Mount Polbearne, the tide was out, and the way was lit, incredibly, astonishingly, all the way to the island with huge proud braziers.

God knows how Reuben had managed it, or how he'd gotten permission. But it looked like a magical winding path leading straight out to sea; a secret golden road, known only to them, that would close as soon as they had passed, sinking back beneath the waves.

The local cars all drove on over. But the wedding cars stopped, refusing to venture on to dangerous territory they didn't know.

So Polly and Huckle, right at the back of the convoy, had to get out of their car, the tiny waves already lapping at their toes, and Polly took off her absurdly expensive shoes and hitched up her skirts, and both of them, floating on champagne and bubbles of pure happiness, giggling their heads off, charged along the causeway as the waves closed over behind them, the flaming torches snuffed out one by one, so that from the mainland it must have looked as if Mount Polbearne was nothing but a mirage in the distance; a lost dream.

Andy was already opening the Red Lion, and the fiddles were starting up, but Huckle simply took Polly in his arms and carried her up the steps to the lighthouse.

And in that moment, as the old year paused before the new arrived, it was as if the world took a breath.

Polly didn't believe in magic, but even so, as they crossed the threshold, in a flash, in a vision, she could see it, feel it all.

Even though the lighthouse was dark and cold and empty, it was as if, suddenly, she could hear her name being called; the bath running; Neil *eep*ing, children charging up and down the stairs—and falling, from time to time—banging and making noise and charging in and out, and it sped up, it went so fast, the oven turning over, and the village children playing together, and friends arriving, and Reuben's new school . . . and it sped up again, and the lamp in the lighthouse whizzed round and round as the boats followed the tide in and out and the freezing winters turned to perfect summers and the children came and went and shouted and grew and the bread filled the air with its scent and the children ran back from school and grabbed great handfuls of banana cake and dashed out again to dabble in rock pools with Neil, tousle-haired, shrimping nets in little fingers, clamoring to be allowed in the sidecar, and Herschel-Lowin, with his bright red hair and freckles, ran around pretending to be in charge . . .

Polly blinked and shook away the vision—far too much champagne, she thought, too much excitement, and tiredness, and emotion. All of those things.

"I love you, my darling," said Huckle. "But I am going to have to put you down. It's your dress that's heavy."

"I know," she said, still half caught in the dream. "It's definitely the dress."

"Definitely," said Huckle. "Shall I go and put the electric blanket on?"

"Yes, please," said Polly.

And as he vanished upstairs, she turned, watching the lighthouse beam sweep over the harbor, the little town, out to the mainland, where the fireworks were already starting to pop, one two three, and just before she switched out the light, she went into the kitchen in her wedding dress, and she laid out the yeast and the flour and the eggs for the morning bread, and kissed Neil, already snuggled in front of the Aga, and put out the light, then ran upstairs, her skirt and a faint wake of flour trailing behind her.

AWESOME HOT CHOCOLATE

NB: Don't add TOO much cream, otherwise it will turn into pudding. But do add marshmallows, even though those two statements contradict each other. Also keep an eye on the chocolate. If it gets above a simmer when it's melting, it's all over.

> One large bar of milk chocolate (the size of one they offer you in shops when you buy a newspaper. The branding is completely up to you.)
> One small bar of dark chocolate (Bournville or similiar but go posh as you like. If you like, e.g., chili flavoring (I don't judge), go for that at this point.)
> Brandy or Cointreau (optional)
> 750ml whole milk
> A dollop of single cream (light cream)
> Vanilla, to taste
> Ginger or cinnamon, to taste
> 2 tsp. sugar (optional)

Melt the chocolate INCREDIBLY slowly, stirring over a very low heat. If you've got small people chuntering around, they may need a distraction whilst you get this together. If you don't, a small slug of brandy or Cointreau is practically *de riguer*.

When the chocolate is melted, add up to 750ml of whole milk—the precise consistency is up to you—and a dollop of single cream. It should be lovely and thick but not dessert.

A spot of vanilla; a tiny pinch of ginger or cinnamon to taste. Some people add a teaspoon or two of sugar at this point, and that is entirely to your taste. I do.

If you have a foamer, use that; otherwise carefully whisk and pour.

Small marshmallows or tiny ones are up to you. I prefer the little ones because it feels like I get more. Don't look at me like that.

Drink slowly. Possibly with this book in your hands.

KNISHES

Knishes are basically the Jewish version of a pasty. You can make your own pastry or just buy it; it should be very thin. They can be filled with meat or potatoes and onion or cream cheese. I don't like the cream cheese one so much, so here's the classic.

2kg potatoes
2 large onions
3 tsp. vegetable oil
Salt and pepper, to taste
Chopped parsley

For the pastry
800g flour
2 eggs
4 tsp. vegetable oil
Cup of warm water
1 tsp. of salt

Boil the potatoes and sauté (softly fry) the onions in the oil. Mash together with plenty of salt and pepper and parsley, and set aside to cool.

Mix the wet ingredients for the pastry, then gradually add the flour until its firm enough for kneading. Knead for a few minutes, then set aside to rest.

You want to roll the dough out as thin as possible, then put dollops of the potato mixture at intervals. Roll the whole thing up like a long sausage roll, but when you slice it up, you should be able to "wrap up" the entire thing in pastry, because the potato mixture isn't touching—they should be round little parcels, if that makes sense.

Brush with egg wash and bake at 375°F for around 35 minutes. Perfect finger food. Dip in sour cream if so inclined.

MINCEMEAT TWISTS

I love making my own mincemeat. It feels like the start of Christmas and it will make you feel better about using puff pastry.

Mincemeat (prepare at least two weeks before)
275g currants
100g sultanas
250g raisins
3 tbsp. lemon juice
Lemon zest
300g suet
300g brown sugar
100g mixed peel
Pinch of nutmeg
2 peeled apples (firm green ones best)
QUITE a lot of brandy

SQUISH SQUISH SQUISH.
Then leave.
After a couple of hours, fill sterilized jam jars (I run them through a dishwasher on a boil setting), make sure the air is out (put one of those little gingham flat hats on it), and lock so they're airtight. Otherwise they will spoil. Stick in the cupboard for two weeks. If I make extra, I give it away as gifts. When we lived in France, I gave it to my French friends and they all looked at me like I was a MANIAC.

I am sure the jars are still in their cupboards.

To make a twist, cut triangles out of the puff pastry. Put a spoonful of the mincemeat at the bottom and roll up. It doesn't matter if they look slightly messy, that's all part of the fun!

Brush with egg wash, sprinkle with brown sugar and bake for 30 mins at 400°F, or until brown.

GALETTE DES ROIS

Where we live in France, the big thing to eat at Christmas is yule log and, after Christmas, *galette des rois* up to the feast of the Epiphany, or Twelfth Night. There are little ceramic creatures, called *fêves,* or favors, hidden in each cake. They can be angels or religious figures, but these days you can also get Scooby Doo. Whoever finds it is crowned the *Roi* with the gold paper crown that traditionally goes around the outside. Then it is their turn to host the next galette des rois. We have found through trial and error it is usually prudent to push the fêve piece toward the youngest person in the room. If you can't lay your hand on some fêves, a coin wrapped in greaseproof paper should have the same cheerful effect in warding off the post-chrimbo blues.

> 1 roll ready-made puff pastry, unless you are a
>   fantastic pastry nut (I worship you)
> 1 egg, beaten
> 2 tbsp. jam
> 100g soft butter
> 100g caster sugar (superfine sugar)
> 100g ground almonds
> 1 tbsp. brandy

Preheat the oven to 375°F. Divide the ready-made puff pastry in half, and roll out each piece into two circles.

Put one of the circles on a baking sheet and spread with the jam.

Whisk the butter and sugar until fluffy. Beat in most of the egg. Stir in the almonds, brandy, and add the *fève*.

Spread the mix on top of the jam, then cover with the second piece of pastry. Seal up with a pinch. You can decorate the top of the *galette* with a fork if you like.

Bake for 25 minutes or until crisp and golden. Serve warm or cold.

Acknowledgments

Thanks to everyone who's been so incredibly supportive of Polly, Neil and the gang over the last three years,
particularly:

Maddie West, Rebecca Saunders, David Shelley,
Charlie King, Manpreet Grewal, Amanda Keats, Jen
and the sales team, Emma Williams, Stephanie Mel-
rose, Jo Wickham, Kate Agar, and all at Little, Brown;
Jo Unwin, Isabel Adamakoh Young, the Amble Puffin
Festival, and all our many dear rabbit friends and relations who were there so staunchly for me during an
unusually tricky time. Love, and a very, very merry
Christmas to you all.